"ARE YOU HUNGRY, JOHN?" SHE WHISPERED

Bea blushed at the possible implication.

"Not for food." John regarded her steadily. "Where is it, Bea?" he asked in his thoroughly seductive voice.

"What?" she said breathlessly, her skin heating in a rosy flush as his arm slipped smoothly around her waist.

"Your bedroom." He lowered his head and began teasing and tasting the contours of her lips. When she eagerly responded, his fiery kiss deepened until it threatened to inflame them both. It was fiercely urgent, desperate, as if he must savor her sweetness quickly or lose it forever.

And suddenly Bea knew this moment was crucial. They were already deeply emotionally involved. It was time for more intimate rewards. But what if she never saw him again? What if she did....

SHARON McCAFFREE

PASSPORT TO PASSION

A SUPERROMANCE FROM
W🌐RLDWIDE

TORONTO · NEW YORK · LONDON · PARIS
AMSTERDAM · STOCKHOLM · HAMBURG
ATHENS · MILAN · TOKYO · SYDNEY

To my husband

———————◆———————

Published October 1983

First printing August 1983

ISBN 0-373-70085-7

Printed in Canada

CHAPTER ONE

THE EARLY DIN of Paris commuters making their daily pilgrimage downtown had long since faded into the July morning when the chartered tourist bus moved smoothly in from the outskirts of the historic city. To Beatrice Allen, leaning her head wearily against the tinted bus window, Paris had an unexpectedly lazy quality. It was as if the Parisians who had been left behind in their neighborhoods after the rush hour were determined to pursue their lives at a leisurely pace. Even the merchants arranging their wares in sidewalk displays appeared more interested in chatting with passing homemakers than in pushing sales. Bea, accustomed to the daylong, frenetic tempo of New York City, found the quiet impression refreshing.

"Lovely Paris," she sighed, enthralled.

"What did you say?" The heavy, middle-aged matron seated beside her roused tentatively from her dozing.

"Nothing," Bea soothed, not wanting to complete the waking process of the formidable Mrs. Bascombe.

"I know you said something," the woman mumbled in her usual bad humor before drifting back into oblivion.

It was fortunate that Mrs. Bascombe had gone to sleep almost immediately after grabbing the empty seat next to Bea that morning, because her loud, incessant complaining would certainly have marred everyone's first impressions of the city.

Bea was surprised at how fast she was falling in love with Paris, for their route had not been through the more glamorous, famous sections of the city. As she glanced around the bus to see if others were equally enchanted, she realized with disappointment that there was no one else with whom to share her initial pleasure. She was one of the few people in her tour group awake enough to even notice their arrival. Although the travelers had not made a particularly early start from their previous night's lodging at a nearby French château, a week of sight-seeing and late-night partying in Spain had taken its toll on all of them.

Bea was tired herself. But she was so excited, both with seeing Paris and with the prospect of meeting Perry soon, that she had been unable to nap.

Perry's right, she thought wryly, settling back into her seat. *For a twenty-four-year-old stockbroker I am alarmingly emotional.* But she couldn't help looking forward to the next ten days when she could explore Paris with him. It had been so long since she had spent time with a close friend. In fact, she had become so engrossed in work the past four years that she had very few close friends left. And of those, Perry was the only one who even suspected she was sometimes foolishly emotional.

Bea chuckled to herself as she recalled a few of

the times she and Perry had had fierce arguments, only to dissolve into laughter together over the idiocy of it all. That was what had been so achingly missing from her life lately, she thought with rising excitement—someone to laugh with. Perhaps someone of her own to love? She tried to squash the thought, but it was there, lurking in her mind as it had been ever since she had left the hectic pace of her office and the loneliness of her apartment to join this tour. Soon she would be on vacation with Perry!

The week's tour without him had not been as bad as she had expected. She had not been a total social dud; she had found things to talk about to the other couples, and she had even formed some casual friendships. But everyone took a second place to Perry Campbell. There was no one more fun to be with—he and Bea were simpatico.

While first one, then another, distinctive architectural setting slipped beyond her vision from the bus window, it occurred to her that she should keep track of some of her favorite interesting neighborhoods, for she could probably talk Perry into bringing her back to visit some of them. Earlier Bea had seen a street lined with art galleries she would definitely like to wander in.

The bus slowed for a slight traffic jam, and she saw several picturesque storefronts on a square just off their route. An old church and a museum dominated the grassy public area, and modest apartment houses filled the rest of the square. Twisting in her seat, Bea tried to identify a street, but the only thing she accomplished was to waken Mrs. Bascombe.

"What are you fidgeting so much for?" the woman snapped, straightening in her seat and apparently readying herself to provide an onslaught of conversation. "Aren't we at the Royal Hotel yet? What's taking that useless driver so long?"

Bea remained turned toward the window as if she had not heard, but predictably Mrs. Bascombe did not take the subtle hint.

"When are you meeting this man everyone's been telling me about?" she continued, undaunted. "It doesn't make sense to me that after you've won this free trip given by our company you would drop out of the tour. You'll have to do so at your own expense, you know, unless of course that man is paying your—"

"I thought it was Mr. Bascombe who worked for the firm," Bea said sweetly, annoyed that the smug woman called the nationwide brokerage chain that employed Bea and all the men on the tour "our company."

"Well, of course he does. Does this...person you're meeting work for us, too?"

Giving up on the woman's supreme arrogance, Bea looked pointedly past her. "I think your husband is awake now," she said instead.

"Well, it's about time!" Thus distracted, Mrs. Bascombe glanced angrily across the aisle at a small man who was just lowering his legs from a double seat. "I can't imagine what got into him this morning, insisting that he had to have a double seat so he could lie down. You'd think he could have just leaned back in his chair the way I did."

Watching without regret as the woman heaved her bulk out of the seat and rejoined her husband, Bea knew exactly what had got into him. He had wanted a rest from his wife's nagging. She smiled sympathetically as she settled more comfortably and allowed the passing scenes to float by her consciousness in alternately hazy and clear patches.

It didn't take much longer to reach the center of the city, and within minutes they had pulled up at their hotel, which was on the rue de Rivoli within sight of the Louvre. Predictably there was so much confusion once people piled off the bus and excitedly began gawking at the famous sights around them, that the tour director had difficulty getting keys assigned. Those people who had slept throughout their drive into the city center were now more interested in making up lost sight-seeing time than in retreating to their rooms.

Bea was invited to join some acquaintances for an afternoon of shopping, but she begged off. Exhaustion was catching up with her, and since Perry did not plan to get in touch with her until seven, after he had settled in at the hotel at his own convenience, she decided to spend a quiet afternoon in her room.

She hadn't planned to take a nap. But after luxuriating in a hot bubble bath and wrapping up in the lush terry coat the hotel provided in lieu of towels, the temptation had been inescapable. She phoned down a message for Perry that they had evening reservations with her group for dinner and a show at the Lido. Abandoning the toweling coat, she slipped naked between the silky sheets and slept several hours.

When she awoke she was so refreshed that she decided to treat herself to an orgy of beauty care. There was still plenty of time, and she wanted to look her best at the Lido; she couldn't wait to see Perry's face when she appeared in her low-cut yellow crochet dress. He usually criticized her taste in clothes, complaining that her fashionable business suits were not necessary to heighten her image of cool competence and that they hid too much of her voluptuous figure. She was certain he would like the yellow dress, for it hid nothing!

Perry did not like her hair pulled back, either, as she habitually wore it. So she first set about correcting that problem. Her mother had given her a French curling iron for the trip, and it worked perfectly to remove all traces of Bea's usually tidy knotted braid and to allow her coal black hair to wave, glossy and free. Bea had done her nails, set out her cosmetics, put on her lingerie and just removed her thick glasses to put in her recently acquired contact lenses when a man knocked at her door, saying he had a cable for her.

Bea was certain it would be a joke from Perry. He did things like that. Hastily she slipped her dress over her head, careful not to mar her fresh nail polish, and made herself presentable enough to receive the message and send the man on his way.

She didn't even open the cable at first. She returned to her chair and let it sit in her lap until she rechecked her nails for damage, her lips curved happily all the time in anticipation of another example of Perry's delightful sense of humor. Although he had told her to pick their first night's entertainment, she knew he could not pass up the chance to make some joke about the Lido. He would probably ask if he had to wear a shirt and shoes to get service. Or better yet, if they could go dutch....

Certainly she had no premonition what the message would actually be. When she did eventually read the cable, she gasped in astonishment.

Surely he didn't mean that he was not coming!

Her creamy skin paled, making her delicate-boned face look even more fragile than usual. Stunned, she sank deeper in the chair, her brown eyes dark with shock as she tried to absorb the implication.

It had to be some sort of a joke. She couldn't believe he would do that to her.

Bea finally absorbed the fact that Perry had indeed left her stranded in Paris. It was little consolation that she was not exactly alone; she would still be with the tour group. She had never felt more lonely. In fact, she was emotionally devastated.

The trouble with loneliness, she reflected as she absentmindedly fastened her delicate, high-heeled sandals, is that it creeps in so gradually, like a wispy cloud. It was so subtle you didn't know what was gathering until the storm hit you without your defenses up.

She thought of her life-style the past four years: the long hours; the prejudices she had had to overcome, both among prospective clients as well as colleagues; the pressures. She had made a success of her work all by herself. Reaching the top also meant she functioned alone, but she had accepted that. Only recently, as she had prepared for this trip with Perry, had she begun to feel that the solitary price she paid for her accomplishments was too high.

"Damn him!"

It still didn't seem possible. Her thick hair fell halfway down her back as she straightened and looked over to the tiny hotel writing desk where the telegram lay among the jumble of her contact lens paraphernalia and cosmetics.

She wondered if she could possibly have misread it.

Thrusting her glasses back on, she gingerly unfolded the telegram and studied it again.

CANT COME TO PARIS STOP HOT DATE NAPLES STOP NOUOK PERRY.

No, she hadn't misread it. And it was no joke. He would have called by now if it was. Perry never left her in a dither for long. He definitely was not coming. He had even been too tightfisted to invest in an apology. Bea knew her old childhood friend had supreme confidence she would be understanding. Undoubtedly his NOUOK was penny-pinching jargon for "I know you will be okay," and the closest thing to an apology she would get.

Well, she didn't understand. He had gone too far this time. How could he cancel their vacation in Paris when her coming had been his idea in the first place?

"You can't turn that European Tour prize down!" he had insisted. "It's an honor to earn such a bonus in a national brokerage firm as large as yours. You have to go!"

Bea remembered the conversation clearly. It had been a few months earlier when she had been in Washington, D.C., spending a weekend at her parents' home, and Perry had dropped by to join them for dinner.

"Bea thinks she doesn't deserve the trip," her mother had sputtered. "She thinks her clients just stay with her because of her dad."

"That's garbage, Bea!" Her father had exploded. "Of course, my friends and colleagues initially gave you a little business because they are so fond of you. After all, you've been following me around my office at the bank since you could walk. But I certainly haven't steered any of my bank's business your way. Besides, in the past four years you've built up a substantial list of your own clients. Neither they, nor my friends, would keep reinvesting with you if you had given them bad advice. I've always said you have a natural business sense, baby."

"Of course she has excellent sense," Bea's mother had mumbled under her breath. "Any girl who can earn her master's degree in business at age twenty...."

"I've looked over your portfolio," her father had pressed on. "Wise investment judgments, if a proud daddy can—"

"All right, all right!" Bea had moaned. "So I've earned the trip. I still don't want to go. All the other winners are men, and they all plan to take their wives."

"Ignore the old biddies."

"Their wives are not old biddies, Perry. The problem is me and my job. A stockbroker has to be so discreet about business matters that I'm even careful what I say to men in my own field because I can't take a chance my remarks will be passed on as tips. The habit is hard to break when you're trying to make social conversation. You know how shy I am."

"I hadn't noticed," Perry had leered suggestively. "Besides, you're a great listener. You let me talk all the time! On the trip just ask a leading question, and the men will talk business to you."

"Oh, beautiful! All the wives would just love having their husbands talk shop to the only single woman present."

"I'm beginning to understand Bea's reluctance to go," her father had said thoughtfully. "I've probably been overzealous in teaching her to be discreet in her conversations. But because she's known so much about my business dealings, I couldn't chance our bank's affairs being spilled by my own daughter. And there's an added stickiness to these business-social situations, Perry. Even I am very careful when Bea's mother can't accompany me; wives and husbands can read too much into an innocent friendly remark. Bea's probably right. She doesn't know any of these other winners, and she probably wouldn't have much fun."

Undiscouraged by her father's long speech, Perry had looked steadily at Bea, his brow crinkled in concentration.

"You say this three-week tour is a prize to twelve brokers across the country showing top profitability last year. You can bring guests at your own expense, but everyone has to go at the same time?"

"Right, the first three weeks in July. But I am *not* going."

"July! Now just a minute." He had drawn a battered note pad out of his pocket. "Where will the group be the second week of July?"

"France. Why?"

"I've got your problem solved." He had grinned boyishly and stuffed the pad back in his pocket. "You don't have to spend the whole time with your tour group. You can drop out in the middle and hole up in Paris for ten days with me!"

"I can't afford your solution, Perry," Bea had laughed. "Or won't, that is. You're saving all your military pay to start your own posh law firm once you get out of the army. The last time we went out for dinner, I had to buy your steak."

"But I gave you lots of kisses to make up for it, remember?" Perry had grinned unrepentantly, not at all embarrassed by her candor in front of her parents. "Besides, I'd pay my own way. I'll be in Europe anyway. I'm the lawyer assigned to defend a soldier in a court martial in Rome early in July, and I've already planned to remain in Europe another ten days. I'd rather spend the time in Paris with you than wander around Italy by myself."

"You'd leave her stranded the first time a pretty face came your way," Bea's mother had observed fondly, not really meaning it. Perry's parents lived next door to them, and his ill-fated loves had been a family joke since he had been a tiny boy.

"Leave Bea stranded? Never."

That's what Perry had said. She remembered distinctly! He would never leave her stranded.

"Never, hah!" she raged.

Restlessly she wandered around her small hotel room, not quite knowing what to do next. Then, horrified that she could feel tears gathering, she flopped down in the comfortable velvet chair near the open window to force herself under control. A warm evening breeze brought in with it the smells and sounds of Paris. The geraniums in her window box had a sweet scent that blended temptingly with the odors of cooking from the hotel kitchen below. Her room was above a courtyard, so the sounds of downtown traffic were muted and almost inviting. Unfortunately these subtle impressions only served to remind her how anxious she had been to set out and stroll through the city with Perry; and now she was alone.

It bothered her that she was so upset by Perry's defection. Until that morning she had not consciously realized how much she had been looking forward to his companionship. But it was apparent upon reflection that just knowing they would be together had made her more relaxed throughout the first week of the tour and had given her a confidence that lessened the awkwardness of being the one person traveling singly.

She realized that she had really let her life get in a rut if this little thing could throw her so much. But she was suddenly so lonely! She tried to recall the last time she had gone out with a man for dinner. With the pressures at work the past four years, it had frequently been easier to retreat to her New York condominium with *The Wall Street Journal* than to summon the energy to accept a date or to renew contacts with married friends. And the invitations had been coming less and less frequently as a result.

Of course there was the possibility she wasn't really lonely—that her pride was just hurt. If she had not told everyone she was meeting a friend in Paris, and even arranged to introduce him to them, she would have nothing to be embarrassed about.

She groaned as she wondered what her acquaintances on the tour would think when she explained Perry's absence to them. Her favorites, an elderly couple named Drake who reminded her of her grandparents, would probably be concerned about her. But that terrible Mrs. Bascombe would be delighted. "What happened to your friend?" she would undoubtedly coo with the false sweetness everyone in the group had come to detest. Bea had never really claimed Perry was a great romantic interest; she had just said she was meeting a friend in Paris. But people had known her friend was a man, and had assumed...and it had been so convenient.

What hurt most was to admit to herself that she had enjoyed having everyone think she had a man of her own. She had even begun to believe her affection for Perry had deepened into something else.

Disgusted, she walked over to the desk and picked up the telephone. The first thing she would have to do was cancel her reservation for the Lido. She wasn't in a party spirit by any means.

Her face burned with embarrassment and dread as she dialed the operator and asked to be connected to the tour director's room. Even though she knew Perry had had no reason to worry about her because she would just remain with the tour, it hurt dreadfully to have to admit to others that her dearest friend had stood her up. And the remainder of the tour would be awkward at best.

But you don't have to remain with the tour!

The idea occurred to her as she listened to the repetitive ringing. She was a more-than-competent businesswoman; she had lived alone, gone most places alone the past four years. Why couldn't she do it in Paris? Everyone said you could always find someone who spoke English.

The idea began to take shape that she wouldn't really have to lie about Perry, just say they couldn't make the show. Then, if she stayed out of sight for ten days and rejoined the group in Brussels, no one would ever be the wiser.

Bea knew such subterfuge was childish, but it became more and more appealing. No one would have to know! In her shattered state of hurt and loneliness she didn't believe she could stand that additional battering to her pride.

"*Madame*, your party does not answer." The

hotel operator finally broke into the line, apparently convinced that Americans must be ignorant of the workings of the French phone system.

Mechanically Bea reseated the phone on its old-fashioned base, panic rising in her throat. She was certain she could carry off the mild deception in a private conversation with the director. But if friends came looking for her when she didn't show up, she knew she might fall apart and blow the whole thing.

With no clear plan for finding the director in mind, Bea hastily grabbed her purse and fled from the room. She turned the huge key back and forth in the lock with an exaggerated care quite unnecessary for the few possessions she was leaving behind. But the door was the ancient kind, which did not lock automatically, and she wanted to be certain the room would be secure when she returned.

She glanced at her watch as she fumbled with the lock and was aghast at how long she had daydreamed in her room since receiving Perry's telegram. It was almost time for the cocktail party that had been arranged for their group in a room just off the lobby. The director was undoubtedly down getting things ready, and there would always be the few habitually early arrivals with him.

It seemed best to take the back stairs; perhaps no one would notice her, and once she'd located the director she could have a bellboy give him the message.

Feeling an increasing sense of urgency, Bea jerked the key from the lock and began following the signs that indicated an exit. Her sandals made a soft slapping sound, emphasizing the surrounding silence. No one was around.

Most people were probably in their rooms, she thought, dressing up for dinner, just as she had done. Her soft crochet dress clung provocatively to the full curves of her body as she moved, reminding her by its very sensuousness that she was a fool.

She had certainly got carried away with the magic of Paris. The romantic atmosphere of the city encouraged her to indulge her feminine nature. And she had responded pleasurably—she'd taken a bubble bath and covered herself in dusting powder, put on the yellow dress she had talked herself into buying because she knew Perry would like it, let her hair fly loose for the same reason....

Eager woman jilted. It was humiliating.

Embarrassment again swept over her in great waves as she carefully made her way down the steep, narrow stairs at the rear of the hotel. When the flight abruptly ended in a corridor at the mezzanine level she was feeling so sorry for herself that her head drooped, and her feet dragged along as if unattached to her body. Moving in a direction she hoped might bring her to the final flight reaching street level, Bea shuffled along, preoccupied with concern about what she would do with herself for the next ten days.

She was not aware that a well-built, sandy-haired man had emerged from a room just a few feet down the hall, a suitcase in his hand. He studied her somewhat suspiciously before setting the case by the open door and disappearing back into his room. If Bea ever heard his movements, she merely instinctively hugged herself closer to the wall instead of looking up.

And it was thus that she did the impossible.

Noisily. With unbelievable clumsiness.

She walked directly into the suitcase and sprawled unglamorously. Her involuntary shriek of outraged pain was only slightly less loud than the thump of her body and the suitcase both falling to the floor.

"Mon Dieu!" a tall, blond woman cried out in alarm as she came running through the open door. Bea stared up dumbly at her. She realized she was being addressed in French and could sense the woman's well-meaning concern, but could not get any sound past the shocked lump in her throat.

"Mathilde?" The man's voice preceded him, but it was not until he reemerged from the room, his attractive face registering disbelief, that Bea became humiliatingly aware of her position. She couldn't seem to untangle her legs from the top of the suitcase. Her skirt was hitched well up her thighs, and the deep neck of her dress had twisted around to reveal much more cleavage than the daring designer had intended.

Dimly aware that the woman was fluttering about, chattering in excited French, Bea couldn't seem to tear her gaze from the man. He was ruggedly handsome, probably ten years older than Bea, tanned and fit looking. He wasn't much taller than the blond woman, but his shoulders were so broad beneath the coarse weave of his tailored suit that from Bea's vulnerable angle he appeared a giant—a very displeased giant, tensed as if ready for a fight.

He kept looking up and down the hall, as if expecting additional troublesome women to arrive.

Bea lay there stunned, thinking incongruously that she wished she had taken time to put in her new contact lenses, because with no makeup and her thick glasses tilted crookedly on the end of her nose, she must look like an old-maid schoolteacher.

Actually she looked nothing of the sort. Her brows were as naturally black as her hair, and her flushed skin caused a glow that highlighted her delicate bone structure. Even the glasses added to her fragile appearance.

The man acted as if he couldn't believe what he was seeing. Finally impatient with the concerned flutterings of his companion, he barked something in French before slipping his hands under Bea's arms. When he lifted her to her feet, it was with such unexpected power that she lost her balance again and collapsed heavily against him, her oversize door key somehow slipping from her fingers to be pressed against his palm as he tried to steady her. For a few seconds Bea was helplessly motionless, enveloped with such a feeling of safety in the stranger's reluctant arms that she couldn't order herself to leave them. Alarmed at her uncharacteristic vulnerability, she began to tremble, and it was then that the man finally settled her firmly on her feet.

He and the woman called Mathilde began ask-

ing her things in French, but she was too be-
numbed to translate accurately in her head. She
mumbled *"Je suis prête, je suis prête,"* which she
thought might mean she was all right, but then
again it might mean she was ready to go. She had
not been very interested in her French course at
college.

That she was not making sense was obvious because the woman was regarding her with puzzled
concern. Bea then began to apologize in English
with a French accent—a totally infantile reaction
that annoyed her, but she couldn't stop.

"I'm fine, really I am, I'm just shaken up," she
stammered, with her compulsive accent. To prove
her point, she stretched tentatively, testing her
tender flesh, not realizing that in her disarray she
was drawing pointed attention to her shapely
body, which was well revealed by the twisted,
clinging dress.

The man was definitely annoyed. His dark
brown eyes raked enigmatically over every detail
of her appearance before he dismissed her with
curt indifference.

"Pour vous," he snapped, handing Bea back
her door key.

The Frenchwoman, obviously his wife, protested when he seemed determined to return to their
room and leave Bea untended in the hall.

"Really, I am all right," Bea reassured her. "It
was all my fault—about the suitcase, I mean."
She pushed her glasses back up on her nose as she
babbled, and the man looked at her as if she were
a bothersome rodent.

"I'll be okay. I'm going now...."

He couldn't have her gone too soon, and with an abrupt nod at Bea, he led his wife back into their room, almost closing the door in Bea's face. As she turned slowly away she could hear the Frenchwoman protesting anew.

Shaken by the fall, Bea regarded this man's indifference as the final insult. Her ego was already hurting from Perry's desertion, particularly because the anticipation of being with him had created such unexpected vulnerability in her. And now came this additional rejection. Bea began to get thoroughly angry. Adrenaline flowed through her system, revitalizing the courage that had sustained her in the four years she had struggled for success in her competitive field. She was a fighter, if nothing else.

I don't have to let myself be treated like this!

Filled with righteous indignation against both Perry and the sandy-haired stranger, Bea altered course and headed directly to the front of the hotel. She couldn't change what had already occurred, but furious as she was, she was certainly equipped to carry off a simple deception that would save face.

When she reached the curving marble staircase that led down to the ground floor, she paused to adjust her clothing and smooth back her hair. Below, she could see that the cocktail party had overflowed into the lobby and that her acquaintances were happily and noisily passing champagne while they took photographs of one another in their elegant evening finery. Picture-taking had seemed a major occupation of the group since they'd left the States.

It was an enthusiastically friendly cocktail party; people not even part of the tour group were joining the festivities, accepting wine and crowding chattily up the stairway.

Deciding against using that route, Bea stepped into the ancient passenger elevator, which was nestled in the curves of the immense staircase. It was a noisy little thing, an open wrought-iron cage maintained, Bea suspected, as much for sentimentality as functionalism. But it was safe enough and even gave an added dash of drama for Bea's purposes, because some of her friends saw her in the picturesque cage and raucously cheered her throughout her descent. There was no way her arrival could go unnoticed.

Conveniently, the tour director was among those clustered in front of the elevator when she stepped out. She made her explanations despite the pandemonium around her, then tried to escape to a rear hall. But her deception was not to be that easy. Someone pressed a glass of champagne into her hand, and someone else wanted her to pose for their picture-taking, and soon she was dragged into the midst of the party. No one seemed surprised her date was not along.

And before long, Bea learned why.

"My dear, we just heard your young man has arrived late." Bob Drake, the man who reminded her of her grandfather, dropped an affectionate arm around her shoulders.

"Late?" Bea squeaked, wondering what garbled explanation the tour director had spread.

"Surely he's not too tired to go out tonight at all?" Helen Drake added her own encouraging pats to Bea's arm. "We'd be happy to wait for you both. We can always skip dinner and take a late cab to the Lido."

"Yes, let's do that! It would be a shame for you two to miss the show," Bob insisted. "I hear they're doing something special because Bastille Day is this weekend."

"Oh, no, you mustn't wait!" Bea protested. "When I agreed we would go along, I didn't think about the timing. I wouldn't want you to miss part of the evening."

"But we want to meet your young man. And it would be no trouble at all. The Bascombes are sharing a table with us, and I'm sure they won't mind holding it."

"What's this about holding a table?" Mrs. Bascombe seemed to materialize from nowhere with her insignificant-looking little husband in tow.

"I just said we should wait for Bea's friend to get ready," Helen explained. "He arrived in Paris late, you know."

"I don't want anyone inconvenienced," Bea said hurriedly. "You see, he's worn out from traveling...." She was waving her arm vaguely in the direction of the crowded reception desk, unable to still her wagging tongue in the presence of the malicious Mrs. Bascombe.

"Are you sure there's a man meeting you?" The

woman's loud, strident question couldn't help but attract attention from those close by. "I've wondered all along. You know, lots of women just plan to pick up a man when they get here."

Bea was speechless at that remark.

But not Mrs. Drake. "That's an unpleasant thing to say!" Her gentle voice edged the closest to criticism Bea had ever heard from her. "Bea's friend just got here, as you can see." The dear lady waved her arm in the same direction Bea had just done, and to Bea's horror, threading his way through the crowd was the broad-shouldered giant she had so recently encountered upstairs. He was apparently heading back to his room for a forgotten item, because beyond him Bea could see his blond wife waiting patiently near the reception desk.

"Surely you don't mean him," Mrs. Bascombe snorted unbelievingly when the impressively handsome man registered recognition upon seeing Bea as he slipped past them to enter the elevator.

And suddenly Bea had had it . . . with the loneliness, with Perry, with Mrs. Bascombe, and curiously most of all with the sandy-haired giant. Why was it so improbable she could attract a man like that? Outraged at the implied insult, she acted without thinking.

"Darling, did you get checked in?" she cooed as she darted into the cage after the startled man. She held the door slightly open so the elevator would not start, while she looked lovingly into his amazed eyes. Confident that the man spoke only

French, she added clearly, "Oh, I must check with the director where I should meet the group in Brussels. You go on, darling. I'll be right up."

"Smile, Bea," someone shouted, raising an ever present camera.

And she flashed an enormous, she hoped loving, smile over her shoulder as she stepped neatly out of the elevator and slammed the door.

Immediately the little cage jerked upward, carrying the incredulous man out of sight. He might not have understood her words, but he had certainly understood Bea's body language, and he was obviously furious.

"He doesn't want to leave you for a minute, Bea," Mrs. Drake sighed romantically. "Now I understand why he doesn't want to rush out tonight. He wants to be alone with you."

"Yes, we will enjoy staying in together," Bea mumbled, anxious to protect herself from any well-meaning visits from tour friends later on. But Bea knew disappointment at parting from her was not the emotion most evident on the man's face. He stared at her with undiminished rage as he was carried out of sight.

Bea scarcely noticed Mrs. Bascombe's jealous sarcasm or the Drakes' placating responses. Mumbling excuses, she somehow worked her way through the celebrating crowd, past the tour director and on to the staircase.

What have I done, she thought in horror as she maintained a breakneck pace up the stairs, determined to reach her own floor before the sandy-haired giant finished his errand and returned to the elevator. The last thing in the world she needed was to run into him again.

She spent the entire, lonely evening in her room, wondering why she had done it. She knew she had only further complicated her dilemma.

CHAPTER TWO

IN HER HASTE to be out of the hotel early the next morning, Bea had left her passport in her room. As she stood at the car-rental desk looking at the empty space in her purse, she was disgusted with herself; forgetfulness was not one of her usual faults. She could visualize clearly just where she had set the document the night before—on the highboy near her bed. And there it remained.

Bea tried all the arguments possible with the agency clerk. He was unimpressed, however, that she had waited a half hour for the agency to open, or that she could produce French francs, an American Express card and an international driver's license. Without seeing that passport he would not let her drive off in his rental car.

Finally there was nothing to do but return to the Royal for the required document.

As she walked the short block back to the hotel she cursed her luck for picking an agency that stuck to its rules. Slipping out of town unnoticed had seemed such a good idea when she had been unexpectedly awakened by the arrival of her breakfast tray.... Stupid mistake she had made the night before, requesting a 6:00 A.M. delivery when she had hung out her menu card. But once the clatter of the tray being placed on the table in her private little entry hall had roused her, she had decided to make good use of her early start. Why not, she had thought, rent a car and resettle in some guesthouse on the outskirts of Paris until her tour group had left town? Then there would be no need to explain the disappearance of the man who was supposed to be her "friend." Bea knew she was just not up to lying anymore.

As long as no one saw her leave, the solution seemed perfect. Bea had collected most of her things in her suitcase, then she'd gone to arrange for a car to be brought to the hotel. But her forgetfulness was now delaying everything.

Still mulling over her plans for the next ten days, Bea was not as alert as usual when she returned to her room. She did not notice that the lock turned much too easily, or that the breakfast tray she had left untouched in the entry hall appeared disturbed. She walked right into the room and tossed her purse onto the bed before she realized she was not alone.

"I see you're packed to leave."

The man's accusing voice reached her just as she heard the inner door being shut and locked. Surprise momentarily closed her throat as she whirled around, immediately recognizing the sandy-haired giant she had claimed was Perry. Warily she watched him, guilt over her own mistreatment of this stranger temporarily numbing the fear she would normally have felt at finding him in her room. He was fully as muscular as she had first estimated, the thinness of his cotton shirt proving there had been no padding under the suit he had worn the previous evening. Her glance moved quickly up the bulging arms and shoulders to his face.

Ice.

No, not a face of ice. More like steam or a well-contained volcano.

His skin was heavily tanned, prompting her critical speculation that he must spend all his time under a sunlamp, lifting weights. Swamped with her own guilt, it gave her strange pleasure to find fault with him.

He was silently examining her in return, his angry gaze registering that her full, trembling lips were the only noticeably vulnerable part of her polished appearance. Her well-cut summer suit hid the voluptuousness apparent the evening before, and her spectacular black hair was tucked severely away from her face.

But even though she now wore her contacts and had put on makeup, he did not seem impressed with what he was seeing.

"You speak English," Bea accused, irrationally on the attack because she did not like the growing feeling of intimidation engendered by this formidable-looking man.

"Californians usually do; we're smart that way." His voice was deep with impatient authority.

Bea moistened her lips needlessly, troubled by the discovery he was an American.

"Why did you let me think you were French?

And how did you locate me?'' she asked, genuinely puzzled.

''I assumed you dropped your key in my hand last night so I would know your room number. Especially since you so conveniently left your door unlocked for me this morning.''

''I forgot the door doesn't lock automatically....''

''Of course you did.'' His tone of voice revealed his disbelief.

Cautiously Bea backed deeper into the room, beginning to feel afraid. ''You've obviously got the wrong impression from my mistake last night.'' She tried to make her voice coolly imperious, but it betrayed her with shakiness.

''Suppose you skip the game and tell me who paid you to do this,'' he cut in icily.

''Who paid me?'' It was not the accusation she had expected. Tentatively she let her hand rest on the desk beside her to steady herself. Something rough littering the surface surprised her, and she jerked her hand away, glancing down to see large bread crumbs stuck to her palm. There was only one way they could have got there.

''You ate my breakfast!'' she shrieked in outrage.

''I hadn't eaten since yesterday morning.'' He was unperturbed. ''Now cut the delays, and tell me who paid you.''

''I don't know what you mean.''

Obviously he didn't believe her, and it was his seething look, rather than any threatening gesture, that alarmed her when he moved toward her.

"Stay away from me!" She shoved him, and he automatically shoved back, his response so overpowering that she stumbled against the bed and started to fall backward. He grabbed her arms, and it was then she panicked completely, striking his face and kicking wildly with her feet.

"Stop it, dammit," he grunted, trying to restrain her flailing body. But her wild struggles pulled him so heavily down on top of her as she sprawled across her bed that her breath expelled in a rush. Absorbing his weight as he fell on her knocked the wind out of her.

"Stop this. You're going to hurt yourself," he commanded harshly, taking advantage of her momentary shock to pin her wrists above her head. Most of his weight shifted to the knee he thrust over her legs as he slightly levered himself up on his elbows. Bea's breath was returning in short, irregular gulps, but her eyes betrayed her. She looked like a trapped fawn.

There was a quick trace of regret in his expression. But only briefly.

"I don't intend to hurt you," he rasped, his breath warming her lips only inches away. "But I have to have some answers from you. Now can you calm down?"

Strange thoughts flashed in confusion. Bea was frightened, and yet she was registering in a calmer part of her mind that his hold on her wrists, while unbreakable, was remarkably gentle; that he was exerting great strength to hold himself above her, sparing her the full weight of his body while still managing to keep her trapped beneath him. She could feel the rise and fall of his chest against hers, could almost measure his steady heartbeat in contrast to the frantic pace of her own.

She was reassured by his apparent self-control, and her change of thinking must have registered in her eyes, for the man gradually began to ease his body off hers, retaining her wrists while still raising himself, then sitting immediately beside her. His weight sagged the bed so much that her thighs rolled intimately against him. She tried to roll away. But he quickly transferred her wrists to one hand and pinned her hip to the bed with the other.

"Hold still!" he ordered. "We have to talk. Tell me why you set me up as your supposed lover last night."

"It was all a mistake." She turned her face away, trying to escape his censure.

His hand on her wrists tightened momentarily, then eased while his other hand left her hip to slide along her jaw, turning her face until she looked at him again.

"Let's try that explanation once more. What were you to get for putting on that scene last night?"

His fingers and palm were rough against the smoothness of her cheek, and even as she tried to fathom the meaning of his question, she was thinking in strange logic that he must indeed either lift weights seriously or do physical work to have developed those calluses.

His impatient snort prompted her to whisper urgently, "I really don't understand what you mean." Any answer more firm was beyond her.

He studied her intently, as if trying to make up his mind about her sincerity, then decisively stood up. Her body almost wilted at this unexpected freedom, so tense had she been, but she remained motionless under his scathing gaze. She knew she was not out of the woods yet.

"What I mean is...this." He pulled a folded newspaper from his back pocket and tossed it to her. It landed with a plop on her stomach, and she felt an acute embarrassment as she struggled to sit and retrieve it.

"I can't read much French," she stammered when she opened the Parisian tabloid.

He took the paper back and shook it out so the front page was squarely before her.

"You're perfectly capable of looking at pictures, though." Any compassion he had felt toward her when she had been trapped against him appeared gone now as his voice resumed the cold stern tone.

Bea leaned back a little to focus her eyes on the page, and as she did so a black-and-white photo stood out—two columns wide and five inches high. The headlines were in French, but she recognized two words: the name John Robertson. The picture was of a smiling woman leaning provocatively against a man, her head thrust back on his broad shoulder, her full breasts and narrow waist almost shrieking for attention from the cameras.

"That's me!" she gasped.

"That's us," he emphasized. "But only my name is used. Why did you do it?"

She glanced up at him in bewilderment before taking the paper from him and looking at it more carefully. There was no doubt about it. They were in the hotel's crazy little elevator, and Bea seemed poured against the man's body, her grin foolishly besotted. The angle of the camera had even altered the man's look of angry surprise to one of eagerness. They appeared to be one step away from bed.

"Who did this?" she demanded hotly.

For a moment he looked uncertain. "Suppose you tell me."

"I have no idea."

But suddenly she did have an idea. She remembered the flashbulbs going off that evening as everyone took pictures of one another; remembered someone yelling, "Smile, Bea." And perhaps more than one flash going off. Perhaps.

"There must have been a free-lance journalist there last night," she murmured. "They've occasionally covered our tour group, looking for a story to sell stateside. Some of our people are rather notably successful and well-known in their own region."

"You're in an American tour group?" He was incredulous.

Her chin thrust up, and she slid along the edge of the bed as far away from him as she could get.

"I wish you'd quit shouting at me."

"Are you actually claiming to be in a tour

group?'' he asked less explosively, but he was just as astounded.

"Yes."

"I don't believe you."

"Well, that's too bad."

"What group?" he pressed.

"Stockbrokers and their wives. We're all annual-incentive winners."

"Whose wife are you?"

"Nobody's. Haven't you ever heard of a woman stockbroker?"

"Why did you give the journalist my name? And what was that, 'I'll be right up, darling,' bit you threw in my face?"

"I don't even know your name, and I don't know about a journalist or this picture. I just told you what probably happened." She hesitated, but as she sensed his continued suspicion, added belligerently, "My date didn't show up. Circumstances were such that it was embarrassing to admit it, and when someone thought you were he, I just acted before I thought."

The breath he expelled was almost a moan as he mumbled, "Do you have any idea what harm your stupid, foolish pride has done? Now people know I'm in Paris with...."

"I didn't think you understood English. Besides, how could my remark have harmed you? Your wife was right there at the reception desk watching us. She knew there was nothing between—"

"I'm not married," he snapped absently, turning away from her and rubbing the back of his neck.

"Oh," Bea breathed softly, the unpleasant implication of what he had just said suddenly hitting her. The woman, Mathilde, was the problem.

The man whirled around, trying to gauge her thoughts.

"I want you out of my room!" she ordered, becoming angry as the meaning of this incident began to make sense to her.

"I have no intention of leaving until I work this out."

"Get out," she repeated firmly as she tried to push past him to the door.

He took no chances of her hitting at him this time. He efficiently trapped her in his arms and pinned her against the wall with his body. "Lady, neither you nor I are leaving until you help me work this out."

"I have no sympathy for you at all." Strangely unafraid now, Bea held her ground verbally even though she couldn't defeat him physically. "If you're going to have an affair with someone else's wife, you should be prepared for the consequences."

"You don't know what you're talking about. I can't have it known I am in Paris."

"It's a little late for that." She tried to squirm into a less uncomfortable position in his arms, since he apparently had no intention of releasing her. "I can't read that caption, but if your name is

John Robertson, there can be little doubt you are in Paris.''

She didn't know if it was her statement or her squirming, but at that he suddenly let her go. She sagged against the wall in relief as she watched him pace around her room, so intent and agitated that she could not doubt he took the incident extremely seriously. She couldn't quite understand why.

"But what harm can I have done you, after all?'' she asked hesitantly, not wanting to indicate she was weakening, but still driven to understand. "Are you worried that the woman...Mathilde was what you called her, wasn't it...that she could be hurt? I assume she has a jealous husband you believe could possibly make trouble?''

He appeared startled at her conclusions.

"But how could he make trouble for her over that newspaper?'' Bea asked. "It would seem to me that the photo proves you are in Paris chasing another woman. If anything, I've helped you both.''

His mind seemed to be changing gears in midstream, and he retrieved the paper to study the photograph's caption again.

"What does it say?'' She looked over his shoulder but still could make no sense of the words.

"Maybe you're right,'' he mused. "I might be able to salvage....'' The idea went unexpressed as he continued to study the paper. Finally he shoved it awkwardly into his hip pocket, then thrust his hand out to her. "I'm John Robertson.''

His change of attitude was hardly reassuring.

She was still saddled with a strange man refusing to leave her room, and she didn't know what he wanted. Limply she touched his extended fingers.

"Of California Robertson, Inc." His look was questioning.

"If you're *that* John Robertson," she murmured pensively, "any broker in our group would at least have recognized your name, and several of my colleagues probably could have identified you to a photographer. I don't deal in agricultural stocks, and even I know your firm." She paused thoughtfully before resuming her slow recitation, as if she was dredging up information from her subconscious. "California Robertson, Inc. The family owns and administers a closed corporation—fruits and vegetables; pays union wages and still shows profit; vertically integrated business from seedlings to canning and freezing; corporation still maintains small, inherited family holdings in fertilizer production and manufacture of irrigation equipment, but the present major thrust is in direct food production and preservation."

She looked up at him to see how she was doing. "Everyone in our industry is speculating on when the family will run out of expansion financing. They'd like your firm to go public so they can get a piece of the action."

"You *are* a stockbroker," he conceded grudgingly, "or else someone has briefed you well."

"I'm not only a broker, I'm a good one," she replied unflinchingly. "And I might add that...."

But John Robertson was no longer listening. He was pacing around her room, so engrossed in thought that he seemed to have forgotten her presence. She had nearly released the night latch when his hand slammed over hers.

"I told you, you're not going anywhere until I work this out."

"I just remembered I haven't eaten since yesterday morning, either," she said haughtily. "I would like my breakfast if you've left any of it."

"I'll get it."

He motioned her behind him and went into the entry hall, making certain the outer door was also latched before he bent down, his eyes on Bea every moment.

"Sit over there," he instructed, not stepping back into the room until she moved.

Bea wanted to hold her ground, but her good sense told her she would never win, that they would both be standing there till doomsday if she made an issue of it. She flounced over to the desk chair.

"I drank the orange juice, but the coffee was already cold when I got here," he explained. "There's a full pot, if you like iced coffee."

"Thanks a heap." Angrily she pulled apart a hard roll and thrust a piece into her mouth, not bothering to open one of the foil-wrapped packages of creamy butter she usually so thoroughly enjoyed. She wondered if she really felt like eating after all. The changing facets of the man's temperament made it impossible for her to know what to expect next.

"How long have you been on this tour?" he asked conversationally as he helped himself to a flaky croissant.

"Oh, how impolite of me," she crooned sarcastically, thrusting the depleted basket toward him. "Do please help yourself to more of my breakfast."

She expected him to be ashamed and to replace the croissant. It annoyed her that instead he said, "Thanks, I will," and almost grinned as he helped himself to the last two hard rolls. With an outraged gasp, she managed to snatch one back before he sat down.

"So how long have you been on this tour?" he calmly asked again between bites.

"One week." Pointedly she moved the roll basket out of his reach.

"I guess you get a little out of touch with the real world on a trip."

"I resent the implication that I am acting in an unbalanced manner."

"Why should I imply that? You made the point so well yourself last night."

"I do not normally behave in such an immature way," she insisted, her face reddening. "I admit it was stupid to claim I knew you. But I don't often feel that . . . rejected . . . and I didn't know how to handle it. I just . . . ."

Her voice trailed off as she read continued criticism in his glance. It was an uncomfortable silence, broken only by the crunching sounds of their eating the hard breakfast rolls, which were impossible to consume quietly.

Eventually he leaned back contemplatively and rather stiffly continued his original train of thought. "Actually I wasn't implying it's your habit to live in a dreamworld. I merely meant one becomes dissociated from current reality when traveling in a foreign country, unless you happen to speak the language of that country." As he talked he brushed the crumbs on his shirt onto the rug.

Bea was having her own problems with the rolls, and she licked off some of the crumbs nestling on her lips. He watched silently as if fascinated by the movements of her mouth. She glared at him, but he was unperturbed.

When she realized he was still waiting expectantly for her to continue his conversation, she decided the man was crazy. But if he wanted everything to appear nice and normal, well, yes—she could play that game, too.

"Foreign tourists do get isolated," she agreed coldly, noticing that he looked annoyingly comfortable in the red velvet armchair by the window. She tried to ease her body into an equally casual-looking position, which was difficult to do in the straight-backed desk chair. "No one in our group spoke or read Spanish well, so we've missed out on a week of media news from home. But then, isn't the purpose of a vacation to get away from it all?"

Bea was merely parroting the words her mother had preached to her as she left the States. "Forget about business for a while, dear. Just have some fun." And Bea had really worked at it. She hadn't even bothered to hunt for an English-language publication.

"So you will be touring France next?" he asked, his alert eyes belying the lightness of the question.

"The group will be touring France in a few days," Bea corrected. "I won't."

"Why not?"

"None of your business."

"Am I going to have to start all this heavy stuff again?"

He hadn't moved, but she could sense the readiness in his powerful body. Feeling slightly threatened, she sat up primly in her chair and abandoned any pretense that they were carrying on a normal conversation. He was not going to give up until he knew everything.

"I was to be met here by an old friend. We were going to see Paris on our own for ten days until I rejoined my tour group in Brussels."

"And he was the no-show date?"

"So to speak." She told him about her firm's incentive prize. "I wasn't even going to accept it until Perry talked me into meeting him in Paris. He's one of the few people I feel completely at ease with."

"What happened to him?"

At the memory of her desolation upon receiving Perry's cable, Bea's self-control slipped. Not quite trusting herself to explain without her voice faltering, she retrieved her purse, which had been knocked to the floor, then silently handed him the telegram.

"NOUOK?" His expression was puzzled as he stood up, reading it.

"I assumed it meant, 'I know you will be okay.'" She tucked the cable back in her purse and watched as he began pacing around the small room. "As I said, he is a longtime, childhood friend."

"Some friend, to leave you stranded in Paris."

"That's what I thought." Her voice broke despite her best efforts to put on an uncaring front.

He was noticeably chagrined at her distress.

"Why don't you feel at ease with people?" he snapped brusquely.

It took her a moment to realize that his harsh question resulted from her earlier remark about Perry. She thought it over, wondering how to answer that. She'd have to be a psychiatrist.

"I'm familiar with your brokerage chain," he continued when she didn't reply. "To win that incentive prize you're obviously extremely successful in a field I know is rough. If you're that good at your work, you must at least appear to be at ease with people."

She was upset that he doubted her word.

"You manage a huge family enterprise and come from generations of businessmen," she countered. "Aren't you careful in your social relationships, discreet in every word you say? My father is a Washington, D.C., banker, and he taught me that lesson before I was even a teenager. I can't imagine your family didn't do the same with you."

"So you depend on childhood friends like that louse when you want to be yourself," he surmised, beginning to look angry again. "Wasn't it out of character for you to publicly announce to a perfect stranger that you'd join him in his bedroom?"

"I told you, I didn't think you spoke English!"

"You didn't think, period. Have you any idea what a disaster you've...."

"Don't moralize! You're hardly blameless yourself, running around with a married woman."

"I'm *not* running around with Mathilde." He noticeably tried to control his temper before he added sarcastically, "Doesn't your sharp tongue ever run down? You're remarkably willing to be yourself with me."

She didn't try to defend herself, to explain that rarely did she ever say harsh things to anyone. Under the circumstances, he would never believe her. She waited silently for him to explain what he wanted with her, watching as he sat on the edge of her bed, his concentration intense. There was little else she could do than wait anyway, since he effectively blocked her way to her door. She wondered if even he knew why he had come to see her.

"Look," he said gruffly. "I believe you had no malicious intent when you set me up for that picture. But you've put me in a bind. One you may not approve of, but pressing nevertheless. And I need your help to get me out."

"The bind you're in is your own fault."

"You owe me," he emphasized quietly. "Your scene in the elevator saves you the embarrassment of admitting your man didn't show up. Now I want you to help me out of the problem you've created.''

"It wasn't your intention to help me."

"But you used me. Now I'm going to use you."

She stared at him belligerently, wanting to refuse him outright. But she had just enough of a guilty conscience about her deception the previous night to make her hesitate.

"What help do you want?" She was finally resigned to hearing his proposition.

"You gave me the idea just now," he said pensively, beginning to pace the room again. "Even though it's already known I'm in Paris, I might still be able to camouflage my reasons. It would help if certain people believe I came here to play around with the delectable woman in that picture—you."

Astounded at being called delectable, Bea stammered, "Certain people like your Mathilde's husband? Don't expect me to believe you weren't running around with her, because I saw the two of you come out of the same bedroom with a suitcase."

He seemed about to deny her accusations, then snapped his mouth shut. She couldn't read his thoughts as he remained silent for some time.

"I am concerned about Mathilde's husband, but not the way you think—he's. . .ill."

"And both you and Mathilde are worried about that," she said sarcastically.

"Yes, we are." He seemed to be choosing his words carefully.

"The three of us have been friends since child-

hood, and I admit Mathilde and I had dated some
before she married her husband. But it was never
anything serious and still isn't. Since he's been
sick, though, he keeps accusing us of resuming our
affair. Their friends in Strasbourg don't believe
anything is wrong because he usually acts normally around them. They don't know he's tried to kill
himself twice. Mathilde asked me to meet her in
Paris because she doesn't have any family left,
and she needs advice from someone who under-
stands him, knows what he was like before.''

"This still isn't believable,'' Bea said stubbornly. "Why couldn't she just have talked with you
long distance? Or even in Strasbourg?''

"I told you, he's depressed and suicidal. He's
upset when she sees any man. She's been staying at
his side almost constantly, except for coming here
supposedly to attend an art preview. But instead,
we saw doctors and described the change in him
over the past few months. They're certain the
cause of this irrational behavior is medical, and
that they can find it. Since he refuses to see a doctor, we're now going through the legal means to
get him into a hospital. But we need time for that
to go through. If he gets a notion Mathilde saw me
when she was in Paris. . . .''

"You really believe he'd commit suicide?''

"I believe he might try it, if he gets a chance
alone. Now will you help me?''

"But why can't she just show him that picture
of you with another woman?''

"He might still think she saw me in Paris and
didn't tell him. And that would upset him. I al-

ways go see him or call when I'm in France, and I haven't this time. I tell you, he's not reasoning clearly. We can't take that chance.''

"I still can't be of any help," she said hesitantly.

"Yes, you could. Be seen in public with me for a few days.''

"In public? You mean, here, in Paris? What would that accomplish?'' It seemed too easy.

"If I call him right away and tell him I'll be down to see them soon, but I'm tied up in Paris with lady business, it might allay his suspicions about Mathilde and me if he saw that picture. And if mutual friends here see us together, they might pass that on to him—or even better, if there's another picture of us in the paper, he'll be more comfortable around me when I do go there to help get him into the hospital.''

"You're saying that even if he had such proof of your interest in another woman as this picture, he might still suspect Mathilde of having an affair with you in Paris? Her husband's dangerous!''

"Only to himself. More accurately, he's ill. Will you help us?''

Bea's eyes narrowed as she tried to analyze the situation. John Robertson's square jaw appeared particularly prominent as he looked back at her unflinchingly, his worry all too apparent.

So the man can feel concern about another human being...just not about me, she thought with a pang. Guiltily she recalled how compassionate the elegant Mathilde had been to her during their brief encounter, despite John Robertson's disinterest.

"If Mathilde's husband is that badly off, she should find a quicker way to get help for him," Bea said, weakening.

"There isn't a quicker way. And she's staying with him constantly until we get this worked out. I don't want to make the situation any more difficult. Now will you help me or not?"

Bea tried to think what procedures might be used in such a situation in the States. But then, French law might be different. She felt confused.

"I don't know if I can carry it off," she mumbled. "I'm no good at acting."

"You did a hell of a fine job for that photographer," he accused, reaching for his newspaper to prove how convincing she had been.

"Don't show me that again," she protested. "I know what the picture looked like. But you'll remember it was your name, not mine, in the headlines. If you're such a jet-setter that you make the tabloids, surely you can set up some publicity without my—"

"I'm not a jet-setter. I don't know why I made that paper—the only publications I'm ever mentioned in are *Forbes* and *The Wall Street Journal*. In fact, I'd hoped your tour director might arrange with his PR man for some pictures of us together...."

"That's a ridiculous idea!"

"I don't care how ridiculous it is if it works!" He had grasped her by the shoulders and was shaking her slightly in his earnestness to convince her.

"All right, all right! I'll do it—" she struggled out of his arms, disturbed at his overpowering closeness "—be seen with you. But for how long?"

"Three or four days?"

"Three days exactly. But I won't ask for publicity pictures."

"That might not be such a good idea after all," he mumbled. "It would probably be more convincing to act as if we're avoiding publicity, as if it were an illicit thing. I'll think about it. Right now you stay here, and I'll go get us a larger room; then you can—"

"Wait just a minute," she objected, running to grasp his arm as he moved toward the door. "I'm not sharing a room with you."

"This has to look convincing. What kind of an affair do you think two adults have?"

"I'm not sharing a room with a stranger. The deal's off."

"Lady, I have no interest in you, but we're sharing a room. I'll get two connecting if I can, separate beds for sure, but this is going to convince the public and Mathilde's husband that we have a torrid romance going."

As she balked at the determination in his voice, they heard the knock at the door. Bea froze. But John Robertson was perfectly in control; he calmly went into the entry hall and began to unlatch the outer door. By the time the confused Bea could reach him, he had flung open the door, and she was face to face with Helen and Bob Drake.

"My dear, we didn't mean to embarrass you,"

Mrs. Drake apologized as she read her own inter-
pretation into Bea's stricken face. "We just wanted to invite you and...your friend to join us on
the city tour today."

Bea couldn't seem to get any words out.

"I'm John Robertson." The giant effectively
intervened and thrust his hand toward the elderly
couple. "It's kind of you to think of us, but actually I was just going to the desk to see if I
couldn't get us resettled in a suite. My room is two
floors down, and I'm not crazy about...her...
being up here alone. Frenchmen do admire beautiful women, you know."

"I thoroughly agree, son." Bob Drake shook
John's hand approvingly, not at all shocked by his
announcement. "You can't be too careful these
days. In fact, we've tried to keep an eye on the little lady ourselves during this trip."

"I appreciate that. And your names are?"

"Drake," Bea squeaked, her vocal cords almost
atrophied.

"It's a pleasure, Mr. and Mrs. Drake." He was
easing the kindly couple out of the doorway even
as he shook Helen's hand. "I'll walk on down to
the desk with you. You say you're going on the
city bus tour this morning? Is there a chance...
she...might do some sight-seeing with you tomorrow morning? I have a business appointment, and
I hate to leave her unescorted."

"We'd love to, John," Helen Drake said enthusiastically, allowing him to take her arm. Bob
pulled the door shut behind them.

Bea was frantically reaching for the knob when

John swung the door back open, hitting her hand with a resounding thud.

"Ouch," she moaned.

"What's your name?" he hissed as he stuck his head inside.

"Beatrice Allen." The response was automatic.

"No nickname?"

"No," she lied.

"Beatrice! My God!"

The door slammed again on his remark.

She stared at it like a zombie, its decorative carving around the knob and center panel dancing before her eyes. *What's wrong with Beatrice,* she wondered belligerently. She didn't even try to run after him; she needed to think. Everything seemed so unreal, as if it couldn't really be happening.

But it is real, she told herself, frustration beginning to replace her confusion. *I have just been tricked into living for three days with a total stranger.*

She mulled the situation over, struggling with her conscience as to whether the difficulties she had caused the man really warranted this solution.

There's got to be a better way to clear this up, she thought decisively, as she gathered up her few remaining things and stuffed them in the suitcase before closing and locking it. There were parts of his story that didn't sound quite right, but she seemed unable to sort it out in his overpowering presence. The thing for her to do, she decided, was to go back to her original plan to rent a car and establish herself in a guesthouse. Once there, she could contact him and have him explain the situation more completely. Hurrying so she could slip down the rear stairs before he returned, she hitched her purse on her shoulder and went to the highboy to get her passport. Surprised that it wasn't there, for she seemed to remember so clearly that spot as exactly where she had placed it, Bea began opening the empty dresser drawers. Then it took her all of five minutes going through the things in her suitcase before she figured out what had happened.

John Robertson must have taken her passport from the highboy before she'd arrived.

A cold logic seized her mind. It was only in the movies that women were forced into situations like this. She would confront him at the front desk and calmly announce she wanted her passport returned, or she would have the clerk call the police. He couldn't refuse. Resolutely she picked up her suitcase and purse and marched to the elevator.

There was one fatal flaw, however, in her plan.

As the open elevator slowly lowered her to the lobby, John saw her descending. He had time to slip behind the large potted plants near the stairway before she could see him. If Bea had realized he was no longer at the desk, she would have been prepared for a private confrontation. But when the elevator stopped, and he popped inside as if from nowhere, she was momentarily speechless. And that was her undoing.

"Darling, you didn't have to come down," he said loudly enough for any hotel guests wandering in the lobby to hear. "It only took a second to get our new room." As he spoke he pressed the up button.

"I want my passport. I'm not staying here with you."

Bea tried to reach around him to stop the elevator, but he grabbed her hand before she could touch the button. Once the elevator jerked upward, she started to call for help, but he sensed her intention and awkwardly pressed his mouth against hers. At first it couldn't even be dignified as a kiss—he was merely chasing and entrapping her lips to silence them while he edged her into a corner where he managed an immobilizing embrace. But when she continued to try to wriggle loose, she found both arms pinned as he covered her mouth with a passionate kiss.

Or at least it must have appeared passionate to the spectators Bea could hear commenting delightedly on the scene. To her it was shocking—particularly because she was so helpless. The pressure of his relentless mouth seemed to go on and on; and when he moved one hand up to hold her head, she was unable to turn away. Angrily she tried to stiffen her lips under his. He sensed her fury, and at that his hand at her neck eased slightly, and his lips moved even more compellingly over hers, urging her to give up fighting him.

She never quite understood how he managed to get her off the elevator without once taking his mouth from hers. Despite her determined struggles he had maneuvered her out of the little cage, then kept her pressed against him until a guest finally summoned the elevator to another floor.

And only then did he stop kissing her. Her mouth and body were so numb she was still trying to catch her breath all the time he was pushing her down the hall and inside a nearby room.

"I admire the way you keep your promises!" His fury seemed to match her own as he carefully locked both doors behind him.

Bea stood in the center of the room, trying to work her throbbing lips.

"My promises to you didn't include sleeping arrangements," she finally said.

"I didn't ask for any. I bought us the closest thing I could get to a private suite." He appeared a bit confused for a moment when he noticed there was only one double bed. But at the front of the room near French doors leading out onto a balcony there was a small alcove. An antique writing desk was visible beyond. "Come on, let's see what we have here," he urged, seizing her arm as he walked around the bed.

Beyond the arch was a small room, also with its French doors to the balcony. Tucked in the back corner was a narrow single bed, well out of sight of the other room.

"So here's your private quarters," he snapped, releasing her and walking past her to throw her suitcase on the luggage rack. "Sorry we don't have a door you can close, but I did the best I could."

Bea wondered how he had managed to pick up her suitcase while he was forcing her out of the elevator. Or had she still been holding onto it throughout the entire unbelievable incident?

Feeling was beginning to return to her persecuted body. "I hurt all over," she blurted accusingly.

"Serves you right. So do I."

Only then did she notice his own mouth appeared to be swelling as quickly as her own. She felt malicious satisfaction that at least he had not come out of his macho demonstration unscathed.

Impatiently he walked over to the French doors and threw them open. The traffic of the busy rue de Rivoli was deafening, and just as quickly he closed the doors. "I suppose these balconies are cool and nice at night. But the sleeping inside may not be the best with the noise. I tried to get us something at the back of the hotel, but this was the only suite they had left."

"Why didn't you look up my name when you took my passport?" She ignored his explanation.

"No time. I found it just as you came in." He didn't even bother denying he had the document. "By the way, the Drakes are nice people."

"I want my passport back." She refused to be sidetracked.

"No deal, Beatrice Allen."

"I can get another one, you know."

"Yes, but it will take a few days. And that's all I need from you. Three or four days."

"I could just walk out. You're going to have to turn your back sometime."

"True. But I'm counting on your sense of justice once you think this thing through. You owe me."

"You sound like a broken record."

"Just think about it. You must sense that I

don't intend to hurt you. But I had to shut you up before you ruined our chance to pull this off. I only dragged you back here just now to make you take time to think fairly. You know you've put me in a position where I need your help...."

As he spoke he was wandering around the room familiarizing himself with everything: the view from his balcony, the bathroom facilities, the telephone table.

"Ah, good. A minibar!" He interrupted his activity when he discovered a small refrigerator beneath the curtained bottom of the bedside table. "Do you suppose they have mineral water in here? I've never learned to drink Parisian water."

Bea watched him rummage among the bottles.

"No water," he groaned, unaware of her amusement. "A Coke will have to do. Want one?"

She shook her head as she watched him open the bottle and take two enormous gulps. The bed sagged beneath his weight as he sat on its edge, leaving the bottle on the table. Then he leaned over and began untying his shoes.

"What are you doing?"

"Our public appearance is going to have to be postponed until tonight. I have an afternoon appointment, and I can't even think coherently anymore. Lord, I'm tired." He kicked off the shoes, drank the remainder of the Coke in two more gulps, then stretched across the bed.

"How do you know I won't leave?" Bea asked.

"I refuse to manhandle you anymore," was his

only reply as he leaned his head wearily against the pillow and closed his eyes.

She stood hesitantly for a few moments, just looking at him. Then for lack of a better idea, she, too, began exploring their quarters. In her alcove she noted that her own satin bedspread matched the brightly colored spread and flocked wallpaper of the room where he lay. The carpeting was a deep-pile Oriental pattern, more elegant than what had been in her single room. She pulled aside the tissue-thin curtain covering her own French doors. Creeping red geraniums overflowed a planter box on the balcony. Two small chairs and a cocktail table completed the intimate setting. Beyond the bulk of the Louvre and its surrounding buildings, she could see the flowers of the Tuileries, and beyond that, the Seine.

Bea sighed sadly. All this beauty. And she had no one with whom to share it. She wondered if loneliness, not guilt, was what had made her even consider helping John Robertson. Things still didn't hang quite right about his story. There had been such an air of understanding and, yes, commitment between him and Mathilde that she couldn't accept his claim they were not intimate. And she wanted no part of a mess like that.

Still undecided, Bea walked back into his room.

She had read somewhere that men looked like little boys when they were asleep—young and vulnerable. How wrong!

John Robertson, asleep, looked fully as formidable as when awake. Her plundered lips throbbed sympathetically as she looked at his swollen mouth—a mouth ruthless even in repose. In fact, the man's body at rest still dominated the room.

It occurred to her that if he and the lovely Mathilde ever worked out their troubles, they should never have a mere double bed; he claimed too much of it.

She walked over to the closet. Empty. Didn't the man even have a suitcase?

Resolutely she picked up her own suitcase and, with her purse over her shoulder, strode to the door, opened it noisily, then walked well out into the hall where she remained five minutes or so testing if John really meant it when he said he would not prevent her from leaving. Eventually walking stealthily back into his room, she discovered him unmoving on the bed, wearily watching her return. His reproachful look made her feel even more confused—and guilty.

"There are things about your story that don't hang true," she blurted, standing angrily over his bed.

"Such as?" he inquired cautiously, not moving from his relaxed position.

"The first thing you asked me this morning was who paid me. If all you're worried about is a sick, jealous husband, why would you assume someone had paid me to set you up for that picture?"

"Why else would anyone have pulled what you did? I had to get it straight. For all I knew you could make it a habit of trying to blackmail tourists. There are women who do that, you know."

She didn't know. She wished she was certain he was telling the truth.

"What's his name?"

"Whose name?"

"Mathilde's husband. The man you're supposed to be so worried about."

He hesitated momentarily before saying, "It doesn't matter."

"I don't believe there really is a sick husband. If you live in the States and they live in France and they only see you occasionally, why would she seek your help instead of friends here? Surely someone in France knows him as well as you; this is hardly a convenient time of year for you to be leaving your business, just for a childhood friend who could get help elsewhere. What's the truth about this husband?"

He didn't want to tell her. She could feel his disgust that she was pressing the issue. Resolutely Bea turned, awkwardly balancing her heavy case as she swung the inner door back open. It was obvious she really was going to leave this time.

"Robertson is his name." The answer was almost mumbled. Grudgingly. "He's my brother."

She dropped her case with a thud and whirled around to look at him. He was staring at the ceiling, his eyes tortured, his jaw clenched as if he was in pain.

"Your brother?"

"Yes! Are you satisfied now?"

"But I thought your family all worked with your firm. What is he doing living in France?"

"He's the only one of us who never took to agriculture. He's a professor of French literature at the University of California and a visiting professor at French universities. When he's working in France he headquarters in Strasbourg because we have relatives there, and it was Mathilde's family home, too."

"I see," Bea said softly. This time she was convinced he was telling the truth. Only a family connection would create such a problem as he described. She wondered, briefly, what it would be like to have a sibling to love and worry about. Her attachment to her own parents and grandparents gave her some idea of the lengths to which people might go to protect a brother or sister. In a pang of lonely understanding she empathized with John Robertson, and the decision seemed out of her hands. Of course she would have to stay with him.

Not saying anything more, she closed the door and replaced her suitcase and purse on the luggage rack in her room. Then she walked back past John, not looking at him this time, to the bathroom just by the inner door. Two lush bath coats hung on hooks. Since the only other toweling was a small fingertip piece, she quickly made use of that to bathe her lips. When she walked back out, she noticed that John Robertson had again closed his eyes. But this time he looked tense, even in apparent repose. And his exhaustion was obvious. She stared, noticing how out of place his dark slacks and socks were on the quilted satin spread. Her sense of homemaking was offended.

"I ought to take that spread off before you sleep."

His eyes fluttered open. "You're kidding!" His speech was groggy.

"It will only take a minute," Bea insisted, beginning to pull at the pillow sham beneath his head.

Her tugging rolled him onto his side, where he eyed her suspiciously a moment before rising shakily to his feet. The action seemed to require a concentrated effort.

Satisfied, she stripped off the cover quickly, easing it into soft folds and placing it on the luggage rack in his closet. As he watched her, he accepted her homemaking flutterings as evidence that she had decided to stay with him and help him out. The sigh of relief he expelled was more expressive than words.

"I'll never understand women," he mumbled almost incoherently before he again sprawled across the bed and was immediately asleep.

She looked down at his inert form before she moved warily into her own tiny alcove.

He wasn't alone, she thought bleakly, pondering the three days ahead of her.

She didn't understand herself.

CHAPTER THREE

ANDRE'S PRODUCE MARKET looked to be an innocuous enough establishment, no different from dozens of other stores sprinkled among the residential streets of Paris.

Only a few of André Clavier's neighbors saw anything unusual about his little market, but then they were *paid* to observe such things. And it was not the fruits and vegetables, fine as they were, that these people observed.

It was the customers.

For André was a former French mercenary, and it was rumored he had far-reaching contacts to make "arrangements" in any troubled part of the world. Underworld figures in Paris, anxious that such arrangements not be made, occasionally offered a good price to learn about the comings and goings at André's market, for that was their means to infer who might be seeking André's services.

In recent days, however, André had apparently been diligently attending to his vegetables, so there had been no contracts out to keep track of his activities. Even the free-lancers were not attempting to watch the market, for André appeared to be taking his produce business seriously and was hav-

ing all his storage bins on the ground floor
repaired or replaced. The job seemed to take forever, with carpenters and laborers going back and
forth in bewildering confusion. And since this was
antique week at the square only a half block away,
bargain enthusiasts were lazily filling the sidewalks and streets of the entire neighborhood,
visiting, looking at the old homes and wandering
into stores with no better purpose than to poke the
fruit or touch the fabrics. It was impossible to
maintain an accurate list and description of
strangers visiting André's establishment, so even
the most diligent free-lancers weren't trying.

John Robertson found the confusion particularly convenient.

As he walked along the streets of André's neighborhood, he was grateful that it would not be
necessary to wait until after dark to see his old
childhood friend. His encounter with Beatrice
Allen that morning had already sorely taxed his
abilities at deception. When he had awakened
from his rest, she had been in her own alcove,
studiously reading a business manual. Mercifully
she had asked no more questions and had seemed
cooperative enough when he said he would return
from his appointment by the cocktail hour to take
her out for dinner.

But he did not trust his luck too far—not with
an agent of André's caliber. So John took rudi-
mentary precautions to avoid attracting attention
to his visit. His taxi let him off at the museum a
block from André's store, and he stayed inside the
musty building an acceptable length of time, look-

ing at the embroidered altar cloths and enameled crucifixes that the museum featured. Then he wandered outside, feigning interest in a sidewalk display, going into a tobacco shop to purchase cigarettes and almost passing by André's market before appearing so fascinated by the window display of fresh plums that he had to step inside.

There were numerous customers, all of whom seemed oblivious of the noise of the rebuilding as they chatted with various members of André's family who were on duty at the time. So it was a simple enough matter for John to move unnoticed to the rear of the store and, under the cover of workmen repositioning a shoulder-high storage bin, to disappear into the stairwell.

As he climbed the narrow stairs, his face like stone even as his nerves crawled with the urgency of his errand, he was confident he had not been observed.

Upon entering the third-floor attic room at the rear of André's building, he saw that the three men, who were already gathered around a small table covered with maps, were being as cautious as he. Draperies were pulled across the lone window, despite the warmth of the July afternoon. They were taking no chance of being seen.

"I knew Louis would be running out of cigarettes by now," John said in French as he reached into his sports jacket for the pack he had just purchased.

"If that's in the nature of a peace offering, brother, I refuse it," Louis Robertson responded in equally perfect French, taking the cigarettes nonetheless. ''After the trouble Mathilde and I went to for you to assume my identity in Paris, how could you goof it up overnight, John? I assume you've seen this tabloid?''

Accusingly he thrust out the same newspaper Robertson had earlier shown to Bea.

''I saw it,'' John said tersely, throwing his jacket over the back of a chair as he sat beside his brother. A year apart in age, the two looked like twins. Both were of average height with physiques almost stocky, unless one could see them without clothes and observe the layers of muscles on their broad shoulders and torsos. Their facial characteristics were similar, but Louis had the expression of a scholar and was indeed a professor of literature. John, on the other hand, had none of the dreamer's look of his younger brother. He was a quiet man in his mid-thirties with tanned skin and sun-streaked hair, which evidenced that he spent much time outdoors. But no one would have categorized him as a mild-mannered nature lover. His expression was pragmatic, and he had a certain presence as he jutted out his overbroad chin in intense concentration, which indicated he was more accustomed to giving orders than to taking them.

''Mathilde and I had checked into that hotel the day before yesterday—'' Louis raised his voice in martyred anger ''—and made it clear I would be staying on to do research at the Sorbonne while she went to Strasbourg for a visit. Then I leave you the simple task of taking my place to put Mathilde on the train before you go about your secret business. But what do you do? Start chasing skirts. . . ."

John didn't answer as Louis pointed to the picture of him and Beatrice Allen.

André Clavier, the owner of the market, had a certain affection in his eyes as he watched the two brothers. Their grandmother and his own family were neighbors in Strasbourg, and the three had practically grown up together. Tall and ascetic, not a weak man himself, André was as unperturbed by Louis Robertson's volatile temper as was his brother.

"Old friend, I've never thought of you as a womanizer—" André focused on John as he broke the awkward silence "—but you have certainly picked the wrong time to begin. I thought we had all agreed it was crucial to keep your presence in Paris a secret. And Louis and his wife had set up a perfect possibility for you to double as him. Why did you go spreading your own name in the papers?"

"I don't believe I've met him." John ignored the question as he looked intently at the fourth man at the table.

"This is Blanco, my Algerian contact," André explained. "We can speak English, by the way. Blanco, meet my oldest friend, John Robertson, who I am presently ready to disavow."

"Don't mind him." The squat, gray-haired man grinned toothlessly. "André disapproves of me, also, because I keep wives in both Algeria and Paris. But he finds my numerous families useful in situations like this. I can help you."

"Don't help him line up a second woman," Louis snapped. "He's caused us enough trouble with one."

"Shut up, Louis," John said, long familiarity with his brother's quick temper leaving him unintimidated. "I know this publicity has fouled up our well-laid plans, but I think I've salvaged something out of it."

"I can imagine what." Louis quipped sarcastically.

"Louis! The woman set me up accidentally last night after Mathilde and I ran into her on the way to the train. Apparently some idiot in her tour group recognized me and identified me to a freelance photographer."

"Whatever happened," André interrupted, "it's only a matter of time now before some American reporter will be over here hunting you. We've all agreed that once the American press knows an employee of yours is being held hostage in Africa, and that you are in Paris trying to arrange his release, our chances of success are nil."

"You know how neurotic Americans are right now about hostage issues in foreign countries," Louis complained. "There's hardly anything that makes bigger news. The most distant of relatives appear daily on television telling what the hostage was like as a little child. Reporters hound all branches of government and speculate publicly on what they might be doing to free the person. Anyone closely connected with the hostage is followed by hordes from the media, the—"

"We know all that, Louis," André said gently,

not wanting to spare the time for his younger friend's harangue. "We also know John's contact in the CIA said we can expect no official help if this thing becomes public, so we'd do better to bypass the government and make our own arrangements right away. But a rehash doesn't help our present situation."

"You say this Harry Ward accompanied a shipment of your fertilizer to North Africa, but has not returned as expected?" Blanco asked. "Instead you have received a ransom note concerning him?"

"The situation is even more complicated than that, which is why Louis was willing to leave his ivory towers and help me out." John glanced gratefully at his brother. "Harry Ward is one of my best friends and my second-in-command with the firm. We were college friends with Nand Towangi, whose family controls a reasonably fertile strip, almost a principality, northeast of Nigeria. They've been trying to introduce modern dry-land ranching methods to help feed their people, and Nand planned to fertilize and irrigate for fall pasturage this year. But his European sources refused to ship to him because of several terrorist incidents in surrounding areas. He finally came to us for help."

"Which you unwisely gave him despite State Department warnings that those terrorists were moving into Nand's territory." Louis had not yet got his temper under control. "They are a fanatical group hoping to unite all of Africa. You should have figured since they have been driven out of all the neighboring countries, some kind of coup attempt against Nand's country was certain.''

"Towangi specifically needed a large quantity of ammonium nitrate. That's why Louis is so upset John decided to ship anyway,'' André explained to Blanco.

"Ahh,'' Blanco sighed pensively. "The excellent fertilizer product that in the last twenty years has also wiped out half the market demand for dynamite. It ships cheaply and safely as fertilizer, but can easily be mixed with oil in the field to become an explosive.''

"It's no comfort to me how quickly you figured out that potential,'' John admitted. "When we decided to ship to Nand, we recognized the danger if terrorists got hold of it. Harry went along to help put it down on the fields properly. If the terrorists moved in, he was to destroy it before some fool started blowing people up.''

"And did he succeed?''

"That's the critical, unanswered question. I don't think so.''

"Assuming the shipment was taken along with Ward, are you so sure these simple natives will recognize its explosive potential?'' Blanco asked.

"This is what scares hell out of us. Ammonium-nitrate fertilizer is used extensively throughout the United States as an explosive in road construction and strip mining. Any professional blaster will know of it. If the terrorists don't understand what a bomb they've got, the people training and supplying them should soon figure it out, especially if news leaks that a large quantity of ammonium nitrate is unaccounted for north of Nigeria. Louis and I won't allow our family's fertilizer to be used as an explosive against human beings. I have to finish what Harry started.''

"Louis figured since he is never active in the family business," André said, taking up the explanation, "no one would be suspicious of his movements in Paris, even if word of Harry's capture or the missing fertilizer leaked out. So John was to pass as Louis while we made the necessary arrangements to get him and a crew into Africa.''

"I object to your going personally," Louis told John irately. "You don't even know where Harry or the fertilizer are. Let André's professionals go; they're trained for these things.''

"I agree," André said quietly.

"If it were just getting Harry out, I'd agree, too," John admitted. "You'd have a better chance of success without me along. But even if you find Harry safe, he won't leave until that fertilizer is destroyed. Getting rid of this stuff isn't as simple as a layman might think. I have to go in myself to be certain it gets done and to convince Harry to come out. Besides, I have an idea where to start looking.''

He hunched over the map the men had spread out on the table. "We had made arrangements at these designations—" he pointed to locations on the map "—where Harry could get messages out to me. The last word from him nine days ago was that the fertilizer had arrived by truck, and they were to begin putting it on the fields the next day.

But we learned the following day that the terrorists had taken over Nand's whole area and had cut all communication in preparation for a coup against the central government. The next afternoon we got the ransom note.''

"And these revolutionaries just asked for money,'' Blanco asked. "No political demands?''

"I think you're upgrading this group to call them revolutionaries,'' John said. "The best information we have on them is that they are a collection of fanatical people with a vague common goal of uniting Africa under one native leader. They do get some funding and training from foreign sympathizers, but they're so fragmented they never organize with specific goals. A few may go off on their own and contradict what the others are doing. That's what makes it so difficult to handle Harry's disappearance now. Whoever has him apparently wants money to finance their cause and grabbed the nearest foreign businessman they could find as a hostage. But they haven't even got organized enough to recontact us on how they intend to collect the ransom money.''

"Could the ransom note be a hoax?''

"I doubt it. Harry was due back in California six days ago. Were he free, he would have found a way to contact me before now. He's definitely missing, and we can't put off going in there any longer.''

"John, I don't want to belabor your love life,'' André said cautiously, "but I'm afraid you've virtually doomed our project. Since your picture's been in the Paris papers, you can bet if any French terrorists are tied in with this African group, someone will be following you by nightfall. They'll want to be sure you're not planning to bypass their ransom demands and will take every means to stop any rescue attempts. You can't risk meeting me anymore, but Blanco and I need at least two more days to arrange for our crews and equipment. Now coordinating with you would be impossible."

"I've installed a scramble phone in my suite for communicating with my office," John argued. "I'll give you each matching incoder and decoder units you can use in any telephone jack. They're small enough to carry in your briefcase."

"In that case I don't think the problem of communication is insurmountable, André," Blanco said thoughtfully. "And if we need to pass anything directly I could serve as go-between. I don't usually do this type of work, so no one should be suspicious if they see me near John."

"Even if we fool the terrorists, the publicity will kill us," André told Blanco with concern. "I've seen those hordes of American newsmen in action before. At best, the American government will fear an international incident and try to stop us. And at worst, some newsman will spread the word about the missing fertilizer."

"Wait a minute—there may be one thing in our favor for a day or two." Louis had miraculously calmed down and was looking over the tabloid again. "Maybe the press only knows Ward isn't home yet; they may not know about the actual kidnapping. Listen to this caption: 'American agribusinessman John Robertson callously cavorts with a luscious woman in Paris—' ''

''I think you're taking a little too much liberty in your English translation of that French,'' John objected, his face reddening.

Undaunted, Louis continued his colorful translation:

. . . callously cavorts with a luscious woman while allowing a trusted employee to rot helplessly in Africa. Mrs. Harry Ward has sought the assistance of her congressman in locating her husband, who was due home six days ago from an African assignment for Robertson's company. The area in which he was working is currently under terrorist siege, and Mrs. Ward fears he is the victim of foul play. Robertson's office has refused to give her any information, and Robertson himself apparently prefers to tend to the needs of Parisian brunettes instead of the needs of missing employees.

''Libelous scandal sheet.'' John showed his first danger of losing his cool.

''But you see,'' Louis said triumphantly, ''there's no mention about kidnapping, and— even better—nothing about the fertilizer. Just that Harry's wife is upset because he's not back.''

''Whatever possessed your office to let this woman talk to the press?'' André asked. ''Surely they could have kept Mrs. Ward properly informed. . . .''

"She's not Mrs. Ward anymore. They've been divorced three years, and Harry never dreamed she maintained any interest in him or his whereabouts. Since he has no other family, we hadn't anticipated anything like this. I was en route to Paris when Carole Ward contacted my office, and they just tried to put her off until they could reach me. By then it was too late; she had talked to her congressman."

"So don't you see?" Louis insisted, "it's probable the free-lancer had heard about Carole Ward's inquiries; and when someone in that tour group recognized John, he probably took the picture and added a juicy caption, hoping the wire-photo service could sell it to a California paper."

"If it made the Paris papers, someone knows something," André asserted.

"But that particular tabloid is a real rag, André," Blanco said scornfully. "They always run a front-page picture of a half-dressed woman. It's possible they just had a light story load this morning and liked Miss Allen's sexy looks; I would guess they had little or no interest in John."

"It isn't the interest from the French press we're most worried about, Blanco. Wire services now know where John is. If news leaks out about the ransom note, the American press will be hotfooting it over here, looking for John, asking what he's going to do about it. We don't have a dream of a chance of passing him off as Louis now. And heaven help us if the press starts speculating about that missing ammonium nitrate. John's only hope of preventing some deaths is for the terrorists to remain ignorant of what that fertilizer can do.''

"Now just a minute!'' John exploded. "Listen to my plan. The American press may know I'm here, but they don't have to know I'm trying to arrange Harry's escape.''

"What else would you be doing, leaving the States at the peak of your business season?'' Louis asked reasonably.

"Chasing that skirt, as you said.''

"I thought you didn't know the woman. How. . . .''

"I've located her and talked her into staying with me for three days. We'll go to every public place I can think of and put on a big show of—''

"How'd you talk a stranger into that?''

For the first time, the rock-hard face of John Robertson had a sheepish look.

"What did you do, John?'' André asked, his concern unexpectedly giving way to amused interest.

"Not what you apparently think,'' he snapped. "Actually she had seen me coming out of Louis's hotel room with Mathilde. When she learned I'm not married, she jumped to the conclusion I'm expecting trouble from Mathilde's husband.''

Louis Robertson burst out laughing.

"You mean she's trying to save you from Louis?'' André was having trouble controlling his own grin.

John looked uncomfortable. "No. She was perfectly willing to let Louis have me—said I deserved it. So I had to think up something else.'' They all waited expectantly.

"You have enough of my plans to go on," John continued, disregarding their unspoken question. "I'll have my office say we shipped dry herbicide to encourage the growth of nutritious pasturage in Nand's region, and that Harry administered its application and has stayed on for a while. They can indicate privately he's on a drinking binge; he won't mind. Since herbicides aren't chemically adaptable for blasting, no one should suspect explosives are missing. That's our biggest concern. If the press here asks me about Harry, surely the woman and I can distract them long enough for you to complete your arrangements and—"

"Oh, no, you don't." Louis was grinning widely. "Not another plan gets made until you explain what you told that woman." Blanco and André quickly nodded their agreement.

"Are we going to get down to business or not?" John insisted coldly.

"My friend, your brother is almost a Frenchman in temperament as well as having a lovely French wife," André said grandly. "He should spend all his time here, for he knows, as any good Frenchman knows, that business can always be conducted. But one has to hear the urgent stories of life first. Don't be so American."

Red crept up John's neck, but the three men were unmoved.

"John, we really should know what you told her, if we ever have to cover for you." André was suddenly serious.

Rebelliously, John stared him down some moments before capitulating.

"I got the idea from hearing my secretaries describe those soap operas," he mumbled. "I told her Louis was temporarily depressed and suicidal and that we were trying to commit him for treatment. She thinks he is insanely jealous and if he learned Mathilde and I were in Paris at the same time he might hurt himself. She agreed to be seen with me to forestall Louis's suspicions until we can get legal papers—"

"She believed that?" Louis and André were both astounded, and interrupted his lengthy explanation. But Blanco was openly enjoying himself. It was his kind of solution.

"She didn't quite believe it. But when I told her Mathilde's husband was my brother, she agreed to go along with my suggestion. I think she's quite family oriented."

"From a soap opera?" Louis was hooting. "Mathilde will never believe this of you, John. She thinks you're too straitlaced."

"Now can we get on with our arrangements," John insisted angrily. "Beatrice Allen is no fool, and I'm not going to be able to keep her at this more than a day or two. I'll trip myself up somehow."

"If you can trust her, maybe you'd be better off to tell her the truth," André said quietly, finally comprehending the extent of his friend's intense discomfort.

"That would just endanger her. I've got Harry and all those potential victims of my fertilizer to worry about; I don't want Beatrice Allen on my conscience, too. She's safer if she knows nothing."

"Then your plan is to party around the city with this woman," Blanco asked, "so if the American press does show up and raise a hostage issue, you will appear uninterested in Harry Ward?"

"That's right. I think my reputation with responsible American media is such that if I appear unconcerned about Harry, they will believe there's no real problem and go home. I might have a few scandalmongers hanging on, but maybe this woman and I can give them enough to gossip about so they forget about Harry. Hopefully I can buy us the additional few days we need without a major hostage scandal or a leak about the missing fertilizer."

"Your hanging around town with a woman should ease any suspicions the terrorists might have that you are going to attempt a rescue," André conceded. "But you can't arrange the necessary bank drafts and currency exchanges with the press or terrorist spies at your heels."

"I have an appointment tomorrow morning to see the family's Paris banker at his home. But he's a friend I call on every time I'm in Paris anyway, so if I'm convincing enough when I'm with Miss Allen, that one visit shouldn't cause too much suspicion. When I see him, I'll get the drafts for the money we know we need now. And I'll arrange for Louis to have access to all my personal funds. He should still be able to travel around Paris without being watched and can take care of our future money needs."

"I hate to take that responsibility with your assets."

"Just do it, Louis. Use every penny I have, if need be. When the time comes, we'll figure out some way to slip me out of Paris undetected. Maybe Louis could take my place here at that point."

"With that woman?" Louis couldn't resist saying with feigned eagerness. "Don't tell Mathilde."

"I'll have Miss Allen safely on her way by then." John was not amused by his brother's humor. "I've already put enough lives in jeopardy."

The others immediately settled back into serious planning, the sense of personal responsibility behind John's concern sobering them all.

They worked more than an hour longer. No one was convinced that they had all eventualities covered by then, but considering the heat, their weariness and John's commitment to get back to the hotel, they were all willing to stop.

"You understand where to meet Blanco to pass on the bank drafts?" André asked John as they walked to the stairwell.

"We'll find the place tomorrow afternoon. I'll have Miss Allen with me."

"And I can probably slip a message to you at the hotel, if necessary. I know the maids." Blanco's grin was irrepressible.

"In a dire emergency, I suppose we could all meet at an office at the Sorbonne," Louis suggested. "They're always willing to make one available to visiting academics, and I could slip André and Blanco in early. It shouldn't seem too unnatural to the press for John to call on his own brother in Paris."

"We'll keep that in mind," André agreed. "In the meantime, John, you do a convincing job with this Miss Allen."

"That should be a pleasant task, old man." Never serious for very long, Louis whomped his brother's shoulder encouragingly.

"Very funny," John snapped.

"If one is to believe the newspaper pictures, she's a gorgeous woman," Blanco said. "You'll probably fall in love with her."

"Among the things I don't need right now," John asserted gruffly, "in fact the very last thing I do need right now, is to fall in love with Beatrice Allen." He nodded curtly to the three before quietly descending the stairs.

CHAPTER FOUR

SINCE EARLY MORNING there had been a peculiar, contained excitement emanating from the masses of people filling the Parisian streets, an excitement not fully appeased by the precision of the parade or the speeches of dignitaries at the one-time site of the infamous Bastille.

The weather was perfect for the all-day celebration—sunny but slightly cool, an unusually delightful combination for France on its most special of days, the Fourteenth of July—Bastille Day!

Bea breathed the words in awe, oblivious of the rush of traffic around the Place de la Concorde as she stood with Helen and Bob Drake before the square's central obelisk denoting peace and harmony. It was difficult to imagine the guillotine atrocities that had taken place on that very site. All morning, since leaving the hotel, Bea had felt immersed in history. The Royal had proved to be an ideal location from which to start the celebration of the French independence day, for it was directly across the street from the original Louvre palace. To the west of the Louvre were the Tuileries gardens, the site of the palace besieged by the Revolution in 1789 and later destroyed, and beyond that was the Place de la Concorde, where they were standing. Just by turning her head, Bea could see the Seine or the avenue des Champs-Elysées.

"Don't you feel we're standing with ghosts from many generations here?" she asked quietly.

No sooner had she said the words than she felt foolish and stole a quick glance at her companions to see if they thought she was too fanciful. But Helen and Bob Drake appeared as moved by their surroundings as she. When Helen spoke, she, too, sounded almost reverent.

"It's hard to believe that Marie-Antoinette and Louis XVI were virtual prisoners in their palace here after the Revolution broke out." Helen looked back over the restored gardens. "Do you realize we've been walking on the very grounds where they fled from the hysterical mob? I have never visualized the Tuileries like this, so...." She groped inadequately for words.

"Normal?" her husband prompted wryly, aware of his wife's tendency to romanticize history.

"I expected it to be dismal." She was unaffected by his teasing. "But have you ever seen such gorgeous flowers? And the grass! So incredibly green and full of life."

"I rather imagine the starving people of Paris saw it otherwise," Bob said grimly.

"I read somewhere," Bea interjected, "that at the start of the Revolution, the nobility and clergy of France owned two-thirds of the land, even though they made up only two percent of the population. That's an unbelievable distribution of wealth and power."

"And in addition to that," Bob added, "they paid very little share of the heavy taxes. It was inevitable that the common people would revolt."

"But the bloodbath they created!" Bea shivered as she looked around at the graceful buildings lining the gardens on one side and the Seine on the other. "Revolution seems such a waste. You'd think people with the intelligence to accumulate wealth would also have the intelligence to find equitable solutions."

"France's problems didn't end with the Revolution." Bob's lifelong love of French history was apparent in the expression on his wizened face as he looked thoughtfully toward the Louvre. "Those old buildings endured centuries of extravagant French kings, but think of the horrors they've survived since then, especially in our century...Hitler...and even back in World War I, the enemy was within artillery distance of this capital."

Noticing the solemn intentness of his listeners, he realized that his train of thought was putting a distinct damper on what had been until then a laughter-filled morning, and his face suddenly broke into a crinkling smile.

"Bea! Did I tell you about my great adventures in Paris in World War I? What an impressive and swinging young man I was then, if I do say so myself. Ladies fought for my underwear on the Champs-Elysées!"

"You're not going to tell that story again, are you?" his wife groaned in mock horror, taking

Bea's arm in an unspoken plea for help to cross the busy Place de la Concorde.

"But Helen, I just have to ask him," Bea gurgled as she tugged the spry old lady safely through the hectic traffic to the foot of the Champs-Elysées. "I can't look at this elegant street and not wonder about that underwear!"

"And more important, who took it." Bob Drake breathlessly caught up with the women. "Ah, it was so nice to be young then, attractive to the ladies, debonair. . . ."

"Don't let him pull your leg like that, Bea. Great lover, my eye. He was a baby. He'd lied about his age to get into the army, of course. I doubt if he was even shaving."

"I was, too! Once a year."

Bea laughed, marveling at how Bob Drake had maintained his sense of humor, as well as his health and business ability at an age when most men had long since retired. He still operated a one-man brokerage branch in a small city in Montana.

"I just have to know the shocking truth about his underwear," she apologized to Helen.

"The only shocking thing about it was that he didn't change clothes for a month," she said, remorselessly forestalling her husband's eager words. "As his unit was being transported through Paris after the Armistice, they hit an obstruction in the Champs-Elysées and his duffel bag rolled out of the pickup truck in which he was riding. His laundry was literally spread out at the foot of the Arc de Triomphe."

"The awful thing about it was the driver wouldn't stop." Bob took over the storytelling. "And once the Parisian women saw all those abandoned clothes, they were fighting the traffic and one another to get something free. I guess they had been deprived of goods too long. My buddies razzed me unmercifully about just who was wearing my underwear."

"I'm sure they did! That's funny, but rather sad, too—for the Parisians, I mean." Bea took both their arms companionably as they began making their way among the crowds along France's most famous avenue where the incident had taken place so many years earlier. "I'm glad we're seeing Paris in happier days. And I'm glad you asked me to join you to watch the Bastille Day parade this morning. Seeing it was much more fun with company."

She flashed a grateful smile to both her companions, then eagerly lifted her face up to the cooling wind, unaware that the breeze ruffled the wisps of hair that had slipped out of her braided knot. In her relaxed enthusiasm, she looked about sixteen years old.

Bob Drake's face softened as he watched the two women, so apart in age but so similar in their childlike appreciation of the holiday carnival spirit around them.

"Seeing Paris with you two girls," he said, "has helped this jaded old man recapture some of the awe he fclt when he first visited France in 1918."

"Thank you for including me as a girl, dear." Helen Drake patted her husband's hand. "It's a shame Bea's John had to leave the hotel so early this morning and couldn't see the parade with us. I know he would have enjoyed it. Don't you think the French far outdo anything in the States?''

"I think you were overimpressed with all those young, handsome gendarmes in their dress jackets and white gloves," he teased his wife. "Bea and John have undoubtedly seen just as many policemen lining the streets of Washington and just as many limousines of diplomats."

"I have seen some spectacular parades," Bea verified. "But I must admit the French have a certain panache. . . . ''

The unique style of the French hardly needed comment from either Bea or Helen. For evidence of it surrounded them in all directions. Everything seemed to attract the women's interest: the red, white and blue banners decorating the broad avenue; the variety of displays in the fashionable shop windows; vendors who offered wares from all over the world on blankets spread on the sidewalk. Many visitors had retired to seats in the numerous outdoor cafés to watch the other people. And that looked like a delightful pastime in itself. But since Bea and the Drakes wanted a closer look at the Arc de Triomphe dominating the far end of the avenue, they resisted temptation and continued their slow progress among the tourists. Helen and Bea set the pace, for Bob was content to let the sun warm his aging back as he kept an eye on his two excited companions.

They had been strolling and stopping, then strolling and stopping again for some time without coming much closer to their eventual goal, when Bea casually glanced at her watch, then gasped in astonishment.

"Didn't you plan to get in line at the Opéra before one? It's already five after."

"I didn't realize so much time had passed." Helen looked anxiously at her husband. "Do you think we'll be too late to get seating?"

"I have no idea how early people line up for these free tickets," Bob admitted. "It's a once-a-year occurrence, and I would guess the French will jump at the chance to see their national ballet perform...."

"I wish it was a regular show, and we had been able to buy reserved seating," Helen sighed. "This is the only chance I'd have to see the interior of the Opéra building. And I did so have my heart set on it. They say the artwork is beautiful."

"It's only a few blocks from here. Get on along, then," Bea urged, leading them toward the corner. "You can probably still get in."

"We hate to leave you alone, dear," Bob Drake replied, hesitating. "Are you certain you won't join us?"

"No, I saw the ballet perform last night. John took me there when your group went to the Crazy Horse, then we went on for a late dinner. I can heartily recommend it; both the dancing and the Opéra building itself are well worth seeing!"

A shadow crossed Bea's face as she recalled how strained the previous evening had been. John Robertson had spoken very little unless answering a direct question. He had been bitterly disappoint-

ed that during their visits to the ballet, a gourmet
restaurant and a cabaret, they had attracted absolutely no journalistic interest, nor had they seen
any of his brother's friends. His fierce preoccupation had ruined any pleasure Bea might have
gained from their spectacular outing.

"You'll not be on your own all afternoon, will
you?" Bob misinterpreted Bea's reflection for
loneliness.

"Oh, no. I'm meeting...him...for lunch."
She tried to force herself to look pleased and anticipatory even as she stumbled over John Robertson's name. She had trouble ascribing a personal
identity to his remote temperament.

"It's already lunchtime. And my dawdling has
kept you from seeing the huge tricolor at the Arc
de Triomphe." Helen looked conscience stricken.
"I was going to guess how many yards of material
were in it. And they only hang it this once...."

"You really must be going!" Bea laughingly
tried to rush them on their way, touched by their
concern. "I'll walk up and see the tricolor by
myself."

But still both Bob and Helen hesitated, torn between their desire to get on to the Opéra and their
reluctance to leave Bea on her own.

"Look, I'll be fine...." Seeing that they were
still worried about her, she impulsively added, "If
your tour schedule allows, perhaps we could all
meet for a drink before we go our separate ways
tonight. John and I aren't leaving to see the fireworks until nine."

Maybe her mention of being with John reassured them. At any rate, her invitation did the trick, and they accepted eagerly before rushing on their way to the Opéra.

Bea was greatly relieved. In fact, she had spent quite some time after their departure sight-seeing contentedly by herself before having second thoughts about the invitation.

She had wandered underneath the awe-inspiring arch built by Napoleon and craned her neck to study the numerous decorative sculptures on it. She had marveled at the immense proportions of the unique French tricolor billowing majestically from beneath the famous monument, then retreated against one wall to study the faces of the cosmopolitan crowd, which mirrored her own contentment with her surroundings.

But as the time approached for her to meet John for a late lunch, she began to worry about her impulsive invitation to the Drakes. If he refused to join the Drakes for a drink, the elderly couple might be hurt, and she wouldn't forgive herself if she let that happen. Their concern about her happiness had been touchingly genuine. Like a family's.

"Me and my big mouth," she mumbled under her breath as she reluctantly left the Arc de Triomphe and began the search for the café where John had asked her to meet him. She was feeling increasingly that she had been a great fool to get involved in this escapade with him.

WHEN BEA AND PERRY had been children playing at their families' summer cottages in Michigan, they had loved guessing games. At first the games were serious and often led to actual fights, which one or the other mother had to stop, for the youngsters were well matched. But later the games had become fun, a shared inside joke between especially close friends. Invariably Perry would be the one to start it all, by unexpectedly telling her some outrageous fact about a person nearby. Sometimes he actually tried to guess something factual about the person under scrutiny and would insist on betting whether he or she was closer to the truth. Since they could rarely verify the facts he chose, Bea would keep the betting low. She always took great pleasure in picking out the dirtiest pennies in her coin purse to pay her losses.

As Bea looked around the busy café after John had given the waiter their lunch order, she regretted that Perry was not there with her. He would have had such a wonderful time, for there were all kinds of people to watch and guess about. Out of habit Bea began cataloging them in her mind. There was the overweight woman with two youngsters all sharing one sandwich. *They've already spent their food budget for the trip.* There was the bald man with the vicious scar over his ear. *A foreign spy. Too easy!* And the extremely sophisticated French woman in her Yves Saint Laurent summer-weight suit. *Stood up by her American lover.* Perry would have picked that description. Bea would probably have countered, *No! Ignored by her executive French husband and looking for an American lover.* And Perry would have liked her idea better and jokingly threatened to volunteer. . . .

She abandoned her attempts to amuse herself. Ten minutes had gone by since John had glanced across the small table and said his only words to her, "What would you like to eat?"

Bea was definitely bored.

"Where did you learn to speak French so well?" She asked the question idly, deciding it was time for another attempt at conversation.

"Ordering lunch doesn't require proficiency," John responded disinterestedly.

"I've heard you converse before, and I can hardly distinguish your accent from a native's. You don't learn French that well in American schools."

"My grandmother was French."

"And you learned from her?" Bea was disappointed at the abruptness of his answers.

"In a way. I've spent many vacations here. You pick up the language fast playing with French children."

"I take it your grandmother's no longer living."

"Of course she's living."

"You said she was French."

"Oh, that. She's an American citizen now; but my grandfather died when I was a baby and since then she's spent summers in France. She owns homes in both countries."

"Is your. . . friend. . . French?"

Robertson had started looking around the café again, but at her question his eyes darted back to her. "My friend?"

"Your sister-in-law, Mathilde. I liked her, by the way."

He hesitated before answering tersely, "Yes, she's French."

Bea had to force herself to continue the line of questioning in the face of his reticence. But she was anxious to know more about a situation that was increasingly involving her.

"Did she live near your grandmother? Is that where you and your brother became acquainted with her?"

"I don't intend to discuss Mathilde or my brother."

His reply was so coldly blunt that Bea didn't bother to pursue the subject further. She would learn nothing. Anger began to well from deep within her. It was bad enough that the man actually expected her to jump at his bidding with so few explanations. But it was insulting that he thought she should do so while at best he ignored her, and the rest of the time appeared bored by her company. She wondered what, if anything, he would be willing to discuss. The previous evening she had tried business topics, the weather, even French history. And nothing had broken the silences for any appreciable length of time. Bea was a quiet person herself, but he carried it too far even for her.

She closed her eyes briefly, not liking the emptiness she felt. She was beginning to think she had already paid back her so-called debt to John Robertson simply by enduring thirty hours of his aloof company.

The afternoon was still cool, and Bea, perhaps doubly chilled by her emptiness of spirit, moved her chair slightly to take better advantage of the changing direction of the sun. Its warmth felt soothing to her body, and she leaned her head back beneath the shade of the sidewalk canopy as she thrust her tired feet into the sunshine creeping under their little table. It felt marvelous.

"It's a good thing I wore low-heeled sandals today. I've never walked so far among such crowds in my life!" She wriggled her toes deliciously.

John evidently heard her remark, for he acknowledged it with an absentminded "Mmmmm," but he was obviously disinterested in learning how she had spent her morning. His great square chin jutted forward as he appeared to concentrate on troubled thoughts.

Under the shade of the canopy his profile was somewhat indistinct, his face very brown. She wondered irrelevantly how he managed to maintain his tan and have any time left for business. But just as quickly she knew he couldn't possibly be neglecting his business, for she remembered reading that he had been running the family corporation for several years. Quite successfully. His father had retired in favor of growing roses, and an older brother preferred the scientific side of the enterprise.

Now that would be something to see, she thought glumly—this stolid, unsmiling giant taking a tour of his father's prize rose gardens. Talk about the bull in the china shop. And yet.... The mental picture intrigued her as her eyes roved over his muscular physique. Occasionally she had thought she had seen traces of gentleness and humor in the man. She watched him thoughtfully, wondering what kind of personality he might exhibit under other circumstances.

For some time he sat motionless, apparently relaxed, but Bea sensed that his body was poised, storing energy until his powerful muscles were needed. When a jovial group of people began moving two tables together next to them and needed more seating to accommodate their party, he had sprung up to help them so quickly that Bea had been startled. But once he had given a squat, gray-haired man in the group the extra chair from their table, he shifted his own chair to Bea's side, then sat motionless, staring out at the street.

Bea watched the new people next to them with envy. She couldn't help but reflect nostalgically that were Perry with her, she and he would be equally jovial, perhaps even playing his silly guessing games about their neighbors. Her mind ran whimsically. Since the people were short and swarthy and spoke French fluently, but with an unusual accent, Perry would probably announce that they were definitely Parisians. Which obviously they were not. She supposed her reply would be that they had to be former colonials, perhaps Algerians, because of their darker skin. And Perry would accuse her of reading too many *National Geographic*s as a child and thus making unsound judgments. He would not be above tapping the gray-haired man on the shoulder and asking. . . .

"Why are you so pensive?"

John's clipped question startled her out of her reverie.

"I don't know. Lonely, I guess," she murmured without thinking. The instinctive answer was too close to the truth. At that moment her feelings were so similar to the dismal emptiness she had been fighting for some months before Perry had talked her into taking this trip, that it alarmed her. Damn Perry—what she'd give for someone she could *talk* to! What was it about human beings, she wondered, that made them need the physical and mental companionship of at least one other like-minded person.

John Robertson was watching her with apparent concern, and that alone seemed so unlike her concept of his character she found herself staring at him. His brows had been sun bleached as blond as the streaks in his hair, giving his dark brown eyes a look of extreme intensity—hard to read. His prominent nose, slightly irregular as if it might have been broken in an athletic injury, contributed a masculine imperfection that heightened the impression of raw danger about him. Bea could visualize the man as a restless eagle ready to pounce on his prey, and yet there was his unexpected solicitude. She looked away in confusion.

"Maybe I haven't been very good company," he ventured.

That was an understatement, Bea thought.

"It's important that someone see us, or that our picture be published again," he emphasized staunchly. "I've had that on my mind."

"It isn't going to work, you know. At least not

the way we're going about it. It's all too obvious we aren't interested in each other.''

"What do you mean?''

''I mean no one would take us for other than what we are: total strangers. We won't stir up any interest among your friends or press photographers.''

"Strangers can still be lovers.''

Her stomach tightened at the throbbing conviction in his voice.

''Not and act the way we do together,'' she reasoned. ''This just isn't going to do it for you. We should call it off.''

"What should I do to succeed? Make passionate love to you on the streets?'' He drew her toward him as if that was exactly what he intended to do.

''I didn't mean. . . .''

His eyes were amused as his hands slid down to her elbows, and his thumbs began a restless, circular motion on the inside flesh of her arms. ''I think this is one of your ideas I might learn to like,'' he said suggestively. Then he leaned closer as if he planned to kiss her.

"Stop that!''

Bea freed her elbows, but he managed to slip an arm around her shoulders so that she could not move completely away.

"Hold still,'' he ordered softly. ''I'm just going to kiss you a little.'' His arm was heavy against her, and she felt the slight roughness of afternoon stubble on his jaw as he began to nuzzle her neck.

''I wasn't suggesting anything like this and you

know it,'' she hissed breathlessly, trying to avoid his roving mouth. "People are looking!"

"Wasn't that the idea?"

He had given up trying to catch her on the mouth, but he was doing an excellent job of nibbling at her earlobe. Alarmed that he was unexpectedly adept at displaying ardor, Bea managed to pull away slightly. "You're making me angry. While I have sympathy with your brother's problem, I think you should give up this idea. You're not going to get your publicity and we're both miserable trying."

"I'm not miserable." He slid his chair closer, still holding her by one shoulder so that she had to fit alongside his body.

"I am!" The words came out louder than she intended. Realizing that the people at nearby tables were beginning to notice them, she lowered her voice and tried to look as if nothing was wrong. "I agreed to help you because I felt guilty,'' she said with thoughtful emphasis, unnerved by his nearness. "I've done my best, but you haven't tried to help your cause along. You've ignored me to the point that I feel...." Her vocabulary of disgusting traits had suddenly left her.

"Feel what?" he prompted gently.

"Like a...nerd!"

She could hardly have picked a more ineffective word.

His face suddenly crinkled into a wide grin, then he laughed out loud.

"A nerd!" His amused exclamation attracted even more attention to them.

"Be quiet!" she whispered, aware of the people watching them with interest. "And quit laughing at me."

But even in her embarrassment she was suddenly motionless against him, only then realizing this was the first time she had seen John actually let a smile reach into his soul and come out in the depths of his eyes. The effect was devastating.

"Surely a nerd isn't too bad?" he said gruffly, his dark eyes sparkling with some secret thought. "I'm glad you're not beautiful. I'd rather have you. . . ."

"You see what I mean?" She was becoming angry again. " 'You're not beautiful.' " Her voice mocked his. "Do you normally feel it's necessary to announce that to every ugly woman you meet?"

"You know you're not ugly." He actually seemed troubled that she had taken offense at his remark, his hands roving over her shoulders and arms as he looked into her eyes. "But beauty is a fashion-magazine perfection I find boring. I. . . ."

"Oh, leave it!" Bea tried to ease her chair away from his. His changes of moods were more than she could handle.

But John was not going to leave things there. He mercilessly drew her back. "I didn't realize you expected this to be fun."

"I didn't expect this at all," Bea corrected. "If you recall, I had other plans for Paris."

"And what had you expected to do in Paris?"

he asked in growing irritation. "Shack up with this NOUOK character?"

"Perry would have taken me sight-seeing!"

"I've taken you sight-seeing."

"I'm surprised you noticed I was along."

"I was very aware you were along. You wear a unique perfume."

"Now you're insulting my scent!" Her voice rose in outrage.

"I'm the one who's been abused." The tone of his voice was accusatory. "That perfume is disturbing, sensuous. Frankly, it's not the sort of scent I want my woman wearing when I have other responsibilities on my mind."

"Your woman apologizes." Her sarcasm did not go unnoticed.

"What are you so upset about? I can't even talk to you without you...."

"Oh! Have you been trying to talk to me? A real conversation? I'm sorry I didn't recognize the attempt." Bea tried again to free herself, by then not caring that the people next to them were gleefully enjoying the scene she was creating.

Robertson apparently didn't mind their audience, either, for he was almost arm wrestling with her until he trapped her fingers under his.

"Let's start at this lover relationship again," he suggested urgently, tightening his grip.

"We're not lovers."

"We're lovers. If I put my mind to it, I can be a good...."

She was never to know what he intended to say, for just then the waiter arrived with their order.

His presence reminded them forcibly of their surroundings, and they both lapsed into silence, John drawing Bea's hands into his lap as the man began placing their food on the table. The young waiter took his job seriously, moving with gallant flourish as he placed the small bowls of steaming soup in front of them, then set out the plate of cheeses, crusty French bread and a basket of fresh raspberries. Bea watched him in amazement, his attempts at grandeur under the circumstances both ludicrous and touching to her. The very normality of it seemed to calm her clouded emotions.

"Shall I pour your wine now?" The man addressed John. But at his polite question the gray-haired Algerian next to them answered with a long French explanation, which the rest of his table found amusing. The waiter grinned fleetingly, and even John smiled broadly before he nodded for the wine to be poured.

"What did...."

John deftly transferred both her hands to one of his before touching her lips to silence her. He drew her intimately closer. "They think I should fill you with wine to make you behave," he whispered lightly into her ear as his fingers ran down her cheek. "There was more, of course. Do you really want me to translate it all?"

She glared at him, but he just grinned and shrugged his shoulders before turning away to sample the wine. Upon his nod of approval the waiter filled Bea's glass, then topped off John's.

"You're going to hurt his feelings if you don't sample his wine." John released one of her hands and cocked an eyebrow toward the man who was poised before Bea.

She hesitated, annoyed that John was pointedly caressing her other hand in his lap.

"I think you'll like this," he explained almost conversationally, his eyes twinkling when he realized his fondling disturbed her.

"The wine, I mean, Ms. Allen. It's a light red, but still dry."

Well aware of the double entendre and also of the deliberate provocation with that Ms. Allen, Bea tried to make her hand rest easily in his while she took a sip of the wine. Her approving smile to the waiter was as charming as she could make it. The man seemed greatly relieved as he moved on.

"Forgive me if I find your change of moods puzzling." Bea tried to sound as sophisticated as possible once they were alone again. "First you don't know I'm around, then minutes later you're calling me Ms. Allen, yet acting as if I'm extremely desirable. I'm not a good enough actress to adjust to such a variety of roles."

"I'm determined to be a convincing lover for you, Al."

Her eyes widened at the nickname, but she refrained from objecting, knowing he wanted her to resist. Calmly she took another sip of the wine.

"Nothing to say?" He leaned over and brushed her wine-moistened lips with his own.

The light kiss caught her by surprise, and when she responded with an involuntary "Oooh," he kissed her again.

"What do you know," he murmured contemplatively. "Wine tastes better secondhand. Care to try it, Al?" He took a drink from his own glass, and she couldn't help staring briefly at his own strong, moistened lips. Tempting!

Insanity. She turned her head away.

"Al is a ridiculous nickname for a woman." She decided instead to accept his challenge of the name.

"It's a logical shortening, Ms. Beatrice Allen," he insisted, looking down at her slender, ringless hand as he turned it palm up and slowly circled her softness with his thumb. "I'll be damned if I'll call you Beatrice. The name sounds like a Wagnerian opera."

"Of course you must know my friends call me Bea."

"I understood you to say you had no nickname." His voice was slyly triumphant.

And suddenly she couldn't help laughing. He was worse than Perry. A little boy having to win his special game. In this mood of his, it was hard not to accept him.

"I concede this match. Please, Mr. Robertson. Please call me Bea."

"So it's Bea and John," he said softly, bringing her hand to his lips and kissing each fingertip. Her face was becoming stormy again, and she was about to insist he stop patronizing her now that he had won his way, when he abruptly released her. "Hungry, Bea?" His polite remark was almost businesslike.

Disoriented once again, she nodded her head,

reaching for some raspberries almost in hopes that the rough texture of the fruit in her fingers would abolish the sensuous tingling left by his kisses.

They ate in silence for a while; but this time, heartened by John's brief show of humor, Bea did not find it as uncomfortable as previously.

"Paris does strange things to one's reasoning," she eventually said as she set aside her soup bowl.

"Really?"

"I can't imagine that I would be in quite this situation if I had met you in any other city in the world."

"How does Paris make it any different?"

"Oh, the city of brotherly love idea, I guess. Maybe I'm more predisposed to trust a strange man here."

"I don't think 'brotherly' goes in there. Wrong city. And am I supposed to be complimented at being called a 'strange' man?"

"You know what I mean. Under normal circumstances, in the United States, for example, I wouldn't consider cooperating with a stranger in a situation like this. Maybe I'm just feeling enough cultural shock to believe in any fellow American, at least in one I've known something about through business. I really think there must be some better way to look after your brother's problem; but I suppose if you insist this is best, I'm willing to trust your judgment. However, you can take it easy on the ardent-lover bit. Just a friendly smile and a little cooperation could do wonders for our image."

John's expression sobered as he listened to her.

"I'll do better, and I appreciate your help more than you'll ever know. But don't be quite so trusting of any other men you see in Paris. If anyone follows you, or behaves toward you in any way that is worrisome, be sure and tell me immediately."

"That's a strange thing to say. Why would anyone do that?"

"Well, you're a lovely woman...."

"Come on, that wasn't what you were meaning at all."

"Just be on the watch for yourself, as you normally would be in the United States. Don't let Paris go to your head."

Bea reached for some cheese and began nibbling delicately at it, more to cover her own confusion than out of hunger. It was obvious he was warning her not to become interested in him, not to take any flirting he might do seriously. And she wondered if she had appeared anxious for his lovemaking. The thought annoyed her, but she refused to stoop to denying the unspoken accusation.

"Just take good care of yourself, and...."

"I do get your point, John. Don't worry about it," she said coldly.

"Now who's destroying our image?" he said gently. "I'm just trying to avoid causing you any problems, and you get mad. As you said, just a friendly smile and...."

"I know—cooperation." She was rather proud of herself that she managed a half smile. As they finished their meal, Bea tried to maintain a light conversation matching his. They were both struggling, but she was determined not to let on how much his warning not to become interested in him had hurt and embarrassed her.

They were working on the last of the wine before it occurred to her that she had not yet brought up her invitation to the Drakes to have cocktails with them that evening.

"Since we're being so polite and cooperative with each other," she said hesitantly, toying with her wineglass, wondering how best to word it so she would get her way. . . .

"I have a feeling I should say no before you begin." He surprised her by teasing with a slight grin.

"Actually I do have a favor to ask," she admitted.

He raised his eyebrows in questioning response.

"Not a big one. I'd just like you to go with me to meet the Drakes for a cocktail tonight. They've been worried about my being alone this morning, and I almost promised. . . ."

"Not the Drakes!" he objected.

"Now there goes our truce!" she said hotly. "I ask one favor—"

"You're not exactly consistent, Bea. You accuse me of not acting romantic enough and then turn right around and suggest we have a public tea party with elderly folks. In our suite would be okay, but not in public. Everyone will think we're vacationing with our grandparents, and my brother and our friends would find it laughable. Don't you know a man in love wants his woman to himself?"

"I'm helping you. Why can't you help me? I don't want those people worried about me."

"I've already helped you. I've replaced this NOUOK character."

"His name is Perry."

"And my name is John. I'm the man you're in Paris with, not NOUOK, not the Drakes. Come on, Bea. You told people that yourself."

She realized that from his standpoint, his reasoning was perfectly logical. But she tried to stare him down nonetheless.

She failed miserably. He was harder to win over than Perry.

"Forget NOUOK, Bea," he said, mischief distinct in his eyes as he drew her hand up to rest against his neck. "And quit worrying about the Drakes. They'll probably be more reassured if you're out somewhere with me than if we see them."

"But I'm the one who made the suggestion."

"So we'll take care of it somehow." He pecked a soft kiss on her slightly opened mouth, smiling at her confusion. "Surely you can do a little pretending? Don't you find it fascinating at all to be seeing Paris with a former Boy Scout, an army veteran, an owner of a secret-decoder ring from a Cracker Jack box?"

He pecked another kiss on her tightly pursed lips at each new listing.

And in spite of her annoyance at his refusal to see the Drakes, she couldn't help laughing. His public ploy was so amusing; she admired his audacity. With a resigned smile she drew away from him.

"I pity your real mistress," she said with wry humor, never doubting that he had one, and almost regretting for a moment that she was not the lady in question. "You must be a devastating lover when you're serious."

CHAPTER FIVE

BEA WAS NOT NORMALLY AFRAID to be alone. In fact, when she first became separated from John as they were walking from their hotel to the Place de la Concorde for the fireworks display, she had appreciated the respite from his disturbing presence. For she was finding that once he had made up his mind to be charming, he could be pretty heady stuff—and his companionship was becoming a habit she would find hard to break.

"I like the man, dammit," she swore to herself as she hunted for his familiar face among the crowds. Not finding him close by, she decided he had probably walked ahead when she had paused to look at a window of Swiss embroidery, so she, too, joined the people moving toward the center of the city. Confident that she would see his great hulking shoulders soon, she had been fearless enough at first, only somewhat annoyed by the ever increasing jostling of the crowds.

Continuing to watch for his sandy hair as she walked, she told herself that liking the man was a losing proposition; he had already warned her away. She had a feeling he didn't settle for half measures like platonic friendship in his relations with women, and Bea knew she was not totally without appeal to men—she had received enough propositions to settle her mind on that score. So she supposed he was thinking that when two adults were thrown together in such intimacy, the situation could easily get out of hand, even if neither of them intended anything to happen.

To Bea, the warning had seemed unnecessary at first because she had been upset with his attitude toward the Drakes. They had never been able to agree on a place to meet the couple, and Bea had been mortified when John had called them to withdraw her invitation. But his cancellation had been so charming that Mrs. Drake had been in raptures, and Bea's own reaction of amused gratitude had threatened to overwhelm her. She changed her mind and decided the man was wonderful.

Insane! How had he put his warning—"Don't let Paris go to your head"?

As she walked along the crowded streets she knew she should heed his words.

But the more sternly she lectured herself about not becoming too interested in John Robertson, the more circumstances made her want to be with him, at least for the immediate present.

Paris on Bastille evening was no place for a woman alone—the crowds were becoming unmanageable.

And it worried her that a man she had seen somewhere before kept coming into view near her, then disappearing. Perhaps under ordinary circumstances she could have explained away the constant reappearance of the bald-headed man with the scar. But the sheer numbers of the Bastille Day celebrants were like none she had ever seen, not even when the Bicentennial enthusiasts had filled New York to watch the Tall Ships. In a crowd this huge it was too coincidental that no matter in which direction she moved, or how many people she slipped around, that particular face stuck close to her.

Recalling John's warning to report any unusual people who worried her, she wished he were with her right now, for she would certainly report. The man had a sinister look!

Bea was finding it increasingly difficult to move independent of the mass of people. She hugged her arms around her to provide some shelter from the jostling and tried to concentrate on keeping her footing as she moved in rhythm with the crowd. The police were closing off the streets to cars and allowing people to walk freely, but additional celebrants were arriving so quickly that the congestion simply increased.

It was the potential danger of the mass of people that frightened her. She remembered her parents' stories of being caught in a runaway crowd at a South American festival in which people were trampled to death. Until now she had not believed such a thing could really happen.

In consternation, she realized that soon she would not be able to get out of the crowd. Studying the faces of those around her, she marveled that the Parisians themselves were unalarmed. Bastille Day was their tradition, and they were having the time of their lives. Unmindful of the sounds of ambulances nearby, many were taking pictures, holding their cameras up over their heads and laughingly snapping everything in sight. Cameras were even hanging out of windows above them, recording the annual event.

John, where are you, she thought wildly. *We could get our picture taken together a thousand times right now. Then we could abandon this farce.*

Bea knew she was not the only one wishing she had stayed at her hotel. On the faces of tourists, who were obvious by their rumpled appearance and untypical choice of clothing, she saw expressions of muted alarm matching her own.

This time when she looked behind her, she did not spot the sinister man, and that made her feel a little better. She tried to rush her pace a little, just to be sure she had lost him, and promptly began to stumble. Only snatching at the clothing of the people in front of her saved her from slipping to the ground. The people whose clothing she grabbed shrugged off her grasp in annoyance, apparently unconcerned that if she had fallen, she could easily have been trampled.

Jostled from every direction, Bea had to fight panic. Noticing that the corner ahead of her was slightly less congested because a vendor had set up a temporary stand near a wall, she worked her way insistently in that direction. She just had to find a quiet place to stand for a moment while she figured out how to get back to the hotel, with or without John.

Normally, wedging herself between a hot nut stand and a wall would not have been Bea's idea of a pleasant haven, but at that moment she was desperately grateful for the small bit of space that kept her from being swept along with the crowd. She could even abide the stifling odors from the caramelized cashews the woman vendor was stirring in her charred pan. Bea could stand anything if it gave her time to look for John.

I wish he were taller, she thought, only then aware that her conception of him as a giant was relative. She scanned the people pouring past her, and even climbed on a narrow ledge along the stone building to give herself a six-inch height advantage. But only an occasional basketball-player type was distinguishable in the mob.

It occurred to her that if she waved something over her head, perhaps John might spot her. Intent on digging a Kleenex from her purse for that purpose, she was unprepared when the man pushed her off her perch.

She recognized the hairless face with its ugly scar just when she completely lost her balance. In a split second of alarm she had a choice of going down under the crowd or trying to throw herself toward the vendor so that perhaps the hot cart would keep her from being trampled. She opted for the vendor.

Reasonable athletic ability from teenage years practicing springboard diving helped her twist her body in midair. She cracked her ribs and hips against the cart, luckily just missing the firebox before she twisted and managed to roll against a small car pulled up on the sidewalk close to the stand. Her head struck a hubcap, momentarily stunning her; but, still horrified by visions of being trampled, she scrambled to her feet and grabbed the door handle to gain her balance.

Coldness swept over her even in her dizziness as she saw the man who had pushed her lose himself toward the center of the people moving away. There was no doubt in her mind that his action had been deliberate.

Shaken, she ignored the angry shrieks of the woman vendor coming toward her. Instead she looked down the side street that was feeding pedestrians into the rue de Rivoli, wondering if there was any chance she could go against the crowd and get far enough off the main avenue to make her way back to the hotel.

She didn't have time to make a clear decision, because the vendor began pushing angrily at her. The woman was heavy and pasty like a Brueghel peasant without the softening umbers of the great artist, and she was forcefully shaking Bea as she shouted French invective.

By then the firecrackers were beginning.

Not officially—by the teenagers.

They were lighting them in their hands and gleefully tossing them directly into the crowds.

Forced from her spot near the car, Bea broke loose from the vendor and tried to move down the side street, raising her hands against her shoulders so she would have some hope of shielding her face if incendiaries were haphazardly thrown in her direction. Half blinded by the flashing of camera bulbs and firecrackers all around her, she concentrated on keeping her panic under control and moving one foot in front of the other, hoping to work her way toward the building side of the walkway, where she would have partial protection. But the natural drift of the crowds seemed to be forcing her toward the street. The noise was becoming deafening, and the pressure of bodies packing the area was so intense that occasionally a screaming person would literally pop up out of the crowd like a cork. *That's what happened to Napoleon's cavalry at Waterloo.* Bea wondered if she was close to hysteria. She forced herself to swallow her fear, even as she felt the curb at her feet and knew that before long she would be forced into the street itself, and all hope of getting over to the building would be gone.

Just then a man's strong hands were around her waist, and she was being dragged along. Her bruised ribs hurt at the pressure, but she didn't cry out. She was not able to turn around as the unseen man was gradually forcing an opening for them, but she instinctively pushed with her feet, trying to help as he threw one arm completely around her waist from behind. Then she was sure it was John. She suddenly realized she would know the feel of him anywhere. His body against hers had been indelibly imprinted upon her memory that morning when they had fallen on her bed in her room.

He found a small indentation against the building. It had a strange decorative brass ring hanging from a goblin face, and he reached around her to seize the ring, his arms encircling her as he protectively forced her against the wall. She pressed her hands against the stones, absorbing the secure feel of them, then slowly turned in his arms, her eyes full of emotion.

"Are you all right, Bea?" he asked hoarsely.

She didn't need to reply. She acted, pressing her mouth eagerly against his in spontaneous gratitude. Her kiss was uninhibited, her smile joyous.

"I'm going to get you out of here." His lips brushed her temple, and he dropped one arm to her waist, holding her tightly against him. "Can you help me?"

"I won't let you out of my sight this time," she gasped, gripping his wrist with one hand. "I've learned my lesson."

The breadth of John's shoulders facilitated his passage through the crowds, and gradually they were able to make a steady path along the wall. A quick glance around John revealed that dozens of other people anxious to leave were taking advantage of his strength and following him.

"You're a pied piper," she shouted into his ear, feeling so safe she wanted to express her confidence in him.

But her euphoria was short-lived.

The firecrackers were starting again. And close to them.

"Stupid kids," John exclaimed as a bundle of Chinese firecrackers popped over the heads of some startled Parisians just a few feet ahead of them. Now people from windows were tossing firecrackers into the crowd.

What happened next was like a bad dream. A stop-action still.

They saw the arm come out of the window with

the big ones. No face, just the arm. The awareness of something being thrown, and Bea's shocked gasp as she realized she couldn't get her hands up in front of her. John instinctively shielded her face and caught the firecrackers just as they began exploding. Bea felt a hot sting across her cheek as he threw the lighted mass high away from them. The resounding bangs sounded like cannons from another scenario. Screams and the never-ending jostle of bodies intensified the tumult.

"They've hurt your hand!" she sobbed as she saw powder burns on the cuff of his shirt. Then horror. As his hand came around, she saw the tip of one finger was missing. Bea began to sob, she stumbled, but he jerked her back to him and shoved his way through the crowds almost like a madman. People had to give way. Quickly he reached a recess just like the one they had paused in before, and his arms came over her head to force her against the wall as he grasped the brass ring.

"Did they get your eyes?" He tried to see her face.

"You fool," she cried. "They blew off your finger!"

He didn't believe her and looked up at his hand. Then suddenly he laughed, an exuberant shout so incongruous at the moment that at first she thought he was expressing pain. But his mouth was curved, his eyes amused.

"What?"

He held up his hand and she cried out, not wanting to look. But he forced up her chin and kissed her.

"I lost that fingertip years ago," he said reassuringly. "My hand is fine. Get hold of yourself, Bea."

And she seriously tried as he pushed her onward again.

Before long, their progress became easier. And once they had gone a few blocks farther they reached a street running generally parallel to the rue de Rivoli down which they could walk reasonably comfortably.

John drew her to his side. "I think we're each going to make it back to the hotel in one piece." He grinned teasingly.

She held on tight to his waist, fighting a wild urge to fling her arms around his neck and kiss him endlessly. Her relief was enormous. The shouts of the crowds and the noise of the firecrackers seemed dim and far away.

They said nothing the rest of the way to the hotel.

But once in their room Bea had plenty to say.

"You've got to let me do something about that hand. Quit trying to hide it under that handkerchief. I saw powder burns."

"You saw a missing finger joint, too, and you were wrong about that."

He had been ignoring her concern, choosing instead to call down to room service for a large container of ice.

"Well, we could clean it before the ice comes; I assume you're going to soak your hand in it?"

"When the ice comes I intend to soak my Scotch in it. Go take care of those powder burns on your face."

Bea started to object again, but he pushed her into the bathroom. Her dark hair had fallen loose from its French knot, and she tugged it completely free before examining her face. There were black streaks across her cheek extremely close to her eyes. Removing her contact lenses, she shuddered as she realized how nearly the explosion had threatened her vision.

After she filled the basin with water, Bea reached automatically for a washcloth. Remembering it was not the French custom to provide one, she dipped a corner of the fingertip towel into the water before opening the small emerald green case that held the hotel's highly perfumed soap.

"They didn't get your eye?"

John loomed over her shoulder, watching her in the mirror as she carefully washed off the remaining black powder. The intimacy of the situation made her uneasy.

"No damage, thanks to you." She tried to hide her nervousness.

"Let me see."

"Would you get out of here so I can finish up?" she insisted.

He didn't give her much time. She had barely splashed the final rinse off her face and put her contacts back in before he was tapping at the bathroom door.

"You should put some salve on that tonight."

"You're the one who should be putting salve on injuries." She opened the door to walk past him, but he led her back into the bathroom where he could examine her face near the lighted mirror.

"I'm a lot better off than you are." Bea pulled free of his grip and looked pointedly toward his wrapped hand. "I know you men probably don't like to use this stinky soap, but that burn should be washed." She knew better than to grab aggressively at him. So she added matter-of-factly as she refilled the basin, "If my face needed care, so does your hand. Quit being so stoic."

He hesitated a moment before carefully unwrapping his handkerchief. His wince of pain was uncontrollable as a portion of the linen stuck to his fingers. Not looking at her, he plunged his hand into the cool water, and Bea heard the grunt he couldn't quite withhold. He seemed to be having trouble even moving the fingers. "The feeling is just beginning to return," he admitted sheepishly, pain evident in his face.

"Let me help you?" It was a question, not an insistence; and when he didn't object, she hurriedly formed a lather and gently rubbed it over the injured area. She wished she had something besides perfumed soap to use; the chemical used for the scent might be an irritant. But it was better than nothing.

She rinsed, then repeated the process several times. Eventually satisfied that she had got all the powder from the burns, she refilled the basin with cold water and settled his hand back into the clean rinse.

A knock at the door startled them both momentarily before they remembered John had ordered ice.

"You don't have to go," Bea insisted. "I have some francs."

Once she had tipped the waiter, she came back into the bathroom for a glass.

"I'll make you a drink first and an ice pack second. How does that sound?"

"You make a determined nurse." He appeared resigned to accepting her help.

"If you'll just keep it as cold as possible, it will probably slow down the burning action. What shall I get from this minibar to put in the drink? Cognac?"

"No, avoid their forty-dollar cognac!" he growled. "What a rip-off in the name of French quality. I have a small flask of Scotch somewhere in my suitcase."

She wondered when he had slipped a suitcase into their room. And where it had come from. But she asked no questions as she opened the small black bag on the luggage rack in his closet. She felt through his underwear and socks and set aside the folded shirts. Eventually opening his shaving kit, she found the Scotch there.

"It is small," she said.

"I just keep it for emergencies."

If he would admit this was an emergency, she felt sure he was hurting badly. Splashing the glass half full and throwing in a couple of ice cubes, she returned hastily to the bathroom. He was trying to see the extent of his injury.

"How bad is it?"

He took a generous drink quickly. "It's going

to hurt,'' he admitted, ''but I can get by without a doctor.'' At her look of doubt, he managed a reassuring grin. ''Stop fussing so much. Like every self-respecting farmer, I keep current on first aid; out in the fields we have frequent occasions to use it. I tell you, I'll be okay.''

Only partially reassured, she went back to his room and redistributed some of the ice into glasses so there would be space in the bucket for him to soak his hand.

''Please come rest on the bed for a while with your hand in this bucket.'' She came back into the bathroom to reason with him.

He frowned at her as if he was going to refuse. Then suddenly he capitulated.

''Only if you take your precious spread off first,'' he said sarcastically. ''This time I won't be shoved off that bed once I lie down.''

She didn't even mind his gibe at her housekeeping mania, she was so relieved he was being sensible. Jerking off the spread hurriedly, she threw it across one of the chairs before fluffing up several pillows.

''It's ready. Come on.''

After he lay back and plunged his hand in the ice, she helped him take off his shoes.

''You have huge feet,'' she said idiotically in her nervousness as she let his shoes drop noisily into the closet.

''I'm a man,'' he snapped, finishing off the Scotch and holding his glass out questioningly to her.

She tossed another ice cube in and splashed the

glass half full again, wondering as she did if the man honestly did not realize how fully, achingly, breathlessly she was aware he was a man.

"I hope this helps," she mumbled. "It finished off the flask, and I didn't see any more in your suitcase."

"It will have to do." He leaned his head back wearily and let his eyes drift shut.

"You should put an antibiotic salve on your face," he said wearily, his eyes still closed. "I have one in my suitcase."

"You need it on your hand more."

"We'll both use it, okay? Spare me the fights."

She was amazed at the variety of first-aid supplies she found in his special kit. It looked as if he had been prepared for a siege.

"Is this it?" She sat down on the edge of the bed and showed him the tube she had selected. At his nod she reached for his hand, but he shook his head and motioned toward the bathroom.

"You first."

She started to argue, then gave up and rushed to the bathroom to smear a small amount of the cream across her reddened cheek.

When she returned he had already set aside the ice bucket and was shaking his right hand dry.

"I hope this also has an anesthetic in it. That looks raw." Gently she smoothed the salve over the injured palm and fingers. Most of the surface was reddened and already some puffiness indicated there would be plenty of blistering. Curiously she lifted his hand to examine his mangled fourth finger. Now, in the light of the room, she could see that the injury had long since healed; the scars were not even discolored.

"How did you lose this fingertip?" Her voice shook a little as she cradled his wounded hand, the memory of her first reaction when he caught the firecrackers still fresh in her mind.

"It's one of my two souvenirs of Vietnam."

"If that's one of the souvenirs, I don't want to see the other one."

"I hardly want you to see the other one." Even though his voice was becoming slurred, she could detect the amusement. "It took a chunk out of my thigh and damned near canceled my contribution to mother's hopes for lots of grandchildren. I was lucky the marksman was off a couple of inches. They tell me I'll make a wonderful father."

Her face was fiery red as she dropped his hand and stood up.

"I can tell you're feeling better. Scotch must do wonders."

He closed his eyes again, apparently content to lie quietly for a while; but he was still smiling. Satisfied, Bea cleaned up the first-aid supplies, then wandered into her own alcove. The noise of the celebrants outside had increased, and she walked over to the French doors and pulled aside the curtain.

"Aaah," she gasped involuntarily as a triple ring of red and blue flares filled the Parisian sky.

"What is it?"

"The fireworks must be starting," she called back to him, opening the French doors to the roar of the city just in time to see a second display, spectacular in its synchronization of golden, whirling flames, rise into the air. Bea began to laugh softly, her voice almost lost in the din coming up from the streets.

John's weight on the bed shifted, and he padded toward her in his stocking feet.

"We should have just stayed here all along." Bea's voice was rich with chagrined humor. "Just look at this view we have from our own bedroom window."

The minute she said "our bedroom" she regretted it, for it made her doubly conscious of the intimacy. But John said nothing about her choice of words as he stood behind her, looking in amazement at the street full of milling people.

"I can't believe this. The crowds go on for miles. I'll swear I don't remember that it was this bad the last time I was here for Bastille Day." He drew her out on the balcony with him, and she dropped into one of the small seats, more to escape from his enveloping arm than with any other intent.

"Ooooh, look at that one." She couldn't help pointing childishly as a blinding white flash preceded a multicolored fountain of whirling light. It was just fading when a second such fountain of different colors exploded. Then a third. Bea leaned forward, the loose neck of her soft, flowered dress hanging gracefully over her full breasts as her chest rose and fell with excited breaths. "Did you see it?" She turned to him eagerly.

He was staring at her strangely. But when she

caught him at it, his glance returned to the sky. They were both quiet then, as they watched the show. It seemed to go on and on.

"Have you noticed that the French are basically silent during fireworks?" he finally asked contemplatively, still not looking back at her. "No ooooohs and aaaahs as we Americans do. I still remember when I was a little boy and came to my first one of these in Paris. The city must not have been as crowded, because we found a little spot rather off by ourselves, my grandmother and I. I remember standing on a rock wall somewhere in the Tuileries. When the big overheads began, I shouted and clapped just as I would at home on the Fourth of July. I was the only one making any noise, and people stared at me as if I was the big show, not the fireworks."

Bea frowned, wondering protectively if the happy little boy had been more embarrassed and hurt by the incident than the grown man's amused voice would indicate.

"Are Parisians this blasé about everything?"

Wordlessly John shrugged his shoulders, watching a circle of white flame fall from the sky, then suddenly disintegrating into whistling, popping rivers of molten noise. It was apparently the beginning of the grand finale, for immediately the horizon seemed to explode with color over and over, each noisy bombardment of flame more spectacular than the last.

Orange balls flared, then withered; streaks of white-hot light broke through the masses of blue, green and yellow twinkling stars; red lightning bolts flamed, then fell to the ground, slowly dying. The noise was almost deafening.

Then silence.

And still there was no spontaneous reaction from the crowd. Nothing.

"We should applaud." Bea seemed disappointed, but her hands remained motionless in her lap.

John's expression was hard to read. "I'm glad you got to see it after all," he said eventually.

She hugged her arms around herself as she moved back into the suite. "In the safety of our room!" she emphasized, shuddering as she walked over to her desk.

"You actually were frightened...earlier?" She heard him close the French doors and move toward her, but Bea couldn't answer, the horror momentarily washing over her afresh. She stood with her back to him, protesting tension in every muscle of her body when she felt his hand settle at the nape of her neck. She was still upset by the experience at the Place de la Concorde, but she wasn't certain she could handle his comforting concern.

He let the back of his injured right hand rest lightly on her shoulder while his left hand slid tentatively down her bare arm. "I should have kept better track of you out there." His breath was warm as his lips touched her hair.

Again she reminded herself that John Robertson was merely a stranger thrown too close to her by circumstances; it was unwise to let herself become involved. But she knew immediately that such reasoning was too late. She was already involved. She and John had passed beyond being strangers from the moment his strong, disturbing body had pinned her down on her own bed that first morning he came to her room. Bea trembled.

"Still afraid?" His voice was worried as he turned her toward him, carefully avoiding spreading the burn salve on her dress or skin.

Bea really didn't know if she was still gripped by the aftermath of fright, but did sense that her present danger was worse. She almost wanted him to. . . . She tried to jerk away.

"Come back here, Bea," he ordered, his one good hand commanding in strength, pulling her to him.

His ridiculous care not to offend her with his messy, injured hand undid her in her weakened state. A one-armed lover? Devastating! Against her will she did let herself sink against him, closing her eyes almost in pain. First she felt their thighs touch, then her breasts soft against his chest. She snapped her eyes open, almost pleading. She wanted him to push her away. She couldn't let this happen. Not when he had already warned her. . . .

But he wouldn't release her. Gently, almost impersonally at first, he kissed her. Soft, feathery kisses on the eyelids closed her dark gaze from his. She gave in to her feeling of security as his mouth played around her ears, nuzzling aside the masses of her dark hair, which curtained softly against his stubble-roughened face. At her sigh of capitulation, when her arms slid around his waist, something in him changed. His lips hardened, sliding hungrily to her mouth, exploring, drinking thirstily.

As she returned his kiss, tilting her head so he could shape his lips more deeply against hers, she could taste the Scotch he had just drunk. They both seemed to like the taste of each other. Again and again their lips clung, seeking every detail of how the other's mouth felt. When they stopped for a needed breath, their lips were still touching, neither of them willing to part completely.

Wanting more, they came together again, this time exchanging a deep, passionate kiss, their lips opening to allow each other's strengths to flow back and forth between them. Bea felt a blaze of desire begin to overpower both her fright and her common sense. John felt it, too.

"I think this is...getting out of hand," he mumbled almost incoherently against her throat; both his hands were fondling her, restless and seeking against her curved hips. He pressed her low against him, his own passion evident.

In despair, Bea realized stopping would have to be up to her. Resolutely she wedged her arms between their aching bodies and buried her head against his shoulder.

He threatened to overpower her, but at her persistent efforts, he, too, regained control. Finally he looked down at her, his eyes tender.

"John, I was so frightened out there," she whispered, her emotions still vibrant and confused. "I didn't realize how much, until I felt your arms safe around me just now."

"I shouldn't have let us get separated." This

time when he drew her back, it was different. He was only comforting her, his arms absorbing her delayed fright with his own strength. And before long his covering, enveloping presence reassured her. She was all right. It was enough for one night.

They shared one last kiss—an affectionate one, long and satisfying.

Finally she slipped away from him.

He stood watching her fiddle restlessly with things on the top of her desk. Both of them needed some method of unwinding from their emotional intensity.

Bea chose to talk . . . about anything.

"You told me to report to you," she murmured wispily, as she repeatedly opened and shut the lid to her powder case, "if I saw anything unusual. . . ."

"Everything's damned unusual right now," he mumbled, almost as if in self-contempt.

"I mean it." She put down the powder case decisively, suddenly realizing she truly did. John should know of the scar-faced man. "For a while out there, someone was after me."

He had started back to his own room, but at that he froze and turned slowly around.

"What do you mean?" His voice was peculiarly casual. Too much so.

"At first I thought I could be mistaken." Bea then began to rummage in her suitcase, delving around for her nightwear, needing the movement to complete the relaxation of her tensions. "But when the same man kept turning up no matter where I went, I knew he was following me."

"And he frightened you?" His face was a careful mask.

"Yes, you could say that," she laughed deprecatingly. "When he pushed me to the ground I was frightened enough! I was certain he'd broken my rib, but I was too afraid of being trampled to sit on the sidewalk and check."

"Broken a rib?" He moved quickly, his hand sliding under her breasts in an examining touch.

"Don't do that!" She flinched.

"I want to see." He began tugging at the back zipper of her dress.

"John, I mean it!" She batted away his hand, thinking that would be all she would need in her vulnerable state—to take off her clothes and let this man examine her.

But he stood his ground.

"I want to know what happened to you. You may be seriously hurt. Either you take off that dress or I do."

"No, you're scaring me."

"Dammit, Bea, take off that dress!" He had it unzipped and sliding off her shoulders before she could even struggle effectively.

"Ouch," she moaned as he brushed against a sensitive spot at her waist.

"Lie down," he ordered, leading her to her bed. Against her will she stretched out, closing her eyes when he flipped on a brighter light.

"The damn...." His foul language faded into angry incoherence as he impersonally ran his hands over her, discovering first one sore spot, then another. Bea tried not to flinch again, not even when he turned her on her side and checked the bruises beginning to show on her hips. She could feel the greasiness of his salve as he used both hands to search for her injuries.

"You're the one who should have been packed in ice." He swore angrily when he eventually straightened and helped her sit up. "It doesn't look as if any ribs are broken, but you're turning black and blue."

"It doesn't matter. I bruise easily. Some of that may be from when I tripped over your suitcase." She tried to mask her embarrassment that she was trapped there in her bra and panties; he had flung her dress to the floor, and she couldn't reach it.

"Probably it was an accident tonight." He seemed to be struggling with something in his own mind. "I don't think you have to be afraid it will happen again...."

"So that man's pushing me was an accident?" she asked, curious to see what he would say.

"Well, sometimes those free-lance photographers can be pretty rough." She knew he was lying, trying to reassure her when he couldn't even reassure himself.

"The bald-headed man with the big red scar over his ear was no photographer," Bea insisted quietly, gathering up the nightgown and cosmetic bag she had dropped on the bed. "He deliberately pushed me."

"You're probably imagining it."

"I was imagining it so much you had to examine my injuries!" she said scornfully. "Make up your mind!"

She was striding to the bathroom, her night-gown draped over her shoulders, when he caught her arm. His face was white.

"Bea, I meant it when I said I wanted you to be careful. Just as you would be at home. But from now on you stick with me and let me watch out for you. My warning is worrying you too much."

"The hell it is! I've just remembered where I've seen that man before." She shook free of his grip. "In that sidewalk café where we went this afternoon. He was watching us and those Algerians next to us. I'm good with faces, John. I'm not imagining it."

She slammed the bathroom door behind her and locked it, then turned on the hot faucet for bathing. Nervously she clutched the nightgown against her breasts as the water slowly ran into the big tub. It was too late to cover her seminakedness, but she tried anyway. Bea was furious at John's conde-scension, but almost relieved that the argument had taken place, for it effectively discouraged her from reading anything serious into the fact that he had caressed and comforted her. No man would refuse to hold and soothe a woman if she obvious-ly needed and welcomed it.

Dejectedly Bea put away her contacts, then stepped into the warm water and soaped her body completely, wanting to rid herself of all traces of his gentle touch. It was a long time before she finally returned to her room.

She was not surprised to find that John had left.

A note on her bed told her not to put on the night latch, for he would be back as soon as he had made a telephone call. For one angry moment she thought about locking him out, wondering what was so important that he had to go elsewhere to make the call. Curiously she went into his room to see if the scramble phone she had noticed on his desk was still there. She had seen those expensive units in a few sensitive businesses and had meant to ask John why he needed one.

It annoyed her to discover he had unplugged it from the hotel jack and taken it with him. Since monitoring by the hotel switchboard could not be a problem with such a phone, he must have left because he didn't want to risk her overhearing. Certainly he would not be calling Mathilde, for Bea already knew about that situation. It occurred to her that he must have a mistress of his own in the States and perhaps needed to reassure her that nothing was happening between him and Bea while he was helping his brother.

The idea of some other woman's having the right to object to Bea's presence in John's arms tore at her cruelly, canceling any understanding she might have had that he would hardly arrange to use a scramble phone for love conversations. She flung herself down on the bed, almost hating that fantasy woman she could imagine hearing John's explanations at that very moment. Resenting a probable discussion of her own fright and need for comfort, Bea considered leaving. She might still have time to get dressed and be gone before he returned.

But suddenly she remembered John's burned hand, and that immediately ended her plan of flight. Recollection of the cruel blisters across his palm and the powder marks so close to her own eyes sobered her.

She owed the man.

She lay back down and tried to relax. But it was difficult; she was so confused. Restlessly she turned over again and again, her nightgown pulling so high up on her thighs as she tried to get comfortable that she eventually gave up tugging it down. Instead, she concentrated on forcing herself to lie still. And that was what her exhausted body needed; she soon drifted into unconsciousness.

She never knew that John Robertson had returned just moments after she fell asleep, or that he had stood over her long moments before gently covering her with a light sheet.

CHAPTER SIX

THE NEXT DAY was uneventful. Bea didn't believe it could have been after the occurrences of the night before. But when she had awakened to find John calmly enjoying his breakfast and a newspaper out on their balcony, she decided she could be as blasé as he. Her determination had worked well for her. John had a morning appointment concerning his brother, so she had taken advantage of that time alone to do some shopping for people on her gift list. Since the Galéries Lafayette, the large Paris department store, which caters to non-French-speaking tourists, was only a few blocks from the hotel, Bea had gone there. The selection of leather gloves, designer scarves and other small items had been everything she could have hoped for, and her tasks had not taken her long. She even had time to buy some things for herself and to browse past the windows of some of the noted Parisian designers before meeting John at a brasserie for a light lunch.

They had spent the afternoon walking. John claimed that was what lovers did in Paris, not visiting museums as Bea had suggested, and she had not bothered to argue with him. And when they passed the Jeu de Paume, she had not even looked longingly in the direction of the lovely museum that housed the Impressionist masters. She was determined to spend her remaining committed time with John Robertson as agreeably as possible, because she wanted to get the man off her conscience.

In the evening they had gone to the theater, not a particular treat for Bea since the show was in French; but she had enjoyed watching the crowds and the colorful costumes of the actors. Afterward they had predictably visited a couple of bistros—*as lovers would do,* she'd thought sarcastically when John had suggested it. But she had been surprised to find that she had enjoyed herself. He had been almost as charming as in the sidewalk café the previous afternoon, and Bea had to keep reminding herself not to take the man seriously.

Her polite reserve had been enough to inhibit any repetition of the lovemaking of the night before. But just to make certain, Bea had pointedly drawn a magazine out of her suitcase after she had taken her turn in the bathroom, had thrust on her glasses and hugged her robe tight around her as she had climbed into her bed. Probably her discouragements had been unnecessary, though, for John had shown no interest anyway, and was breathing so deeply by the time she had read the first three pages that she could hear him from her own room. She assumed he had fallen immediately asleep.

It occurred to her as she settled down in bed herself, that she had not been able to help the man much. As far as she knew, no friends of his brother had seen them together, nor had their picture been taken again. But he had mentioned that he thought his arrangements for his brother would be completed within another twenty-four hours, so that took some concern off her mind. She felt that when her commitment to him was over, she could leave with a reasonably clear conscience.

It was not until the next morning that she learned she had been more helpful than she'd realized.

"WE MADE THE PAPERS! And your name is in the headlines."

Bea rushed back into their hotel room excitedly waving the newspaper she had picked up at the corner kiosk. Only moments earlier she had left for a morning walk while John was shaving, needing some time alone to sort out her thoughts, but this development had driven all other worries from her mind.

"You'll like the picture," she called out, assuming he was still in the bathroom. "I'm not sure my mother would approve, but we look rather passionate. Enough to convince your brother, I think."

"Are you serious? Someone photographed us?" John's shirt hung unbuttoned over his underwear as he stepped out of his closet.

"They caught us that night at the fireworks when—" she hated to admit it "—when I kissed you, up against the wall. I can't make out the French caption. What does it say?"

His face reddened angrily as he scanned the story. "They say I'm chasing around after you all right, among other things. Where did they get *your* name?"

"You mean they identified me, too?" Bea tried to see around him, but he tossed the paper onto his bed and strode back to the closet, buttoning his shirt as he went.

"Damn! I wanted your name kept out of this mess."

"What does it matter? My clients couldn't care less about my private life as long as their stock goes up. And I can eventually explain to my family. I thought the whole point was having people know you're in Paris with someone other than Mathilde."

"They don't have to know I'm with you."

"Thanks a lot," she mumbled under her breath, feeling strangely deflated. She walked thoughtfully into her own room.

"At least now I can send you on your way. My other arrangements have all worked out, so we can proceed."

Moving out immediately was the exact thing Bea had been planning, but oddly enough it irritated her that he was so anxious to be rid of her.

"I think the best thing would be to get you on a train out of here today." John's voice sounded far away as he shuffled things around in his closet. "Did you say you were meeting your people in Belgium at the end of this week? We could get you on an express to Brussels this morning if you like."

Automatically Bea began to repack her suitcase, not bothering to answer. She had been planning to resettle in another hotel in Paris, but perhaps Brussels would be better after all; she would prefer not to run into John Robertson again.

"On second thought, there's no need for you to rush away this morning. Tonight will be soon enough, and there are plenty of trains available." John was thumbing through a train timetable as he strolled into her alcove, fully dressed in a suit and tie. His efficiency appalled her.

"Probably the best would be to get you on the 20:30 Trans-Europ Express. You'll be in downtown Brussels before midnight. Shall I pick a hotel for you? I can have you met."

"Oh, I suppose so." Bea shrugged her shoulders disinterestedly, then decided to assert herself. "But make it near the EEC headquarters."

He looked surprised.

"The European Economic Community is a strange choice for a tourist. Wouldn't you rather be close to the Grand' Place?"

"I'm a broker, remember. I might as well research the international business climate while I'm killing time. What better place than the Common Market headquarters?"

He appeared disconcerted by her cool determination.

"I don't want your vacation ruined. The Amigo is a nice hotel right on the Grand' Place."

"I prefer the European Economic Community area." Not looking up, she could feel that he was watching her, but eventually he returned wordlessly to his own room.

In relief Bea sank into her desk chair, only half listening as he began to make a series of phone calls. If they were getting along this poorly already, what, she wondered, was she going to do with herself until 8:00 P.M.? She didn't believe her battered emotions could stand another whole day subjected to the whims of John Robertson.

Resolutely she marched into his room.

"I'd prefer to take the next train to Brussels."

He rudely waved her to silence and continued his phone conversation.

Disgusted, Bea went back to her desk and began filing her nails unnecessarily. She was still at it by the time John had made several more calls and returned to her room.

He leaned silently against the archway looking at her, but she refused to acknowledge his presence.

"You're going to have stubs for fingers if you keep that up," he finally barked.

"I prefer my nails a practical length," she lied.

"Everything's set for the 20:30. We can't get reservations this late, but they assure me you'll have no trouble finding a first-class seat. I'm having someone purchase your ticket and bring it 'round to the hotel."

"Hmmmm." Still not looking up at him, she dropped her emery board into her purse and turned toward her desk.

"Don't you want to know what we're going to do the rest of the day?"

"We?" Her sarcasm prompted his irritated, explosive sigh. Ignoring him, she began arranging her cosmetics neatly in their case. She absorbed herself in the activity, trying to shut out his presence, concentrating on the fascination of making the tiny plastic bottles fit into their exact locations. Her face cream was slightly too small for her first choice of placement. If she put it in there, she thought dully, something else would not fit. The case was like a child's toy, in which every shape had to be placed in a particular slot.

"Stop that!" He laid his hand over hers.

She looked at him angrily. "Do you mind? I'm trying to pack."

"You can pack later. You're practically ready anyway."

"I want to finish now."

"The Drakes will be disappointed to hear that."

"The Drakes?" She watched him suspiciously, not knowing how to interpret his boyish look of self-satisfaction.

"I thought you'd like to spend your last day here with them."

"But the Drakes already have plans for today."

"Their group is visiting the military museum," he scoffed. "I convinced them a trip to the gardens at Versailles with us would be better."

"But I want to take the next train!"

"I felt the vibes emanating from you when we passed the Jeu de Paume," he admitted. "I'll make up for that another time. But you'll love the fountains at Versailles, Bea." His voice was cajoling. "They're only turned on a few hours each year. And this will be one of the afternoons. We can have a nice day together, drop the Drakes off here and still have time for a light sandwich before I put you on the 20:30. No one will have to know you've left town alone. I'll be careful your tour group doesn't see me again. . . ."

It disconcerted her that he was going to so much trouble for her benefit.

"But why did you ask the Drakes, too? Night before last you refused to have a cocktail with them."

"You have that a little wrong. I suggested inviting them up to our suite for a drink, and you refused."

"Having them up to these bedrooms was hardly proper. What would they think?"

He laughed out loud and pulled her to her feet.

"Bea, you are the most inconsistent woman I know. We're ostensibly living together. And they know it. What difference would it make to them if we all had a drink in our bedroom?"

"*You're* the one who's inconsistent. At first you didn't want us to be seen in public with the Drakes, but now. . . ."

He shook her slightly, his look amazingly carefree.

"That was just because of the photographers. Now that our sexy picture has been in the papers again, surely I can have one day of fun?"

"And you call going out with me and the Drakes fun?" She didn't quite trust his jubilant behavior.

"It's fun having this public-relations and legal

problem concerning my brother behind me,'' he corrected. ''Now I'd like to do something you would enjoy.''

Her throat felt tight as she backed away from him.

''I'm glad you're as relieved as I am to have this charade over,'' she said coolly, fumbling on the desk for her purse.

He pulled her hard against him, his eyes blazing. ''Bea, we only have this last afternoon together. Let's treasure it.''

He seemed to be trying to tell her something, but she couldn't understand. Her lips parted in confusion.

''Why did you have to come along right now?'' he groaned, pressing her head into his shoulder and holding her tightly, urgently.

It was irrational, but she wanted him to kiss her. Badly. She needed it. She buried her face against his jacket, trying to quell the compulsion.

But he did not kiss her. Instead, he pulled her with him as he strode toward the door.

''My purse!''

''You won't need it.''

''It has my comb.''

''You're wearing your hair pulled back.''

''But strands keep coming loose,'' she insisted.

He stopped and looked at her, shaking his head in disbelief, then went back to pick up her pink macrame clutch bag.

''Women!'' His voice was not entirely angry as he finally followed her out the door.

The delicate purse was a perfect match to Bea's

What made Marge burn the toast and miss her favorite soap opera?

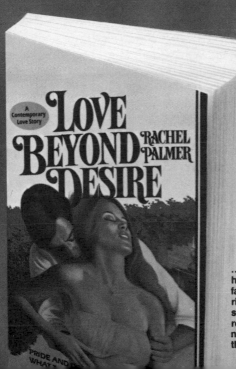

A compelling love story of mystery and intrigue... conflicts and jealousies... and a forbidden love that threatens to shatter the lives of all involved with the aristocratic Lopez family.

← Mail this card today for your FREE gifts.

TAKE THIS BOOK
AND TOTE BAG FREE!

Mail to: **SUPERROMANCE**
649 Ontario Street, Stratford Ontario N5A 6W2

YES, please send me FREE and without any obligation, my **SUPERROMANCE** novel, *Love Beyond Desire*. If you do not hear from me after I have examined my FREE book, please send me the 4 new **SUPERROMANCE** books every month as soon as they come off the press. I understand that I will be billed only $2.50 per book (total $10.00). There are no shipping and handling or any other hidden charges. There is no minimum number of books that I have to purchase. In fact, I may cancel this arrangement at any time. *Love Beyond Desire* and the tote bag are mine to keep as FREE gifts even if I do not buy any additional books.

334-CIS-YKB9

Name	(Please Print)
Address	Apt. No.
City	
Province	Postal Code
Signature	(If under 18, parent or guardian must sign.)

This offer is limited to one order per household and not valid to present subscribers. We reserve the right to exercise discretion in granting membership. If price changes are necessary you will be notified. Offer expires April 30, 1984.

PRINTED IN U.S.A.　　　　　**SUPERROMANCE**

**EXTRA BONUS
MAIL YOUR ORDER
TODAY AND GET A
FREE TOTE BAG
FROM SUPERROMANCE.**

Mail this card today for your FREE gifts.

Business
Reply Card
No Postage Stamp
Necessary if Mailed
in Canada
Postage will be paid by

SUPERROMANCE
649 Ontario Street
Stratford, Ontario N5A 9Z9

Canada Post
Postes Canada
021

pink silk shirtwaist dress. But it looked ludicrous in John's masculine grip. During the slow, noisy descent in the elevator, Bea stared at him carrying it.

Finally she ventured meekly, "Pink macrame is hardly your style, John."

He glanced down at the bag, startled, evidently having forgotten he had it. Embarrassed, he thrust it at her, but at her amused grin, he laughed out loud himself. Then without any real reason, they both began laughing headily together and couldn't stop. Their voices were exuberant, unexpectedly carefree as they descended into the lobby.

As ONE MIGHT EXPECT on a holiday weekend, there were long lines at the gates of Versailles as people paid their entrance fees and made choices of the language guide needed for the tours of the magnificent palace. At John's suggestion, however, Bea and the Drakes withstood the temptation to run through the restored portions of the edifice and instead concentrated on the gardens. But even those were too large to see in one visit, especially once the fountains began to play, and visitors were tempted to pause longer.

"Spacious. No, immense! Magnificent, spectacular, ah. . . ." Bea ran out of words trying to record in her mind what she was seeing.

"Bea looks in awe," John observed quietly, making her aware that he and the Drakes had been watching her in silence for some time as they all stood at the Latona Basin centered before the sun-goldened palace that had been the envy of every seventeenth-century ruler in the western world.

She could feel the coolness of the spray without the droplets of water actually touching her, could hear the splashing, singing sounds of the many fountains gracing the large basin banked with flowers. The blossoms' sweet perfumes added another dimension, difficult to describe.

"Even the world's greatest writers have been left speechless by Versailles, Bea," Bob consoled her. "They've found adequate descriptions for the individual sculptures or for the thousands of blooming plants and varieties of trees meticulously chosen to provide just the right color, height and density to frame the fountains. But the whole *mood* of Versailles leaves them devastated. It's more than beauty. It's a symbol."

"Bob does pretty well with words, even if you don't." John smiled at Bea, and he laid a hand companionably on her shoulder. "Liking it?"

Her answering smile was uninhibited. "I'm so glad we came."

"I think you're right, dear, about its being a symbol." Helen slipped her arm inside her husband's as they moved closer to Bea and John to avoid being separated. For although there were two hundred fifty acres in which tourists could wander, once the fountains were turned on in sequence, crowds naturally congregated around each new major display as the intricate sprays began to take shape.

"A symbol of what?" Bea asked over the chatter of those around them.

"France's strength," Bob explained. "Louis XIV intimidated his own nobles and everyone else in Europe with the grandeur of Versailles. It was well-known that his engineers and architects conquered this dismal, swampy area just as France conquered half the civilized world."

"This area was a swamp?" Bea looked around in disbelief. In every direction was a manicured path leading through well-kept woods or landscaped gardens to another enticing focal point, each centered with a gorgeous bronze, a stone sculpture or flowers. And always a fountain. Dominating the whole was the sense of order, with the major north-south axis extending the visual line of the immense palace and terminating in magnificent basins, each framed by its own unique landscaped setting.

"Louis's engineers tried to talk him out of this location," John explained, "but he was convinced Frenchmen could do anything, so they dutifully drained the swamps." His explanation was cut short by a number of children plowing right through their small group. "Since the Drakes want to see the Neptune Fountain, why don't we walk on down there now?" he suggested. "It should be less crowded, and we'd have a place to sit and talk comfortably until the fountains start to play."

"You mean all the fountains in the gardens don't work at once?" Helen asked over her shoulder as she and Bob led the way, following directions in their guidebooks.

"Hardly, dear," her husband responded before

John could answer. "Can you imagine the expense of pumping that much water? It would bankrupt France in a month. As it is they only turn on selected sections a few hours on rare Sundays."

"But Louis XIV managed it."

"No, he didn't," John corrected her gently. "The fountains were never turned on all at once. The engineering problems to divert enough rivers and construct enough reservoirs or wells to provide gravity flow to them were insurmountable in the eighteenth century. Even just before the Sun King died in 1715 they were only turning on sections of the gardens at a time, trying to keep up with him wherever he was wandering around."

"This book says Versailles is not as spectacular now as when Louis was alive." Helen was glancing down at her publication while Bob guided her along the broad walkway.

"I can't imagine this place any more beautiful than it is now," Bea sighed.

"Well, it used to be," John assured her. "Louis had many more bedding plants brought in than are used now. And he had fourteen hundred fountains. Only about six hundred remain."

"*Only* six hundred!"

"You have to remember that Louis kept his thousands of nobles and their entourages living here with him," John said humorously. "He didn't want them to be bored."

"Bored? Unbelievable!"

"But you're easy to please, Bea. Give you a little beauty, quiet, art and nature mixed, and you seem happy."

She was surprised that he had so quickly sensed her private interests. Most people thought all she lived for was business.

"And why not? Especially here. Every time I turn my head there's another path through the gardens, and ahead of me I see a little haven just demanding to be explored. And there is always the woods beyond. I can't imagine anyone would ever be bored with it."

They had paused in the middle of the sidewalk to talk, but it was immediately obvious that they were interfering with the flow of the crowds, so they huddled closer together and resumed their walk. Almost unexpectedly they emerged over a gentle slope and could see the Neptune Basin, largest on the grounds, spread enticingly before them.

"See what I mean?" Bea gasped in surprise. "One could never be bored!"

Indeed, if one had any interest in the god of the sea and his watery creatures, the Neptune Basin alone could occupy one for hours. The sculpted figures presided over a miniature lake tucked into a virtually private setting. There was room, however, in the open amphitheater design for hundreds of people to be seated.

"Good, we've beaten the crowds here," John observed, helping the Drakes to an excellent vantage point. "We'll be able to hear ourselves talk. And we'll have plenty of time to argue over the mythological symbolism of all those cherubs and their sea god before they start spouting water."

"Spouting water? You sound like my father,"

Bea objected. "Couldn't you describe the fountains more artistically?"

"Nope," he grinned, throwing a friendly arm around her shoulders. Bea let him draw her close as they settled into silence. She didn't want to think beyond the next few hours and leaned contentedly against his shoulder, treasuring, as he had suggested, their time together. Her elderly friends also seemed to be enjoying the respite for they sat quietly, hand in hand. They both appeared tired. Only when other people began drifting in did Helen stir.

"I'm almost ready to skip the tour of France and spend all this week in Versailles," she said lazily. "We're not going to begin to see the gardens today, Bob. In fact I don't know that I want to run around and try. I could look at this one fountain for hours. And there's the palace itself."

"You could spend days in there, even though only part of it has been refurbished," John warned. "Remember, it took fifty years to build, and it housed about five thousand people."

"Normally I would say when you've seen one palace you've seen them all," Bob mused, "but I would like to come back some day and see Versailles. It's one of a kind. You know, President Wilson was active in the peace talks here in 1918."

"Here's another good excuse to bring Bob back to Europe next year, Helen." Bea smiled as she and John stood to make room for some tourists passing to seating beyond them. Soon the amphitheater was filling so fast there was little opportunity for conversation. At almost the exact time scheduled, an expectant hush came over the large audience as they felt the preparatory vibrations of the fountains coming to life.

Dozens of jets of clear, icy water rose in a puff, then fell back momentarily. It was not an ostentatious beginning for the great basin. But then the water pressure stabilized, and the intricately designed fountains began to work in earnest. Cherubs and dragons exchanged arrows of spray, their dazzling water shapes mingling with the unexpected eruptions from other parts of the basin. The picture varied constantly: heights changed, shapes rearranged. And above it all Neptune presided, seeking glory in his watery turbulence. Even the children watched in wondrous quiet, only murmurs breaking the whooshing sound of the fountains as first one, then another spent itself. The careful placement of the fountains' elements to please the eye gave proof of the genius of Louis's engineers. In fact, every detail enhanced the overall effect. Even the trees planted some distance back had been chosen carefully, their unusual dark foliage providing the perfect contrast to make the myriad water shapes more dazzling in the rainbow effect of the sunlight.

When it was all over, there was no applause, but the excited chatter of the crowd gave evidence of their enjoyment.

John discouraged Bob and Helen from joining the throngs anxious to leave first.

"Are you folks in a big hurry to see more?" he

asked casually. "I hoped you wouldn't mind waiting for us just a few minutes. There's a thicket near here I used to love as a child, and I'd like to show it to Bea if I can find it again."

"Take as long as you like," Bob said almost in relief. "Of course we don't mind waiting."

"It will feel rather good to sit a while longer," Helen admitted, crossing her trim little feet in their sturdy walking shoes.

"You're sure you don't want to come, too?" Bea asked politely.

"I think we'd better not." Bob grinned as he saw John lecherously shaking his head discouragingly over Bea's shoulder. Her face reddened when she saw John's antics.

"And fittingly so, dear," Bob reassured her. "If I were a young man, I'd want to be alone with my woman for a few minutes myself."

"What's wrong with an *old* man being alone with his woman?" Helen squeezed his hand. "You two go on. We'll enjoy the sunshine."

Bea seemed to hesitate, but John tightened his arm around her waist and drew her toward the most remote exit near the great basin.

"I was afraid we'd hurt their feelings," she tried to explain as he led her into a deserted, densely wooded area of the park.

"We'll hurt them a lot more if we don't force them to rest a while longer."

"That was your reason for rushing off? I didn't realize you had noticed how tired they looked."

"I noticed."

As they walked along, Bea looked curiously at

the dense canopy the trees made as they met overhead, cutting out all but occasional patches of sunlight. This area of the park appeared deliberately cultivated into a wild state. The deeper they worked their way into the woods through the various side-branching paths John chose, the more isolated they became. Before long one could not even hear sounds indicating others were nearby.

"Is there really some place around here you wanted to see?"

"Actually there is a little clearing my brother and I discovered years ago. I didn't think of it until I realized the Drakes were tired, but I think I can find it again."

"Did your grandmother let you children wander around Versailles alone?"

"No, we usually had Meghan along."

"Meghan?"

"Our French housemaid. I know—" he held up his hand "—Meghan is an odd name for a Frenchwoman. She said once that her mother and father had visited Ireland on their honeymoon, and that's where they got the idea for the name. She didn't look like a Meghan."

"What did she look like?" Bea tilted her head back against his shoulder to see his face. He seemed so different when he talked about his childhood and his family.

"Meghan? She looked like a Brünnhilde." He grinned down at her. "And she acted like one, too—very 'scrubby dutch.' But she was French about one thing."

"Oh?"

"Sex. In her lifetime she had three husbands and two lovers. She thought Americans were much too Victorian, and she used to enjoy telling us three boys shocking stories just to 'Frenchify' our education."

Bea stumbled against him in surprise. "Didn't your grandmother object? How old were you?"

"Not old enough to understand half of what she told us." He smilingly helped her regain her balance, then moved her in front of him so they could walk single file down the narrow path he had just chosen.

"Are you sure you know where we are?" She was beginning to feel she had entered a lush, green, magical world inhabited only by the two of them. The silence in the midst of what she knew must be thousands of people was eerie.

"Not really."

"John, we'll get lost!"

He had his hands around her waist, and as he drew her closer she could almost feel his chuckles against her back. "Trust me, little Bea. I know what I'm doing."

"Tell me about Meghan," she demanded, letting herself slip into the nostalgic mood.

"We loved her. She was a character, and we didn't dare tell grandmother half the crazy stunts she let us get away with."

"So your grandmother didn't know about the sexy stories?"

"Oh, she knew. Grandmother had a way of knowing everything. But she figured whatever we could understand we could handle. And if we worried about what we didn't understand, she knew we'd ask her. I remember one time here at Versailles Meghan got on a kick about the personal habits of some of Louis XIV's relatives. Much of the gorgeous woodwork at Versailles is hopelessly stained because King Louis and his friends used the halls as public bathrooms. That infuriated her. And she didn't approve of the blatant homosexuality that apparently went on at Versailles. She kept raving about how those men had missed out on the best part of life."

He was smiling at his memories. "My younger brother and I were afraid we might miss out on the best part of life, too, so we did ask grandmother about that!" His hands moved idly, almost caressingly, along her back as he talked. "Grandmother discussed everything with us, but it wasn't until I got older that I understood what she meant about this man-woman thing being the essence of life."

"Man-woman thing?" Bea's breath caught when his hands brushed her breasts, and he pulled her against him and buried his face in her hair.

"Mmmmm. *This* man-woman thing." His hands curved to her shape as his lips roved restlessly around her neck.

"John, someone will see you."

"In all our years here, no one ever found this place." He nuzzled her throat.

Bea wanted more than anything to melt in his arms, to turn, raise her chin and give him full access to her lips. She wanted to burn with his kisses. Surely it was harmless enough to share a few kisses in a public place; she would be gone before night-fall. Yet still she was afraid. Of him? Of herself? She didn't know.

John sensed her hesitancy. He gave her a moment more; and when she continued to hold back, he reluctantly released her.

"This is the last stretch," he said lightly as if nothing had happened. Guiding her with just the heel of his hand, he directed them along yet another branching path, this one so narrow and unkept it could hardly be seen.

"We're here?" Her voice was wispy, barely in control.

"I'm going to be one disappointed man if, when we part those darker green ferns to your left up there, we don't find...." Gingerly, expectantly, he held back the thick fronds for her to pass through.

"Oh, John, it's beautiful!" She stepped into a tiny, circular clearing lined with lush blue green moss and feathery ferns. The surrounding trees were lacy thin at the top, letting in just enough snatches of golden rays to give a cathedral effect to the hushed place. As the fern doorway swished back, she felt herself enclosed in a green world of magic—a private, wooded world, cool and sweet smelling. Whimsically Bea slipped off her sandals and walked into the center of the clearing, careful to avoid the few white wild flowers, which lifted their tiny heads greedily to the specks of sun.

"I can see why you and your brother loved it," she sighed reverently, stretching her arms until her fingertips reached soft leaves on each side of her.

She and John reaching together would probably span the clearing. But it must have seemed a large secret world to a child.

"I always wondered what this area had been designed for." John loosened his tie and walked slowly around the edge of the undergrowth, his eyes trained downward. "Somewhere in here is a tiny statue. Of some mythical god, I think. My younger brother and I found it once, then never could locate it again."

"Did you and your brother play mythology games here? You'd make a formidable Thor."

"I hate to disillusion you," he grinned, picking at a moist pile of leaves with the toe of his shoe, "but we played cars. We made Indy 500 racers out of bark."

"What a waste of this setting! Meghan should have 'Frenchified' you some more."

He looked at her strangely, then gave up trying to loosen the pile of leaves and instead strolled toward her. Her breathing seemed suspended as she saw him approach, read the desire in his eyes.

"That was when we were quite young." His voice was thick as he took her hands and raised them against his cheek. "Later, during those frustrating teenage years when a boy needs lots of time to think, I came here alone. That was when I vowed someday I'd bring a woman here with me."

"And did you?" Bea moistened her lips nervously.

"Not until now." His words were almost lost against her lips. She sank into his body as comfortably as if she had been born to fit there. It was what she had been waiting for all day, wanting, fighting. *Just one kiss,* she told herself. *I can give myself that farewell gift.* But the idea of a limit faded when he kissed her a second time. And then she kissed him back, clinging to his lips as hungrily as if she had never been touched before.

And she hadn't—not like this. Never like this, not even after the fireworks scare. There was a fierce urgency in his seeking mouth, a desperation, as if he must take her sweetness quickly or lose it forever. She let him force her lips open, liking the way he made her share herself with him.

A determination ran through her like an urgent crusade that he mustn't forget her. She would be leaving him in just a few hours. She couldn't bear to step out of his life unremembered. She wanted herself indelibly imprinted on his memory, wanted him to *know* it was Bea Allen he had brought to his secret hiding place. Only Bea. His Versailles woman. The need to be remembered was an obsession.

A slight breeze entered the clearing, faded, then reentered, stirring her soft pink skirt around John's legs. They were wrapped in each other's arms, in their garments, in their needs.

He was covering her face with little exploring caresses. And she could feel some of her hair blowing loose and spreading lightly across his mouth. She drew back slightly, wanting to spare him the irritation, but he laced his fingers into her elegant chignon to keep her still while he lifted his strong face close to hers and smilingly let the wind brush the sooty black strands across his lips.

"Not a bad idea," he muttered, thrusting both hands into her hair and beginning to loosen the neat coil.

"No, John," she objected shakily, trying to regain her composure. She was so mesmerized by the place, so gripped by the knowledge they would soon be parted forever, that she didn't trust herself. Making him remember her was one thing. But what if she let it go too far, if she let him imprint himself too poignantly on *her* memory? She sensed he had the power to make her subsequent loneliness insurmountable.

"John, I'm only willing to accommodate your nostalgia up to a point...." Her tone of voice was not as detached as she would have liked while she tried to redo her hair.

"Hush, Bea." Ruthlessly his elbows pressed her hands away as his fingers unwound the coil, pulling her long hair out across her shoulders. The breeze immediately caught the tangled curls, enveloping his head as he leaned into her open lips.

"No! I...." She got no further, for he was kissing her passionately, absorbing her, transforming her.

And she was swept up in it. There was only his desire and passion in that kiss—desire she matched, passion she felt, like Eve, that she deserved.

His hands roved over her hair as if he adored the feel of it. He caught at the curls and wrapped them close to his neck, imprisoning himself. She was excited by the gesture and pressed closer to him, wanting to enslave him completely, not caring about anything but that he never, never forget her.

In a reaction so natural it was beyond seduction, she rubbed her breasts against his chest. His hands fell motionless in her hair, then moved down her back to her hips, urging gently. Sensing what they both needed, she eased away from him slightly to loosen his suit coat, then slipped her arms around him.

"Ah." That was better. Beautiful feeling, the heated strength of him against her. Again she began that instinctive movement with her breasts, and he shuddered, kissing her deeply with an almost guttural moan against her breath. His mouth moved on to her throat, one hand holding her head against his shoulder to facilitate their pleasure as the other pressed her hips against him.

She knew when he spread his suit coat and lowered her to the ground. She couldn't say later that she wasn't aware, or that it "just happened." She knew they weren't being seated merely for a quiet rest in the shade. She felt it happening, felt his hands at the tiny buttons of her dress, sensed the cooling breeze flitting against her body as the garment slipped off her shoulders. And she did nothing to stop him. Not even when it occurred to her that people might arrive, that she would be leaving him tonight; not even when she remembered the unknown mistress he must surely have. Today, this moment, he was hers.

He was fumbling with the back opening of her bra until, frustrated, he just slid it awkwardly down. The straps partially pinned her arms to her sides as his hands eagerly closed over her pulsating, swollen softness. She sighed with pleasure, adoring the texture of his rough palms against her skin. With a stab of mental pain she identified the contrasting texture of his injured right hand where it had been blistered, sensed the little area where one fingertip was not there to caress her. Shuddering, she pulled her arms free of the hindering straps and drew his mangled hand to her lips.

"It's all right, Bea," he comforted her soothingly. Then he lifted her hair into a web on the moss as he stretched out beside her. His face was close to hers, and she pecked little kisses on his brows and temples. For a while he accepted her play; then he drew away, leaning up on one elbow so he could look at her as his hands explored her body. She reached for him, wanting him close against her. But he quieted her, then slowly pushed her dress and bra farther down to her hips. Delicately he ran his hands over her full, erect breasts, his eyes caressing her while he watched her body react to his touch.

She somehow sensed that he was trying to plant her in his memory as surely as she had tried to be implanted there. She was swept by a feeling of satisfaction so intense it was almost as if they had already made love. She lay unmoving before his gaze, anxious, hoping he found her beautiful.

Although he didn't speak, he seemed to find great pleasure in looking at her. His eyes roved over her face, the hollow of her throat, her full breasts, both swollen in his hands. With a groan he slid low beside her and rolled almost on top of her, his mouth moving to one demanding nipple, then the other. With a cry of delight, she sank her fingers into his sandy hair. She felt as if she were melting from deep within her.

But suddenly, cruelly, he was moving away from her. And not returning, pulling at her hands, abruptly raising her to her feet.

"John?" She was disoriented, crushed.

He was fumbling with her clothing, tucking her arms back within her bra straps and trying to rearrange it properly. "Someone's coming." His breathless warning was frustrated and angry as he tried to cover her nakedness.

"I don't care." At that point she would have believed anything. She wanted him to make love to her.

"You'd care." His gruff answer was protective. But she still stood unmoving.

"Bea, help me," he urged, more awkward with replacing her clothing than he had been in removing it. Automatically she slid her bra back in place. He took over from there, getting at least some of her dress buttoned up as voices approached. Then he pulled her against him to shield her, just as the chattering children came tumbling in. There were three of them: two look-alike boys and a curly-haired little girl. Their excited voices suddenly fell into silence when they learned someone was in the hidden clearing.

"You found our place," the eldest of them, a boy about ten years old, finally accused in French.

"No, you found *my* place," John answered gently in their own language. "This has been mine since I was younger than you. But I'll share it with you next time you come."

They had stared at him, wide-eyed, for just a brief moment before popping under the ferns and disappearing as quickly as they had come. It was only for a few seconds after they had left that their retreating footsteps could even be heard.

Bea was trembling against John, reaction at how close she had been to losing her head just beginning to dawn on her.

"What did you tell them?" She tried to make her voice firm.

"That this man-woman thing is terrific, and that one of them must bring that little girl back here when they are grownups." He was kissing her hair lightly.

"At least now you have brought a woman here. You can close that unfinished book." She sounded bitter as she slipped from his arms.

"Bea, it wasn't like that...."

"Shhh, John. Please don't say anything. I know it was my fault." Still embarrassed, she took her fingertips away from his lips and turned to complete the adjustment of her dress. Then her hands went nervously to her hair.

But his hands were there, sifting through it. "You were right to bring your purse," he said. "You will need a comb after all."

"I left my purse back with Helen." She tried to move his hands away.

"My fingers make a pretty good comb." He closed his elbows around her shoulders, drawing her against him as he continued to stroke her hair.

"John, this has to stop." She got the words out jerkily, but her seriousness was evident.

John's hands fell to her shoulders, not content yet to leave her body, and it took all of her determination to not lean against him and leave everything to his judgment.

If John sensed the fragility of her resolve, he did not take advantage of it. With a muttered imprecation he released her and knelt to retrieve his coat, shaking it off before shrugging into it and walking across to get her sandals.

"You're right, of course." His face expressionless, he knelt to grasp her ankle and help ease her foot into the shoe. Even that light touch was provocative to her, and she could hardly tolerate his helping her with the other sandal. When he finished fastening them and stood up, she shied away from him, but he reassured her immediately.

"I'm just going to brush you off. You work with your hair." His touch was impersonal, his face almost icy as he carefully removed the bits of moss and bark that clung to her delicate pink dress.

She was still fussing with her long hair when he finally moved away.

"You look fine," he snapped.

"I'll feel foolish going back with this braid down my back. The Drakes will know. . . ."

"They'll be delighted for us," he said huskily, momentarily revealing that he had not been able to completely discard his previous passion.

"John, I'm sorry that I...."

"There must be some of your hairpins around here somewhere." He knelt and started rummaging around in the moss. "Ah, here's a few...." Realizing that he was not going to let her talk about it, would not let her take the proverbial cold shower verbally, she snatched her pins from him.

"There might be more." He moved searchingly to his left and felt around the ground.

Roughly she coiled up her hair and began stabbing the few fastenings into place, only halfheartedly watching him continue his search.

"Well, I'll be," she heard him say slowly, his voice strange as his hand struck an obstruction buried under moss and leaves.

She saw him carefully lift debris away from a tiny statue firmly implanted in the soil, its minute bronze features covered with the grit of time.

Delightedly she knelt beside him, her own jumbled emotions momentarily unimportant in her realization of what this rediscovery must mean to the grown man, what childhood memories must be sweeping over him while his huge hand touched the outlines of the little god so long hidden. The moment, she thought, must be especially poignant with his younger brother so ill. "You found it!" she breathed almost reverently, her heart lurching at the brief look of boyish awe she surprised on his face.

"I'll be," he repeated huskily, gradually recovering his adult composure. He took a cigarette lighter out of his pocket and flipped it on, close to the tiny figure.

"Can you tell what it is?"

"Not really. It's too dirty. But it's still as ugly as Louis and I first thought it was." His voice held satisfaction.

"You and. . . Louis?" Her lips quirked.

"My brother Louis—not the Fourteenth!"

It was the first time she had heard his brother's name, and she liked the fond, indulgent way he said it. "Who knows, maybe the other Louis thought it was ugly, too," she said quietly. "And loved it anyway, just like you two. King Louis must have known this place and this statue were here."

"No!" he chuckled. "Only Meghan, my brothers and I knew. . . and now of course, dearest Bea. Only we know." He clicked the lighter closed and grinned at her. "And don't you forget it."

Forget it, she thought wildly, carefully following him out of the clearing. She had already foolishly made certain she would not forget this place. Her legs felt like jelly, and unfinished desire still ground hungrily within her. She hoped the man never chose to exercise the subtle, alarming power he seemed to have over her.

"It's a good thing I'm leaving tonight." Unknowingly she blurted the thought aloud.

"Lord! I'll be so relieved when I get you on that train and out of my life. I don't need this right now."

Bea didn't find his shared revelation as satisfactory as she should have. But it had one positive effect. By the time she and John rejoined their companions at the Neptune Basin, the urgent heat that had been surging continuously over her in demanding waves had settled down to a desolate, frozen ache in her soul.

CHAPTER SEVEN

JOHN FOUND IT CONVENIENT that Bob and Helen
wanted to go to a restaurant in the St-Germain dis-
trict, where they were to meet friends for dinner.
As he explained to Bea after they had dropped off
their elderly companions, it would be easier for
him to get Bea out of the Royal unnoticed if the
Drakes were elsewhere.

"Since the parking lot is at the rear of the hotel
anyway," he said as they approached the rue de
Rivoli, "I can slip your bags to the car from the
back stairs just as soon as you're packed. Then
we'll eat in the hotel coffee shop before I bring the
car around front. People seeing you leave will just
think we're going out for the evening."

"Whatever you think," Bea said absently.
Maintaining an image for her tour group no longer seemed particularly important. She was preoccupied with the frozen ache inside her. It alarmed
her that she was so reluctant to leave John Robertson, particularly in light of his own hurry to be rid
of her.

"Bea, I'm trying to help you. I promised I
would give you a good cover in place of your
friend who didn't show up."

"I really don't care if the whole tour group sees

me walk right out the front door by myself carrying my suitcase. I want my passport back, by the way."

He reached inside his suit coat for the document and handed it to her.

Pointedly she examined it.

He was annoyed that she had felt the need to check her passport. "I haven't changed anything or substituted fake papers," he snapped. "If you're upset after what happened at Versailles, I'm truly sorry I let it.... Well."

"It was my fault, too. Forget it."

"That's impossible!" he exploded. "I hadn't planned that love scene—it was a monumental mistake on my part."

Bea had been thinking the same thing about her own role. Instead of forcing the man to remember her, she had let him get under her own skin, making her body and soul actually hurt with her need for him. She had never felt this for anyone before, never been sad when it was time for an association to end. But it didn't assuage her deep, empty ache when he seemed to be experiencing the same regret.

"John, forget it! I intend to. All I want to think about right now is boarding the train."

After her chilling reply, he had remained silent until they had arrived at the hotel. His instructions to her once they pulled up at the lobby entrance were brief and firm. "The rear door will be locked from the outside, so I'll let you off here and drive on to the back to park. Wait for me in the lobby."

She resented his order, but hopped out quickly without arguing, fully intending to disobey him anyway and go on to their suite. She had a key. She was convinced the less time she spent in his presence these last few hours, the better for her. She hoped she would be able to talk him into just dropping her off at the train station instead of seeing her into her compartment.

With those troubled thoughts running through her head, Bea had absolutely no premonition of the ordeal that awaited her inside the hotel. She had walked quickly to the entrance, taking no particular notice of the unusual number of people milling in the lobby as she pushed open the revolving door. Perhaps she would have been curious had she not been so distracted, but her attention was further diverted when a small child came charging from a corner of the glass-enclosed foyer and bumped into her.

"Careful, you're going to get hurt...." She hadn't finished her sentence when the boy grabbed hold of Bea's hand and intentionally pressed a scrap of folded paper into her palm.

"This at you, him," he whispered urgently in butchered English. Then he scampered away. Bea automatically closed her fingers around the paper, intending to glance at it when she got inside the lobby, expecting to find a religious tract or advertisement for a sleazy sex nightclub. But such reading was quickly forgotten once she entered the hotel.

Because pandemonium broke out.

"It's the Allen woman!" Someone shouted.

"Where's Robertson?"

"Doesn't he feel any concern about the missing man?"

"Does he know Carole Ward got a ransom note last night?"

"Why was it necessary to send Harry Ward along with that herbicide?"

She was surrounded by screaming people waving microphones under her nose and popping flashbulbs that gave her spots before her eyes. She could hear the grinding of a TV camera as crewmen tried to force a path toward her with their bulky equipment.

In astonishment, Bea backed away from the mass of reporters, at first not comprehending that they were actually talking to her. She kept thinking that if she just got out of the way, the people would move on to whomever they were trying to interview.

"Has Robertson been with you today, Ms. Allen? Is he really unaware Ward has been kidnapped?"

That question drove home to her the horrible reality that she was the actual target for these newsmen. Confused, she shook her head and tried to skirt around a large chair blocking her retreat.

"Were you with Robertson when he was hiding out at his ranch last week? Has the government been in contact with him?" This time the TV cameramen were ahead of her and the ugly lens stared mercilessly in her face, cutting off her escape.

"I have nothing to say." She tried to appear composed while the yelling people completely surrounded her. Her knees were pressed against the back of a huge overstuffed chair and the glass window of the hotel was behind her. There was no place to run. Cameras were flashing and grinding from all angles, and reporters, shoving from the rear, were forcing others to crush against her. Bea looked around in baffled alarm.

She could see a hotel clerk trying to reach her, but he was having trouble himself. Desperately she grabbed the top of the chair and braced herself as the shouting reporters continued their onslaught.

She realized later that it would have taken several policemen waving clubs to get her out of there, had not John arrived.

"There's Robertson," someone yelled from the edge of the melee, and everyone was diverted. As John strode purposefully into the lobby with two burly strangers at his side, the newspeople descended on him like locusts, and that gave her enough space to rush toward the hotel clerk.

"I'm taking you to the back freight elevator," the man said as he grasped her arm. "We have our security staff trying to keep them off the upper floors. And the police have been called."

Gratefully she let him lead her away, but unfortunately they were spotted by a woman who had been unable to get close to John Robertson. Her shriek of "Wait, Ms. Allen" reinstituted a minor swarm in Bea's direction. She could hear questions being thrown at both herself and John.

"Carole Ward says Robertson won't help her. Isn't he actually here to arrange...."

"How long have you two been having an affair? Are there any marriage plans?"

"Will you appear at the hearing called by Congressman. . . ."

"Was it really herbicide that was shipped?"

"Mr. Robertson, have you received a ransom note similar to. . . ."

Bea's mind stuck on the ransom note query. The piece of paper in her palm seemed too hot to hold. But she clutched it in her fist and followed the man who was trying to open a path for her.

The rest was a nightmare. Even when the pushing crowd made her stumble over furniture, her one thought was not to lose her grip on the note. With her purse in the other hand and thus unable to use her arms effectively for balance, she went sprawling sideways across a red velvet couch. But the photographers had no mercy for her helpless position. Gleefully they snapped pictures while she struggled to rise. Some unknown man, perhaps one who had come in with John, forced the crowd apart and helped her up. Then the hotel clerk literally dragged her along with him, holding up his free hand to try to stave off the picture-taking. Glancing over her shoulder, Bea saw John being helped similarly, horror in his eyes as he shoved against reporters to try and reach her. Eventually they gave up trying to get Bea to an elevator and led her up the huge curving staircase with John and his entourage close behind.

By then, policemen had arrived to hold the media back. The hotel clerk actually came into their suite with Bea while other hotel staff talked with John in the little entry hall. They were incensed that he had not prepared them for the possible influx of newsmen. Such things were usually predictable, they claimed.

Half listening to John's assurances that he would get his own security staff in quickly to handle the press, and that he would pay the expenses of the necessary hotel protection, Bea sat dazedly on the edge of her bed and smiled weakly at the hotel clerk. Only gradually did it dawn on her that John had anticipated this—it had not been the shock to him it had been to her.

He's been lying to me all along, she realized bleakly. It was incredible. The whole thing about his brother and this Mathilde had to be a sham. Bea burned with embarrassed fury as she recalled how easily she had been duped, what a ridiculous story she had actually believed. At first she had thought it too complicated, unreal; and yet because John had seemed concerned about his brother, she had been all too ready to accept it, to feel she was obligated to straighten out the mess she thought she had created.

And then she had continued to believe in the deception because she had learned to like John Robertson much too much.

The hotel clerk was watching her with concern, and she realized she probably appeared to be in shock. She reassured him that she would be all right, and insisted that he go on to his other work. But he left rather reluctantly.

It was not much longer before John got rid of the remaining hotel personnel and hurried into her room to kneel by her side. She just stared at him when he asked her how she was doing.

"Bea, did they hurt you?" he repeated, running his hands anxiously over her arms.

She cringed away from him, abhorring his touch. She felt betrayed.

"Do you even have a brother?" she asked woodenly.

"Answer me, Bea. Are you all right?" His face was worried as he drew her to her feet despite her protests.

"Oh, I'm just wonderful." She broke free, but stood resolutely near him, watching him unflinchingly. "Of course, a little honesty might have been helpful. It would have saved you the trouble of buttering up the lonely tourist so she would go along with your game."

"It wasn't like that, Bea."

"You expected those newsmen," she accused.

"No! Not today. Or I would have put you on that morning train to Brussels. I didn't know Carole had received a ransom note...."

"Are you going to tell me what's really going on?"

He was pacing the way he did when troubled, and she knew then that he still had no intention of telling her the truth.

"Now I can't put you on that train tonight." He seemed to be thinking aloud instead. "Those newsmen would eat you alive. You'll have to stay here until I can work something better out."

Bea didn't argue about that. She was in no hurry to go back and face that public absurdity again. It was when she sat back down on the bed that she realized she still had the piece of paper crumpled in her hand. Carefully she spread it out and tried to read it. Predictably it was in French, but she had no trouble making out a name and a group of figures with a dollar sign. Quietly she folded the paper up again and watched John continue his preoccupied pacing.

"Who is Harry Ward?" she demanded.

He whirled around. "What did you say?"

"Who is Harry Ward?"

"How much did you hear down there?"

"Not enough. Who is he?"

"An employee."

"And he's been kidnapped?"

"No. His wife thinks so, but...." His expression was guarded as he seemed to be groping for words. "Actually, he's embezzled some money and run away with another woman. That note the reporters say his wife received must be a blind he thought up."

"I don't believe you."

"Bea, it's not your concern."

The note felt hot in her hand. "I think it has become my concern," she said carefully, holding up the paper. "A child handed me this just before I got inside the hotel and told me to give it to you. Even without French I can understand words like Harry Ward and $100,000!"

John's distress was evident as he took the message from her.

A NIGHT'S SLEEP did nothing to relieve John's anxiety.

"I want Bea Allen out of this! You can't protect

her." He swore as his fist banged the tattered note spread out on the desk in Louis's office at the Sorbonne.

"Keep your voice down, John," Louis ordered. "Do you want those newsmen who followed you to know that Blanco and André are in here, too?"

"And quit ranting about your woman and those reporters yesterday." André appeared unmoved. "We know that those media people were waiting for you after Carole Ward received a ransom note, and we were outside the hotel, ready to warn you. But did you tell us you had rented a car? No! Your lady friend hops out and runs in before. . . ."

"At least we know to coordinate better." Blanco tried to soothe them both.

"I should never have let you talk me out of sending Bea back to the States after someone harassed her at the fireworks display."

"John, I still think that the incident with Blanco's scar-faced friend was a flyer," André said reassuringly, "a warning. They are competitors. The man regularly does such things. Remember that three others Blanco was seen talking to at that sidewalk café were also harassed Saturday night. The man was just discouraging people from using Blanco's services."

"We have a feud going over a little activity in the Middle East," Blanco explained sheepishly.

"Your argument at the café with the woman. . . ." André continued.

"Her name is Bea Allen!"

"With Mademoiselle Allen," André corrected smoothly, "was most convincing to observers. As was the making up. A very good move on your part.''

''Back off, André.''

''All right, old friend. So the café scene was not planned. Anyway, I had observers there, and they did not suspect you as Blanco's contact. They saw you two as lovers, exactly what you had hoped. That image is the best protection she has.''

''But someone targeted her to receive the note about Harry. I don't want Bea targeted by anyone, for any reason.''

''John, accept André's word that he will protect her,'' Louis advised. ''His agent kept good track of Ms. Allen when she went shopping on her own. You're losing sight of your primary problem.''

John slumped down in his chair, and there was a strained silence as the four men pondered their present crisis.

''We have a hell of a job cut out for us,'' André mused aloud. ''We seem to be dealing with three conflicting factions: the one that sent John the original million-dollar ransom note; one that has demanded Carole Ward mail ten thousand dollars to a Liechtenstein postal box; and this group that gave Mademoiselle Allen the note offering only information.''

''Did you tell everyone that yesterday my office finally received instructions for paying the million dollars?'' John asked André.

''Couldn't it be the same group that contacted Carole?'' Louis ventured.

''We don't think so—this last message to my office included a list of some equipment Harry had taken with him. Carole's note had nothing like that to validate it and could possibly be a hoax. And we had different instructions than she: we are to transfer the money to a Swiss account within a week.''

''At any rate, we're going to have to accept that at least one of these groups has Harry Ward held prisoner,'' André pointed out. ''Now, do we also accept that Ward was not able to destroy the fertilizer?''

· ''Definitely,'' John agreed. ''I *know* Harry was in on that note Bea was given for me.'' John pointed to the roughly printed letters. ''See this phrase, 'We can tell you where to find Harry—SME, 17'? That SME code identifies the person writing the message as having actually cleared with Harry. A number more than ten means Harry has not yet destroyed the fertilizer. The closer to ten, the less concerned he is about its future use; the closer to twenty, the more critical the problem.''

''I'm glad you weren't in charge of our wartime coding,'' André shuddered.

''It works for us,'' John snapped. ''None of the other notes had Harry's code in it. He must have found a bribable person and figures if we get there soon, we can take care of him *and* the fertilizer. I'm prepared to pay the hundred thousand tonight and hope we can get Harry out before the week's deadline is up. But if my office gets a followup on that ransom note they're going to try to buy us some time.''

''Frankly,'' Blanco said, ''my experience indicates these kidnap-ransom projects have a way of going wrong, and you'll have a better chance of rescuing Ward with bribes anyway. It will be expensive, you'll have more palms to grease before you can finally get him out, but it just might work."

John nodded in agreement. "I plan to meet these people tonight and try to discover Harry's whereabouts. In the meantime, you two activate the arrangements for us to enter Africa."

"Everything's already set up within Africa, assuming Ward is in the vicinity of Nand's plantation," André mused. "But we can't leave from France now; our authorities get more careful when publicity such as you are receiving begins circulating. We'll have to shift our flight to Belgium."

"Not Belgium! I'm sending Bea Allen there by chauffeur this afternoon."

"You can't do that," André objected, pointing to the paper on the desk. "These extortionists demanded that she go to that bistro with you tonight."

"I won't take her. They'll have to settle for me."

"You're letting yourself get emotionally involved," André barked.

"Right! I'm emotionally involved. My decisions have already endangered Harry, and God knows how many innocent Africans. I'm not adding Beatrice Allen to the list."

"You'd better be thinking of those innocent Africans again," his friend pursued relentlessly. "We've been lucky so far; the press and the terrorists don't seem to know about that fertilizer yet.

But I wouldn't trust your luck much further. Ward's concerned enough to give it a 17. We can protect one person whose whereabouts we know, but we can't protect random citizens when those rebels learn how to blow up your fertilizer.''

"Damn you, André!" John's face reflected his anguish.

"You can't take a chance those extortionists might panic if you don't follow their specific instructions," Louis warned his brother with uncharacteristic sympathy. "And you have to find Ward right away because only he can lead you to the fertilizer. You've got to take her tonight."

"Tell her the truth," André advised.

"No! She'd be in worse danger if she gave any indication she knows what's going on."

"I think you're making a mistake, but I don't care what methods you use if you just get her there tonight."

"I'll ask her to go," John finally said reluctantly, "but I won't trick her or force her. If she refuses, she's out of it."

"And you're hoping she refuses." André started to argue further, then, seeing the set of John's chin, sighed in resignation. Shrugging his shoulders, he pulled his chair closer to the desk, and the others gathered around him attentively.

"Those two security men your office has sent over should be arriving within a few hours," he said matter-of-factly. "We'll place them at the hotel to assist you and Mademoiselle Allen with the remaining newsmen. That will leave our own men undercover where they can be of more use.

Once Mademoiselle Allen helps you get your information tonight, we can let her go on to wherever she wishes. We'll arrange cover for her until this is over.''

John dejectedly nodded his understanding.

''Now, about our flight into Africa: depending on what John finds out tonight, we'll probably still go in over the desert via Algeria and. . . .''

The men settled deeper in their seats, taking no notes, their concentration extreme. No one doubted that they were at a point where mistakes would be disastrous.

''THIS MORNING you said you didn't want my help.'' Bea's response was guarded as she wrapped the tie of the toweling robe more tightly around her dripping body. At first she had thought John's banging at the door was newsmen, and she had rushed out of her bathtub to be certain the night latch was secure. Now she ignored her sogginess because she was curious why John had returned early from his meeting and why he was asking her to accompany him to the bistro. ''When I offered to go along tonight as that note demanded, you refused! You insisted that I take a chauffeured ride into Brussels this afternoon.''

''I've had to change my mind. You were right. I might not get the information otherwise.''

''And you still won't tell me what this is about?'' she asked. Contrary to John's, Bea's disposition had improved after a night's sleep, and in a perverse way the problem of Harry Ward fascinated her. ''Your story last night that he's embezzled some money and run off with a woman was as lousy as the insane-brother farce.''

"So just accept that it's worth $100,000 for me to locate him.''

"Carole or Mathilde don't fit in, huh? I don't understand any of this. Those newsmen said you called the man a drunk.''

"I said he'd turn up when he's sober. There's a difference. Will you help me or not?''

"Why would newsmen be interested in a drunk?''

"If you're not going to help me, just say so. I won't make you come. But spare me the inquisition.'' He strode over to the closet and Bea padded barefoot after him.

"Just don't make up any more stories about Harry Ward. What are you doing now?''

"Undressing. Do you mind?''

She retreated from his closet door. "Are you going out again?''

"These questions! Are you never satisfied? As a matter of fact, I'm taking a shower. Are you through in the bathroom?''

"I was going to curl my hair and do my makeup. You could go ahead if you won't be long.''

"Thanks so much,'' he said sarcastically, moving past her in just his underwear. At her surprised look because he carried no clothes, he snorted impatiently. "I'll dress back out here so you can have the bathroom.''

While Bea waited on the edge of his bed, she examined her stubby fingernails; she had really made a mess of them. Even putting on a coat of fresh clear polish had not helped much. Sighing, she crossed her naked legs, idly turning her bare feet to watch the afternoon sunshine sparkle off the polish she had frivolously applied to her toenails. She clutched at anything that could distract her from her troubled thoughts.

"He probably hates the womanly smell of the bathroom," she thought with satisfaction, recalling that in addition to doing her manicure she had dusted herself liberally with scented powder and spread cosmetics all over the glass shelf above the sink. Thinking he would not be back for hours, it had felt good to linger over freshening up, because she had gone to sleep in her clothes the previous night.

Bea shivered a little as she recalled how terrifying the situation had been then. Assuming that the newsmen had left after she and John had been in their suite an hour, she had slipped out while John was engrossed in a phone conversation, intending to look for an English-language newspaper in the lobby. She wanted to understand what was going on. It had irritated her that the security people in the hall insisted on accompanying her, but once she had reached the mezzanine and a horde of newspeople had started up the stairs toward her, she had been glad the two men were along.

"Don't you dare set foot outside that door again without my help," John had ranted.

"I thought they would have left by now."

"We'll be lucky if most of the better ones have left by tomorrow. But you can be certain the worst and most obnoxious ones will be dogging us for a long time."

"But how am I going to travel alone on a train tomorrow?" she had shrieked.

"Obviously you're not. I'm going to have to work out private transportation for you."

"I don't want your help!" Bea had insisted illogically.

But John had just gestured toward the door. "Go ahead by yourself, then," he had offered. "Some rag reporter will ask how I am in bed, so think up a good story. But remember, they'll print an answer whether you give one or not. And they'll follow you all the way to Brussels."

The probability that he was accurately describing what she would face had sobered her. She had retreated listlessly to her room, eventually lying fully clothed across her bed, trying to shut out John's voice talking on the scrambled phone. She wondered why she hadn't been suspicious of that specially installed phone earlier; while such communications devices were not uncommon in sensitive-research businesses, she should have realized they would be unusual for a firm like California Robertson, Inc.

Later he had come into her room and suggested she should change into her nightwear before she fell asleep. But the concerned tone of his voice had somehow annoyed her, and she stubbornly had refused to comply.

Thinking about it as she waited for John to finish showering, she regretted her obstinacy; her pink dress would never be the same. Restlessly she swung her leg over her knee, wishing John would hurry. She was tired of sitting naked and soggy on his bed, trying to decide whether to leave or stay.

"Finish up with that war paint you have scattered all over in there," he ordered, padding wetly out of the steaming bathroom. His eyes narrowed when he saw her waiting on his bed, her shapely legs quite exposed beneath the short robe. "And get dressed."

"I couldn't before," she said haughtily. "My clothes were in with you."

"I saw them on the hooks," he admitted gruffly. "That lace bra is indecent. I hope your blouse is stouter fabric than it looked."

"Go to hell," she snapped.

Just as she entered the bathroom she heard the phone ring and was surprised to hear John say quite clearly, "All right, you'd better let him come up. In fact, bring him yourself so the security people will let him in."

Quietly she closed and locked the bathroom door behind her, wondering who their visitor would be. John had been so secretive about the people he was doing business with that she had yet to meet anyone he knew in Paris. She could not imagine his letting anyone else up under the circumstances, and it felt almost sinister to anticipate the arrival of one of his colleagues.

Bea hoped the man would not come soon. She needed some quiet time to ponder this new development. The previous night when she had rashly offered to assist John in getting the information about Harry Ward, he had furiously insisted he did not want her help; and even now he seemed ambivalent in his reluctantly tendered request. She wished he would make up his mind.

Restlessly she put in her contact lenses, then stared at her pale reflection. She looked terrible. Worried. And she knew what was wrong. Illogically she wanted desperately to help John Robertson in any way she could. But she was afraid of making a fool of herself, of being tricked yet again. A decision would have been easier had he come off as macho as he had the first day he barged into her room. She would either have been furious enough to say no, or challenged enough to say yes. As it was, she simply didn't know where she stood.

If I didn't have so much pride I'd go with him tonight and say to hell with being a fool, she thought.

Pride had its value, though, she realized as she reached for her makeup. At least being armed with a reasonable appearance gave you more confidence in your decisions. And she had a feeling she would be needing all the confidence she could get.

As she stepped back to look at the first swipe of makeup across her face she stumbled against something soft. It annoyed her to discover that John had left his underwear in a heap on the floor, and she kicked the garments out of her way, determined she would not be the one to pick them up. It was probably a Freudian thing with him—getting even with her for spreading her woman-stuff all over. Hurriedly she finished patting the foundation onto her face, grateful now that she had left her clothing hanging neatly in the bathroom. Her bra and blouse might be indecent to John's puritanical eye, but at least she could be fully clothed if she had to meet their visitor.

She had done her eyes, dotting on a light splash of beige tones in shadow above the lids and lengthening the deep black of her lashes, when she heard the man enter their suite. She regretted his prompt arrival, for the bathroom was steamy from John's shower, and she would have liked to crack the door open a few moments because her skin was picking up the moisture. In compromise, she loosened the belt of her toweling robe and eased back the deep neckline, letting a bit more air flow across her damp skin. Anything would help.

Then she began on her rouge. She was frowning at her reflection, annoyed that the humidity in the room gave her complexion a flushed, almost rosy hue—not at all the sophisticated effect she was trying to achieve—when it dawned on her there was something familiar about the voice of the man speaking with John.

Too familiar!

Intrigued, she listened carefully. The man's voice was quiet at first, then raised in anger to match the rumble of John's fury. It couldn't be! She flung open the door in excitement.

First she saw John across the room, his powerful body apparently naked beneath his loosely belted toweling robe. Droplets of water still clung to the hair covering his chest. The shoulders of the other man were familiar to her, and she knew, even before he whirled to face her, who he was.

"Perry!" An ecstatic smile was on her face.

But his expression was grim as he watched her move toward him. The question that was poised on her lips went unsaid because he brushed off her touch on his elbow and strode to the door. At her cry of alarm, he glanced back at her.

"I'll call you in the morning, Bea," he grunted brusquely before slamming the door behind him.

The suite was deathly still after Perry Campbell had gone. At first Bea couldn't actually believe that he had left so precipitously. Then her belated dash to the door to catch him was cruelly cut off by John. He half carried her, struggling, back into her own room.

"But I might not be here tomorrow."

"You mean you *still* want to see that bastard?"

"Don't call him that."

"He's a bastard! Any man who would leave you stranded alone in Paris.... I won't have you seeing him again."

Bea's mouth dropped open at the forceful way he filled the alcove, barring her exit.

"You can't stop me."

"I won't have it, Bea. He's no good for you."

"You won't have it? You have no say in it. Perry is my oldest and dearest friend."

"You can still say that after what he did to you?"

"I'd trust him with my life!"

John was so obviously taken aback at her statement that Bea realized with a warm flush that his concern had been genuine; for one brief moment he had been protecting her interests, not his own.

"What did you say to him?" she asked tentatively, her eyes huge.

"I told him to leave you alone—that he'd had his chance, and he'd blown it."

"Why did you let him up here in the first place?"

"If I hadn't seen him, he'd have made trouble. And I already have all the trouble I can handle."

"I'm surprised he took your orders lying down." Bea was troubled. Such docility was not typical of the Perry she knew.

"Actually, he didn't," John admitted. "He insisted on seeing you and hearing from yourself that you were all right. We were about to square off for a fight when you bounced out of the bathroom."

"But why did he leave then?" Bea was bewildered.

"Are you that dense?" Angrily John pushed her in front of the mirror over her desk. "Look at us," he ordered, gruffly calling her attention to the two of them in matching toweling robes, both obviously fresh from bathing. After she had loosened her robe from the heat, Bea's breasts were partially exposed, and the rosy flush of her skin made a vulnerable contrast against John's browned hands at her shoulders. She stared at their image, her breath uneven at the erotic, intimate picture they made together.

"Do I need to spell out for you what conclusions he drew?"

"I'm going to call Perry and explain."

"Suit yourself," he barked, returning to his closet where she could hear him beginning to dress. She averted her head as she moved toward the telephone.

"Is he staying in this hotel?"

"I haven't the foggiest."

"You didn't ask?"

"He wanted to take you with him, and I wasn't having any of that. We didn't get past that stalemate before you danced ecstatically out of your hidey-hole."

"Don't talk to me that way." It was clear from her shaking voice that she was confused and hurt.

With a muffled imprecation John thrashed around in his closet, then walked toward her, buckling up his belt as he came.

"Bea, we've got to talk this out." His remorse was evident.

"I have nothing to talk out with you. I must make Perry understand."

"You mean you actually still care for this NOUOK character?"

"Don't you understand anything? Perry's apparently seen this publicity and rushed up here in his protective mood. He's very tenacious when he decides to be protective."

"I am, too. I take care of my own!"

"I don't need either of you fools," Bea said hotly.

"We'll go back to my original plan." John was

unbothered by her assertion of independence. "We'll have the car pick you up this afternoon, for Brussels and—"

"Quit arranging my life!" Bea objected. His macho presumptuousness had forced her into a decision.

Bea hesitated, conflicting impressions raging for dominance in her confused emotions. There were John's lies—so many of them. But there was the tenderness, too, the reality of his gentle touch when he comforted her. Worst of all was his changeability—the humor, but the silence, the passion, then withdrawal. She was a fool to trust him, and yet instinctively. . . . A memory gushed warmly through her, a memory of his fury with Perry and his protectiveness toward her. Nothing added up to make any sense.

She stared at him curiously, unable to find any answers in his implacable glare, and she desperately wanted answers, both about the Harry Ward affair itself and about John Robertson, the man.

"I'm not going to Brussels this afternoon," she remarked coldly, tossing aside her pride and trusting her instincts. She was thinking absolutely clearly, all her senses tingling with her judgments. If she were to be a fool again, so be it. At least maybe then she would know.

"I started in this problem with you, whatever it is, and I'm seeing it through. I intend to go to that bistro tonight and help you get the information you need. Then you'll be off my conscience."

"I don't want you!"

"Make up your mind. Ten minutes ago you said you wanted my help."

"I said I *needed* your help."

Bea pondered a moment, watching him closely. His hands were clutched in tense fists, his eyes troubled.

"Then I suggest you accept it for this one last night," she said finally. "After that, we can stay out of each other's lives."

CHAPTER EIGHT

THE INSTRUCTIONS in the note handed to Bea had been specific. To learn Harry Ward's location, a messenger must place $100,000 in a storage locker at the Gare du Nord, then wait by an assigned pay phone with the key. John and Bea were to stroll a two-block area on the city's Left Bank for a half hour before taking a seat at the Bistro d'Oiseau. At exactly eleven-thirty John was to use a pay phone at the bistro to call his messenger at the assigned number.

It was the requirement that Bea remain alone at their table during his phone conversation that worried John.

At first Bea had belittled his concern; but once on the Left Bank, she began to share his misgivings. The neighborhood was incredibly shabby, and its noise and stench shattered the senses— hardly the place a woman would choose to be alone. Roaring motorcycles shared the sidewalks and streets equally, forcing pedestrians to dodge them or be hit. Bea's differences with John were pushed to the back of her mind as they weaved their way through the crowded, littered streets, and she was grateful for his protective arm around her waist.

They had been walking about fifteen minutes when they came upon the elderly man lying in front of a deserted tobacco shop, his scrawny legs stretching halfway across the narrow sidewalk. He had obviously not bathed for days, and his dirty face had the unhealthy color of the advanced alcoholic. His eyes were glazed, and he was too far gone in his drunken stupor even to lift a hand to beg as had apparently been his intention when he had positioned himself against the rotting doorway. An empty, rusted container, which at one time in the evening might have held some coins, was turned over near his listless body.

Although Bea had encountered the occasional panhandler lying around New York without becoming overly concerned, something about this man tore at her heart.

"The police will notice him soon. You can't rescue every drunk you see." John's quiet observation broke through her horror as he guided her around the man's feet.

"I could leave some francs for him. He might use them for food."

"Bea, he'd never get them. Someone's already pilfered his collection can."

She knew his observations were accurate, but it hurt her to walk on. "If only everyone didn't look so...amused by him."

"It's the absurdity surrounding him that gets you. The Left Bank isn't what you expected, is it?"

She frowned nervously. "The ultimate place of freedom, to which Hemingway and Stein fled to create? No, it isn't as I pictured it."

"They headquartered several blocks from this area; there it's a bit more sophisticated."

"I expected avant-garde music on the streets by starving musicians, original poetry recited on the corners," she admitted wryly, moving closer to John as a large group of unwashed adults in togas shuffled toward them.

He drew her close to look in a tiny food shop while first that group, then a number of young couples shouting exuberantly at one another moved noisily by.

"I feel as if I'm in mime heaven," she observed once the outlandishly dressed young people had passed. "Everyone seems to be acting out a role, complete with costume and stage makeup."

"And our role is bumbling tourist—we stand out like sore thumbs," John grunted as they walked on again. "Why did I worry about discretion? I could have allowed the reporters to follow us here after all; there's no way we can be given a message unobserved."

Bea glanced up at him. He was so handsome she drew in her breath, almost in pain. His powerful face showed none of his worry; in fact if anything he looked bored. His well-cut brown sports jacket hung casually open at the waist over his tailored oxford-cloth shirt, and his slacks fitted equally well—softening but not completely masking his muscularity. He had the look of a man one might well avoid tangling with.

Nervously Bea smoothed down the skirt of her yellow crochet dress, wishing John had not insisted that she wear it. Until they had entered this neighborhood, she had not been aware quite how insistently it clung to her curves. Never before had strangers looked her over with such cold, leering assessment.

"Are you all right?" He had felt her shudder against him.

"I wish I'd worn a business suit."

"Now I wish I had let you," he admitted gruffly, drawing her even closer against his side. "The dress seemed a good idea to make reporters think we were just going to an expensive restaurant for dinner. Then they were easier to shake. But if we should get separated, don't go it alone. My security men must be somewhere nearby."

"I'm sure they're fitting right in with the scenery." She tried to appear confident so at least he would not have her fears to worry about. It had been worrisome enough eluding the press just to get this far.

The press numbers had diminished since John's brief news conferences had convinced major media that there was no real hostage story developing. But the scandalmongers were hanging on, and some had followed Bea and John earlier that evening to an exclusive café. A few even realized they were slipping directly out the back door of the café and had tried to follow them again. John's driver had exhibited some wild street maneuvers before getting them to the Left Bank without an entourage of newshounds. Bea could tell from John's withdrawn demeanor that he was still concerned something would happen to blow the whole secret meeting.

"The Left Bank would not have been my choice for a meeting of this type," he muttered, his hand spreading over her upper arm as if trying to increase his protection of her. "Puts us at a distinct disadvantage."

"Have you been here much?" she asked weakly.

"A good bit the year I studied at the Sorbonne." He halted her so they could feign interest in a menu posted outside a restaurant. "This neighborhood attracts a different crowd now. But the Left Bank has always been a place a person could come and 'act out' while he tried to 'discover' himself."

He glanced at his watch.

"This is it! Our spot is the next one on the right." Tense excitement roughened his voice. "We'll check out the menu, walk on a few doors, then return."

She nodded imperceptibly.

It was after they had turned back toward the Bistro d'Oiseau, which had been their goal all along, that the three young men wandered noisily out of an intersecting alley.

"I hope your visits here as a student never took that drunken form," she said softly. The raucous trio almost blocked the sidewalk and were making suggestive remarks to every woman who passed.

He didn't answer, but she could feel his arm move defensively up to her shoulder.

"Look at that! The American Establishment has arrived," one of the three derisively shouted at John and Bea.

Deliberately ignoring them, John led her to walk in the street, as all others nearby were doing to get by the group. He acted as if he did not understand the remark, and only his strong grip on her shoulder hinted at his annoyance.

"I want her." One of the three men pointed to Bea, his slurred voice and dilated pupils evidence of the drugs he had consumed.

Confused thoughts whirled in Bea's head as the man continued to make lurid remarks. She wondered if this was planned, if somehow the extortionists intended to get the money in the train station without ever giving John the message. Or could it actually just be an incredibly unlucky coincidence?

"I think we'll go back to the Bistro d'Oiseau. That food sounded pretty good, don't you think?" John spoke in cold calm, apparently having opted in his own mind for the "coincidence" explanation for the obnoxious trio. He seemed determined not to let any insult make him lose sight of his primary goal.

At first it appeared they would be able to avoid a confrontation, but perhaps the fact that other people were watching the situation with amusement encouraged the trio to actual aggression. The three men wobbled crazily into the street to block John's way to the bistro.

Strangely, Bea's greatest concern was time. It was almost eleven o'clock; they couldn't afford this problem. She tried to ignore the suggestive gestures of the one who weaved toward her.

"What's the matter, lady?" he sneered. "Don't you like the crepes at your fancy hotel?"

Graphically insulting in his manner, he reached out a shaky hand toward Bea's well-exposed breasts.

She couldn't help herself. Her stony aplomb left her, and she jumped back in horror.

The repulsive man lunged toward her and she screamed, but his fingers never reached her body.

She didn't even see John move. One moment the challenging man was reaching for her breast, the next he was lying on the sidewalk, the victim of John's stunning karate attack. The other two took a shocked glance at their fallen companion and quickly ran back to the alley from which they had come.

"Come on," John said, guiding her toward the bistro. Others watching the scene climbed over the unfortunate man on the sidewalk with unconcern, their faces deliberately vacant.

Bea was trembling when they stopped just inside the entry of the Bistro d'Oiseau.

"Are you all right?" John was unconsciously rubbing his right hand as he looked her over carefully.

She was unable to speak, her breath still coming in short gasps, and John's eyes darkened in anger.

"Did he touch you?"

She shook her head, her skin crawling with the sheer memory of the near intimacy. She realized she had probably not been in any real physical danger, but she was still shaken.

"Please help me," she mumbled almost incoherently, grateful that his large bulk shielded her from the patrons inside. "I feel...dirty!"

Not even aware of why she was doing it, she clutched at his wrist. John seemed suddenly to understand her need for cleansing, and he solemnly opened out his palm, allowing her to place his hand full across the dipping neckline of her dress. He let his fingers rest warmly against her body until his touch healed her revulsion.

"I'm so sorry, love," he murmured when he finally drew her into his arms for a brief moment.

THEY WERE SEATED in the most brightly lighted section in the center of the bistro. John did not argue with the assignment, for the host had seemed to recognize them and go unerringly to that particular table. But to Bea it seemed an odd location to select if one wanted to pass on a secret message worth $100,000.

They had to do something to pass the time until eleven-thirty, so although John rejected the menu, he did order champagne.

He had made his selection carefully from the wine list. But when the waiter poured his glass, John had declared the wine unsatisfactory after merely raising it toward his lips. Bea watched in amazement as the waiter apologized profusely and scurried back with a second bottle, which did meet with John's approval.

"What was that all about?" she asked after the waiter had poured her own glass and hurried away in apparent embarrassment. There had been no instructions in their note regarding a ploy over drinks.

"Taste your wine."

Carefully she took a sip, finding the flavor satisfying almost beyond words.

"It's delicious."

"It had better be." John's voice was rough with contained anger. "Since the management here seems to be in on this extortion I'll tolerate their charging me a hundred and twenty-five dollars for what should be a forty-five-dollar wine. But I'll be damned if I'll let them slip me an inferior bottle."

"But how could you tell? Did it smell like vinegar?"

"No, but it should smell superb. My grandmother's cousins produce grapes for this maker."

"So that's why you didn't want the cognac in our hotel minibar, either; you're a spirits expert!" She found the interest unexpected.

"Robertson grapes go into several California varietal wines. I know fruit better than the finished product," he explained as his eyes roved the room restlessly.

"What time is it?" Like John, she couldn't keep her mind on much except the job at hand.

"About 11:10, I think. I don't want to look at my watch again just yet."

She followed his gaze toward the dance floor, a small area that was decorated with hanging plants and crystal balls not too different from decor used in some American bars. Watching the dancers, Bea realized she and John had not been so unwise in their choice of clothes after all; the bistro seemed to cater to English-speaking tourists dressed much as they were.

"Slumming for local color," she mumbled to herself.

"What?" He didn't look at her as he absent-mindedly responded to the sound of her voice. His eyes were narrowed and hawklike, as if he were braced for any eventuality, and only his thumb, rubbing occasionally across the edge of the table, betrayed his anxiety.

"John, people will begin to think you're up to something strange if you don't start acting more like a carefree tourist," she said gently.

He thought about her remark only a moment before standing up abruptly. "Let's dance, then."

"At least act as if it's not a duty," she hissed as he grimly held out his arms.

His answering smile was pained at best. But he held her very close—probably, she suspected, because the small floor was quite crowded. It was not a particularly pleasant way to pass the agonizing minutes left to them. The music, while better than most Left Bank fare they had heard in snatches during their walk, was raggedly irregular in its rhythm. She had to concentrate to match her steps to John's.

"Damn band!" he mumbled when she almost stumbled against him after the musicians skipped several complete measures of a familiar American tune.

She giggled.

"What's funny?"

"I was just remembering the last time I went dancing."

He pulled her almost too tight in his arms. "Do you always laugh at your dates?"

"What's wrong with you? I was feeling sorry that I'm stepping all over your toes. My last dancing date was a pompous man who didn't stop talking about himself the entire evening. I felt it served him right that I wasn't the world's best dancer. But with you...."

"I hadn't noticed." His hold on her relaxed. "I think we'll do better if we just ignore the music completely."

They moved together rather well several minutes before she began to get worried. "Do you know what time it is?" she whispered.

"We're okay. I've checked my watch. Now who's ruining our tourist act?"

"I just don't want you to be late."

"Be quiet and let me hold you a little longer." It seemed a strange response, but she melted against him willingly. "Actually, you dance well." His lips were tantalizingly close to her cheek.

"In this crush of people I think I'm becoming a rubber stamp of you," she said with greater lightness than she felt. "If we get any closer you'll never get me brushed off."

"Maybe I won't want to."

She was wondering what, if anything, he meant by that remark when the band stopped playing abruptly, with no retard or fade. Bea laughed nervously.

The announcement came blaringly over the loudspeaker. "Ladies and gentlemen, it is almost 11:30, so we will take our break. Please enjoy yourselves, and we will be with you again in a short time." The remarks were repeated in French and German.

"Isn't it suspicious that he announced the time first, plus used English before French?" Bea asked.

"So the band is in on this plot, maybe the whole restaurant," John commented quietly as he led her back to the table. "Take special care, love."

He was gone as soon as he'd seated her.

"You say there's nobody at the Gare du Nord?"

"There are thousands of people at the Gare du Nord," André soothed in French. "But no one has approached me. And speak up a little; I'm near the railroad tracks and can hardly hear you."

"I can't talk louder. These phones are right across from the headwaiter's post." John held the receiver closer to his mouth and turned away from the small black woman looking up a number in the booth next to him. He was startled when she immediately touched his arm.

"Sir, you are to tell the gentleman to give the key to the boy in a green sailor's uniform who comes up to him and asks for fifty francs." The woman's French was heavily accented.

"How do I know you have any authentic news for me?" John demanded harshly, holding the receiver against his chest.

"Your Harry Ward said to tell you he has updated his SME number to 19." She looked apprehensive, as if not certain the message meant anything.

John blanched as he raised his receiver. "André, I'm in contact now with the group that helped Harry get that note to us. This woman says he's raised his concern to 19. Do you understand?"

André grunted his acknowledgment.

"Is there some boy near you in a...don't laugh at this...in a green sailor suit?"

"You were right to warn me." Ever unflappable, André spoke wryly. "Let me look. No. Wait, yes there is—about twenty feet away."

"When he comes up and asks for fifty francs, give him the key instead."

"You'd better get your information first."

As if anticipating André's response, the woman touched John's arm. "I remain with you," she whispered. "When my son calls from the phone near the locker and tells me the money is really there, I will tell you what you need to know."

John repeated the message to André, and the passing of the key was quickly completed, but waiting for the boy to contact his mother seemed interminable. The plan within the bistro had been well coordinated to the advantage of the extortionists. John could not lean far enough around the corner to see Bea's table and check on her safety without dropping the phone, thus risking losing contact both with André and the woman. His stomach was churning madly as he bitterly waited it out.

Once the woman finally received her confirmation she rapidly gave John the name of a village some thirty miles east of Nand Towangi's plantation, where the terrorist headquarters was located, and where Harry was imprisoned. She expected the terrorists to be at the location some time, for they felt safe from discovery and had their arsenal there.

The information did not relieve John's mind, for with an arsenal there was frequently a blasting expert. He felt sick.

"The name of the village alone is not enough," he insisted. "We would risk discovery while wasting time trying to find Harry's specific whereabouts." He moved slightly to block the woman's exit.

"Your lady has been told a street number. If you do not let me leave here safely we will see to it that she cannot tell you."

John's rage was almost blinding. He would not tolerate Bea's being exposed to any more risk. His response was to hang up on André and seize the woman's wrists. "Shall we check on her present safety, then?" he urged threateningly.

The woman's eyes revealed fear, but she did not object when he pulled her with him just far enough into the bistro so he could see his table. The lights had been turned down and smoke was filling the cavernous room with a blue haze. But once his eyes adjusted he could make Bea out. She was sitting with her back almost to him, apparently agitated as she drank hastily from her wineglass. John's hand on the woman's arm tightened in fury. But when Bea lifted her chin in recovered poise, he realized she was all right. His relief was instantaneous.

"Get away from me," he commanded, shoving the woman away with disgust. She scuttled off, her own relief rivaling John's.

Mechanically he placed one foot in front of the other, conflicting thoughts whirling crazily through his mind as he worked his way toward Bea—fury that anyone would dare threaten her; pride in her calm acceptance of this impossible situation; adoration.

She's gorgeous, he thought. She was sitting erect, her lovely head tilted slightly to one side, her waving hair trailing down her back as she watched some movement beyond his vision. She appeared to have all the time in the world. But he didn't! He couldn't wait to reach her side.

He thought he was trying to run to her. But he was sluggish, his feet seeming, in his frenzy, to be ploddingly slow. As he approached he believed that he saw her heart pulsating temptingly beneath the outrageous neckline of that dress. He could almost forgive the dirty youth's attraction to her peach-tinted skin, for her cool beauty was enough to drive a man wild, and he felt an increasing urge to caress her himself. Then he forgot about forgiveness, his rage returning. If he could arrange it, no one would ever touch her but himself.

It seemed to take him forever to reach her table. When she glanced up and saw him, her eyes became hugely round, her face flushed. He knew, then, that she had indeed received the other half of the message.

BEA WAS TAKEN BY SURPRISE when a new waiter approached their table after John left to make his call. She had been nervously pleating the tablecloth, wishing either that she smoked or that she had worn glasses she could take off and clean—anything to fill time during the interminable waiting.

"Perhaps *madame* would like to sample our batter-fried cheese and vegetables served with hot French sauces." The uniformed man interrupted her mental searching for things she might do with her hands. Suavely he set down a large, steaming tray. She looked at him intently, wondering if some particular answer was expected from her. Then, telling herself that she was foolishly anticipating intrigue from every person she saw, she glanced down at the tray. At least food would give her something to look interested in.

"Perhaps you should advise me what to select," she responded. "You seem to have several choices."

"I would suggest a few of each," he said as he began to pile various golden fried tidbits on a large plate. He leaned toward Bea, and she looked at him expectantly, thinking he would explain what he was serving her.

"Continue to look as if we are discussing the food," he said firmly, his hand pointing out something on the plate. Automatically Bea's eyes followed his fingers, his words not quite registering. "You are to tell Monsieur Robertson the street is Loglum. L-o-g-l-u-m. The number is 28. Two eight. Do you understand?"

His manner did not change at all as he began to fill a small bowl with steaming sauce.

"But I have no money to pay..." Bea stammered when she realized what had taken place.

"Your man has taken care of it. Did you get the message?" the waiter insisted, deftly placing the food in front of her.

"Loglum 28," she repeated in a hushed voice. He nodded imperceptibly.

"This sauce is quite spicy, so use it sparingly," he said more loudly as he straightened. "You might also enjoy the grated cheese on top." No sooner had he placed a silver canister near the other plates than he had walked off.

Bea's first inclination was to follow him. What if she had misunderstood? *Loglum 28*. She tried to repeat it over and over in her mind, desperately hoping John would return soon, for she dared not write it down. Unthinkingly she fiddled with a piece of fried vegetable, dipped it in the sauce and delicately bit off a piece.

Hot!

The spice tore at her throat and burned deep within her. Desperately she reached for a water glass, but finding none, drank a huge, sputtering gulp of wine. Someone at a table nearby laughed indelicately at her predicament, and she glared at him, barely overcoming an urge to choke noisily. She did manage, however, to recover her self-possession, and it was only when John's shadow fell over her table, and she looked into his eyes, that her poise momentarily faltered.

"I ORDERED US SOME FOOD," she blurted out breathlessly, hoping her smile looked convincing to those around them. "The waiter had some interesting explanations. I told him I didn't have any money, but he said you had taken care of it."

John knew she was wondering how much they could safely say to each other.

"Which waiter did you buy the food from?" he asked as he seated himself beside her. "I'll make certain it gets on my bill."

She looked toward the tables at her left where she had last seen the man serving someone else. But he was no longer there. In fact, as she scanned the whole room, she could not locate him.

"He seems to be gone." She looked back at John in confusion.

He shrugged his shoulders as if he had expected as much. They stared at each other in strained silence. Finally he reached for one of the cheese balls.

"Don't try that stuff—it's more Mexican than French." He pointed to the sauce. "It'll burn holes in you."

"I found that out," Bea returned stiffly.

By then the band had returned, and the musicians were making their absurd tuning noises, which signaled a new round of dancing. Once the music began, John reached for Bea's hand. "Let's join them," he said abruptly.

Bea was more than willing to fall into his arms. She needed his strength.

"Are you all right?" was the first thing he mumbled in her ear as he gathered her against him.

She nodded, even as she spoke.

"Loglum 28."

"What's that?"

She pulled him back against her and raised her face closer to his ear.

"I'm to tell you the street is Loglum. The number is 28. Loglum 28."

She could feel his hand tighten briefly in reaction, before clasping hers even more firmly.

"I regret ever dragging you into this mess." His whispered apology was urgent.

"Shh," she murmured against his rough chin. She had her own regrets, but not for the same reasons. Somehow she felt physical danger was easier to face than her aching heart.

She had no awareness of what tunes the miserable band was playing; mercifully the set was quiet enough to be ignored, and she could move easily with John, gaining strength from being held by him. She didn't want to think yet of what was to come.

It was John who ended the mood.

Bea could sense the tension in him through the tightening of his arms around her, even before he began his muffled cursing in her ear.

"No! I thought we'd have a few more moments together before...and there's another.... Damn!"

"What is it?" She drew slightly back, trying to see his face.

"The reporters have tracked us down. My men have three of them cornered just a few feet from our table."

"At least we already have the information you needed."

"Yes, we have that," he said strangely, burying his face in her hair.

"Are we supposed to be putting on a good show for these reporters?" she asked breathlessly, trying to quell the curious longing his mock passion was stirring in her. "You should warn me first."

"Forget the reporters," he mumbled huskily, tucking her hand against his chest before putting both arms around her and drawing her intimately against him.

They swayed together long moments, and Bea shamelessly indulged her need to absorb his closeness. But again it was John who eventually broke the mood.

"Bea, I have to get you out of this mess."

Her hand slid down his sleeve to be captured again in his firm grasp. "You mean—" her voice was husky with affection for him, and she stopped in annoyance "—you mean, these reporters...."

"That, immediately. Yes." She saw that his eyes were clouded with intense feeling. He was not pleased that she had sensed his own vulnerability, for he quickly masked his expression, his lids half closing as he generated steely determination.

"You've got me the information I wanted. Now I have to figure a way to get you home to New York."

His dictatorial turnabout was shattering. She wondered how he could turn off his emotions so easily.

"I will not go back to the States just because of this publicity," she whispered. "Running, after being caught living with you, would be the worst thing to do. That is, if you're thinking about my reputation."

"I'm worried about more than your reputation," he admitted.

"I'll worry about my own reputation and anything else concerning me."

"Then suppose you tell me how you propose to continue this idyllic vacation of yours without reporters making your life impossible?"

"Simple," she snapped, crushed that he insisted on pursuing the issue so soon. She could have done with a little more time in his arms before she had to face what was ahead of her.

"I'll maintain a sophisticated facade as if I'm not ashamed of what I've done. But I'll let it be known I find the hassling by the press unacceptable. Even media people will believe that no woman would enjoy living with you for long with a pack of vultures in pursuit."

"How do you propose to put this plan into motion?" His clipped question showed he did not believe her capable of carrying it off.

"Since they're here now, we can have our fight, and I'll walk out on you. They may follow me around Europe for a while, but they'll drop me soon enough once they realize their interest has scared me away from you."

At that she broke free of his arms and pushed her way through the dancers back toward their table.

"Bea!"

His agonized call of surprise was, she thought, more convincing than anything they could have planned. She had grabbed up her purse and fought her way past the reporters to the entrance, where she was insisting that the doorman summon her a taxi, before he caught up with her.

"You're not going without me!" As he grabbed her arm, he canceled her order for a taxi and gave his own order for a car to his security people, who had hastily clustered around them.

"You do something like that again," he hissed, pulling her tight against his chest, "and I'll lock you up."

"I have my departure story set up for the press, don't I?" she said defiantly.

"Bea, you don't know what you're getting yourself into," he started to warn. But the media people were creating such a disturbance in the bistro that the manager interrupted the couple, urging John to leave the building. Apparently his private car had been cruising close by, for the

driver had pulled up by the time they stepped
outside. John unceremoniously pushed Bea in the
back to sit with him; one man hopped in with the
driver, and the others, who she hadn't even
known were accompanying them for the evening,
boarded a second car behind them. They were
away in seconds.

The ease of the operation unnerved Bea. She
had seen enough security arrangements around
the president of the United States to recognize
professional tactics, and it troubled her to realize
that the skill of these men was beyond what a
small-corporation executive like John Robertson
would normally maintain. The Harry Ward problem had to be much more serious than John was
admitting.

They were silent most of the ride back to the
hotel. But the man in front talked quietly into his
two-way radio, and Bea gradually realized he was
speaking Spanish.

"Aren't your men going to a lot of trouble to
cover their tracks?" she demanded.

"Speaking Spanish is a necessity for anyone in
California agriculture," he seethed. "If you want
every reporter in Paris to know that I've asked
your NOUOK boyfriend to go to Brussels with
you in a chauffeured car in the morning, we'll
speak French and English, too."

"You did what?" she almost shouted.

"We're not going to argue about this," he said
wearily. "I admit I'm full of admiration for how
you got our separation set up. It's the best solution we can hope for. But I'm taking over now.

There's a late flight back to the States tomorrow that you two should be able to make before some free-lancer locates you in Belgium. I have too much at stake right now to let your pride and stubbornness foul everything up. I'm not playing games anymore.''

She felt as if her heart had exploded.

Playing games! Was that what he thought she had been doing all along...that she was a bored career woman looking for a lark in Paris? She wanted to hit him, to say something inexcusably foul, to hurt him as much as he was hurting her. Her anger was so complete she froze.

"Did you contact Campbell?" John held both her wrists in one hand as he leaned forward to talk with his man.

"Yes. I gave him your message, and he agreed to be at your suite with his suitcase at 5:00 A.M.''

"Damn you! Passing me on to another man!"

John whirled toward Bea, his face flushed.

"And damn *you*!''

He suppressed any insults she might have thrown at him by sinking his free hand into her hair and pulling her lips against his in a crushing kiss. She fought him bitterly. The struggle ended when they fell against a side window and almost slipped onto the floor. They broke apart, horrified at the uncontrolled rage behind their reactions.

By then they had reached the hotel. Their car was immediately besieged by two cameramen shouting their old questions about Harry Ward, and it must have been obvious to them that Bea and John were furious with each other. However John seemed to regain his control better than she.

"Get out of our way," he insisted coldly as he shoved a path for Bea. "I've already told you that Harry Ward will turn up when he's sober."

"You still insist you're just on a...recreational trip." Two other reporters stationed inside the hotel joined the commotion.

"Don't you care what happens to Ward, Ms. Allen?" a woman reporter asked in apparent disbelief.

"Leave me out of this!"

Bea raised a hand to shield her face from the cameras.

"You mean you're leaving Robertson?" someone else shouted at her.

"I'm leaving *you*!" She shouted back, grabbing hold of the sleeve of John's sport jacket as they fought their way into the hotel. Astoundingly her brain was clicking like a computer as she tried to grasp the developing situation and react accordingly. John was right about one thing: this was not the time for her to argue with his plans. No matter what he thought of her motives, she must help him because...she loved him.

"But I can't!" Her shocked protest at the recognition was verbal.

"Can't what?" The woman pounced on her mistake.

"Can't take this," she snapped back in disgust. No one seemed to doubt that she meant the circus world of the scandal media. She tried to force the discovery of her developing love from her mind as she and John struggled through the rude group.

It was not as difficult getting to their room as it had been the previous night, probably because the number of newspeople had so diminished. But the hotel was prepared for them, and John's men did their work well, too. It didn't even surprise Bea that one guard was waiting inside their suite to guarantee safety when they arrived.

By contrast, once they were alone, the relative quiet was unsettling. Bea could hear every little sound—the clank of the water pipes when someone above them turned on a shower; the reverberations of the ancient elevator down the hall; the rustle of John's coat sleeve; the padding of her shoes against the deep carpet as he led her to her own alcove.

"I want you to go to bed and rest," he ordered, releasing her arm.

"There's no need to be macho," she said coldly. She hoped desperately her heartache did not come through in her voice. She could not really be in love with this man. Not after knowing him just six days.

"Bea, don't push me," he warned.

Infatuation. That had to be it—infatuation of a lonely fool already disappointed in her dreams.

She started throwing the last few things she had left unpacked into her suitcase with total disregard for care. John watched her with hostility but did not move to stop her recklessness. Aware of his disapproval, and not wanting to give him the satisfaction of knowing he unnerved her, she forced herself to finish the task in a reasonable manner.

"I assume you have not taken my passport again," she said when she was done.

"I have not."

"I'll just check on that." She could not stop the vindictive devil that was driving her. She opened her purse and carefully examined her passport before tucking it back inside.

"What was this whole exercise about?" He indicated the closed suitcase.

"Since I'm returning to the States anyway, I'll just go on now."

"In that dress? You're a menace—the airline won't let you aboard."

She didn't like the appreciative curve of his mouth as he looked her over thoroughly.

"Wearing this dress tonight was your idea. I'll manage." Manage, indeed! She'd do anything to get away from him. She had to think.

"You're not going anywhere until five o'clock tomorrow morning." He was intractable as he blocked the archway.

"John, you can't stop me."

"You think I can't?" He walked menacingly toward her. "You're going to lie down on that bed and rest until 5:00 A.M., if I have to sleep with you myself to keep you there!"

She backed away from him.

"I would never want to force that dreadful fate

on you,'' she said stiffly, her head lifted proudly. ''Get out of my room!''

His eyes filled with pain for only a second, then he turned on his heel and disappeared into his own quarters.

CHAPTER NINE

THE MUFFLED ACTIVITY in John's portion of their suite sluggishly entered Bea's consciousness as if through a haze. Turning slightly in her narrow bed, she tried to see the travel alarm clock on the nearby table. Its luminous hands glowed, but they blended into a blur, and it was not until she had fumbled for her glasses that she could be certain it was almost four o'clock.

At first she was incredulous that John would already be up. She could visualize him striding about, gathering together his clothes for the day before going to the bathroom to shave. He was probably still in his underwear; because they had been living so closely together it had been impossible for her not to notice that he shunned pajamas. Bea settled deeper into her mattress, slipping the narrow strap of her pale cream nightgown back up on her shoulder. Her body felt dead, which was not unexpected since she had only been sleeping a bit more than two hours. Groggily she questioned the wisdom of John's insistence that she get some rest. It might have been better had she stayed up.

What she wanted most in the whole world at that moment was a good hot cup of American coffee.

She heard a case being zipped, then John's measured steps moving across the room, and a door being eased shut. Days of knowing this routine, although it usually began at a later hour, helped her pace herself. She could count on about fifteen minutes of gurgling noises while he spread lather on his face and shaved. When the water was finally turned off, she would have to start moving, for it would not take him more than another five or ten minutes to dress and be out.

Wearily she sat up, trying to force herself awake, wondering if just this once she could slip into her robe and not have to rush her dressing as she usually did when John Robertson was around. But one look at the ruffled chiffon wrap convinced her she could not lounge about in that. Briefly she regretted her perverse femininity, which always had her buying soft and fluffy personal wear that no one would ever see. If she had bought a practical cotton robe instead, she wouldn't have to worry about what John Robertson thought. To her right, neatly laid across the back of the desk chair, was her fresh lingerie and the summer suit she had worn the first time John had come to her room. There was no sense in prolonging the inevitable, for that morning Bea did not believe she could rush if her life depended on it. Even before she heard the water turn off she had slowly stepped out of the nightgown, pulled on her bikini panties, fastened her bra and eased into her full slip.

Usually she would have gone ahead and put on the suit, too, but since she knew she had a little more time before John would be wandering around the suite, she decided to put in her contacts first. Before going to bed, she had put water in the miniature pitcher provided with a matching basin on her desk, so it was possible to freshen up her face even without having first crack at the bathroom.

The water felt wonderful! Although it was at room temperature, it still made her feel tingly and alive again, more ready to face the day. So this was it, she thought as she perched on the edge of the desk chair and reached for her contact-lens case—the day she would leave John. And then?

The problem would have to be tackled later— she wasn't *that* awake.

She dropped some saline solution on a lens and dried off her fingers, forcing her attention to the job at hand. She loved the freedom wearing contacts had given her, but she was still a little awkward about getting them in and out. As she balanced the flexible lens on a fingertip, she thought she heard John coming out into the suite, and she involuntarily jerked her head toward the alcove entrance. It was much too soon for him to be ready. Self-consciously she glanced down at herself. The filmy bra she was wearing was the same style as the one he had called indecent the previous day, and her slip was not much better. Hurriedly she brought her finger toward her eye.

"Oh, no!"

She didn't even know she'd spoken the words aloud. She stared down at her empty finger. Where had the lens gone? Frantically she looked for her glasses until she realized she had left them on the bedside table by the alarm clock. Then she sat still, afraid the slightest movement might flip the lens into an even more obscure location.

"John!" She called sheepishly, hating her eyesight, which left her so helpless.

He came running in as if she had shouted.

"What's happened?"

"Stop!" She did shout then, halting his headlong rush to her side. "You'll step on my contact!"

"What?"

"My contact. I've dropped it." She was like a statue as she stared in his direction, her blurred impression of him telling her only that he had pulled on slacks, but had not made it as far as a shirt.

"I thought you were hurt!"

"I will be hurt if I don't find that contact," she insisted, aggrieved. "I can't see a thing."

He was looking carefully at the floor before taking each step that brought him closer. "Were you sitting there when you lost it?"

"Yes, I haven't moved. I had it on my fingertip and just turned my head a moment...."

He knelt beside her, looking first on the desk top, then all around her bare feet. His gaze moved to her lap, then slowly up.

"I'm sure it didn't drop there," she protested, able even in her visual haze, to sense his eyes traveling slowly around the insets of lace along the top of her slip.

"How can you be so certain? My little sister has even found them in her hair."

His eyes moved toward her long curls, still tangled from sleeping.

"Hah!" Triumphantly he held her still with one hand on her shoulder, while the other carefully stroked the long, black waves.

"It was in my hair?" In disbelief she watched him carefully transfer the little object back to her container of soaking solution.

"Your hair's so long, it must have brushed your finger when you turned," he explained, gently swirling the container. "The lens looks folded, but it should open in a few seconds." His hand dropped to her knee to balance himself from his awkward crouching position.

She couldn't even thank him. There was something too touchingly intimate about the moment. His other hand still rested on her shoulder, and his face was almost on a level with her own. He seemed caught in the tension himself, holding as motionless as she, his fingers increasingly warm against her lightly clad body.

Involuntarily she laid a hand on his forearm, wondering if it was just her eyesight that seemed to be putting everything in a golden glow. And then he was gathering her against his bare chest, and she buried her head against his shoulder.

"Bea, I wish..." he started brokenly, then stopped himself. But he did not release his hold on her.

She lay weakly against him only a moment, absorbing the strange tension, even if she didn't quite understand it. Then she recalled how he had held her so lovingly and gently just a few hours earlier in the bistro, only to ice up and reject her. She remembered her rage that he had actually passed her on to Perry as if she were a bargainable item. Slowly she drew away, unsure, despite his warm encouragement, that she would not suffer yet another arbitrary rejection.

"I'd better get dressed," she said hoarsely.

His hands dropped to his sides as he rose. She sensed him standing above her as if he couldn't quite make himself leave, and it took all her will-power to turn back to the paraphernalia on her desk as if unconcerned.

FIVE O'CLOCK APPROACHED all too quickly. Somehow John had managed to convince the hotel kitchen to send up hot coffee, and Bea had indulged too long in her addiction to the warming liquid. The last minutes before her scheduled departure were rushed and frantic.

When she brought her suitcase out to the entry door, John's small case was already there. It surprised her that he intended to check out of the hotel, too.

"Might one ask," she said with mocking humility, driven by the same self-destructive devil that had temporarily dominated her the previous evening, "where you intend going once you have gotten rid of me?"

"One may not," he said curtly, his narrowed eyes revealing that he resented her manner.

"I see—John Robertson is responsible to no one?"

The wording was disastrous. Right after speaking, she braced herself for the scathing rejoinder, "Not to you." But it never came.

"Don't do this, Bea."

His terse entreaty steadied her recklessness. She backed away from his approaching closeness, but the wall prevented her from going very far. She wondered what he still expected from her.

"I wish you luck, John," she said sincerely. "And I do regret that my impulsiveness caused you these problems."

He was standing so close to her by then that she ached with love. She hated the helpless longing.

"I'm sending a security man along with your driver." His voice was taut, and he caught her by the shoulders when she would have moved away from him. "They'll get you safely installed in a hotel so you can rest until plane time, but I'll have to pull them off immediately. Otherwise they might attract press attention to you...."

"Don't worry, John. Perry and I are not exactly babes."

His look hardened at her mention of Perry. And his face became even more unreadable when they heard the knock. A second knock on their inner door and a muffled call by the guard stationed in their entry hall confirmed that Perry had arrived. John acknowledged the message but still did not release her. Instead, his arms moved across her shoulders and he turned her toward him. In dismay she watched his eyes wander to her lips and stop, felt his approaching closeness.

Oddly, despite her love, Bea did not want him to kiss her. He was like the forbidden fruit. She knew the more she tasted, the more she would desire. And she did not want that to happen. Her struggle against his embrace was genuine.

In the end his body trapped her in a corner near the door, and he grasped her face in both hands. Ignoring her moaned protest, he kissed her almost frantically, his lips pressing urgently against her eyelids, her cheeks, across her mouth, along her throat, then back to her mouth.

She both wanted and hated him.

At yet another knock he pulled back. Bea's eyes snapped open, and she breathlessly looked into his, unable to hide her anguished longing.

Fleetingly his lips curved into a pleased smile as he correctly interpreted her expression. And this time when he leaned toward her he expected no protest. Nor did she offer one. What use would it be, she thought, since he *knew* she wanted him so desperately? This time when he tipped her chin, her mouth was soft under his. The caress was light but insistent, sadly ardent, as if he thought he might never touch her again.

Fear churned inside her as she tried to understand what the strange moment meant.

"That wasn't necessary to impress Perry," she murmured brokenly, still afraid to trust his motives.

"It was necessary for me," he groaned against her hair, tightening his embrace one last time. Then he swung the door wide and literally pushed her into Perry's arms.

"Take care of her," he ordered gruffly. "My men will get you into a hotel in Brussels and give you tickets for tonight's flight. Make her stay out of sight in her apartment until she hears from my office.''

"I understand," Perry returned calmly, his expression as inscrutable as John's.

"Damn you both!" Bea understood, too. John didn't trust her—not even to take care of herself. And traitorous Perry was agreeing with him.

She brushed past them and marched toward the elevator. There was muffled confusion as the guards picked up suitcases and rushed after her, and she knew the exit was childish. But she didn't believe she could handle saying goodbye to John. She would not even have waited for Perry had not a guard gently restrained her from entering the elevator alone.

At the last moment as the elevator descended, she could not resist one final look down the hall. But it was a fruitless indulgence. John and the remainder of his staff had already returned to his room.

THEY DID NOT CATCH THE PLANE to the States after all. Perry had argued, raved and threatened her with bodily harm. But once in Brussels, Bea had been adamant. Although not giving her reasons to Perry, she was overwhelmed with a feeling of doom and could not bear to leave Europe without knowing where John was or what was happening to him. Her only recourse seemed to be to remain until things *felt* right to her.

Perry had been livid. He seemed to feel she was in some sort of danger but denied her accusations that John had told him more than he had told Bea. So in the end he had given up on her. Making her promise not to step outside her door without contacting him first, he had arranged a second room for himself and gone off to catch some sleep.

Bea had tried to rest, but it had been impossible. She spent most of the day going over and over things in her mind, but coming up with no new explanations for John's erratic behavior toward her. The sad conclusion seemed inescapable that, despite his occasional physical attraction to her, he simply didn't care deeply about her.

It had been hard to accept. Just being separated from him those few hours was tearing her apart. She had never believed that love such as she felt for John Robertson could develop without being reciprocated.

But once over that hump, she still was not ready to leave Europe. She couldn't explain why, even to herself. And she certainly couldn't to Perry. So they didn't talk about it at all. When Perry met her for dinner that evening, he had suggested she at least follow John's advice to stay out of sight. But sensing her obstinacy, he had instead bought her a huge meal at a café across the street from the hotel, and then he'd walked with her for an hour before seeing her back to her room. Bea had never appreciated her old friend more than during that lonely strained evening.

THE NEXT MORNING was overcast, not the best sort of day to view the Belgian countryside. But when Perry had suggested a visit to Waterloo, Bea had not had the heart to resist—Perry had been a military-history buff since childhood, and she knew he never missed a chance to see a battle site. They had caught a bus near the hotel and with only one transfer were soon approaching the famous farming village where Napoleon had met his final defeat. Even some distance away they could see a curious mound around which many little shops clustered.

"That must be the Lion's Mound monument," Perry said, looking at the tourist book to which he had referred several times during their ride from the hotel. "I can tell you the dimensions of the lion's statue on top, if you want to hear them."

"Thank you, no," Bea said with the same lack of interest she had shown to the other tourist tidbits Perry had been spouting ever since they left. The dreariness of the day suited her disposition to a letter.

"Okay, then I'll tell you how many steps we'll be climbing to get to that statue of unknown proportions."

"What?" That woke her up. Once the bus turned the corner she leaned to get a better look at the height of the hill.

"There are. . . ."

"Oh, hush, Perry. You're not really planning to make me climb that thing?"

"The walk will do you good. I've had enough of your gloom."

Guiltily she realized he was justified in his lack of sympathy. She was being abominable company.

And surprisingly, the walk did make her feel better. Perhaps because of the cloudy skies, very few tourists were willing to brave the climb, and Bea appreciated the relative privacy once they reached the top.

For a while they just strolled hand in hand around the stone walkway of the monument. There were plaques at various locations on the perimeter, directing visitors' attention to battle points in the fields below, and Bea dutifully stopped to look at each one, knowing that Perry would want to read them.

Then they took seats along the huge steps that flanked the entire monument, letting the eerie peace of the fog-washed countryside absorb them. The haze was patchy, and some of the old farmhouses and ancient trees could be seen, while others were lost in a swirl of gray masking the healthy green of the farmland.

"I have a feeling you're not thinking about Napoleon," Perry said gently when the few other people on the mound with them had moved to the opposite corner.

Bea glanced at him, startled that he had not given up on her after all, but was, in his own way, encouraging her to talk about what was troubling her.

"Tell me what you know about this situation with John Robertson and Harry Ward," she blurted.

"I repeat, he told me nothing. And you know nothing to tell me. So do you mean, what do I know from the newspaper reports?"

"The newspapers, yes. I haven't seen any English-language publications since we left New York."

"You won't like this—the media have been brutal in their criticism of John."

"Tell me!"

"Apparently Harry Ward is a high-ranking executive with Robertson's corporation. This Carole Ward claimed her husband, or ex-husband I guess he is, was due back from an assignment in Africa more than a week earlier and hadn't shown up. Some kind of revolution has broken out in that area, and she was afraid Ward was caught in it. When Robertson's office refused to check on him, she went to her congressman."

"John wouldn't help her?"

"Honey, your John wouldn't give her the time of day, not even after she'd received a ransom demand. He was too busy running around Paris with you."

"Is that what the papers have been saying?"

"Some of them. I called one of my army buddies at home this morning, and he said the story has died out on television and in the better publications. But the yellow-journalism sheets are making a big deal of this, especially since you're involved. They're harping on the fact John refuses to interrupt his vacation with you to look into it. They quote Robertson as saying Ward makes it a habit to go on a drinking binge after an assignment and that he'll turn up when he's ready."

Bea pondered that information, knowing it

didn't make sense. John had set her up to promote his uncaring image.

"Once I got his picture in the paper by mistake," she said slowly, "he insisted on being seen with me, deliberately cultivating a false impression. That was even before Carole Ward got her ransom note. Perry, he's got to be trying to buy this Harry out of Africa and doesn't want the media to get wind of it."

Perry didn't seem surprised by her conclusion. "Quit thinking about it so much, Bea," he advised, leaning back against the stone step. "If Robertson had wanted you to know what he was doing, he would have told you."

"I can't get over how you keep supporting that man. And you claim you came to Paris to protect me from him!"

"And I can't get over how you keep defying him. This situation is too complicated for you to interfere with. I think Robertson was trying to do what was best for you, and that you should get out of here. I should have thrown you over my shoulder and forced you on that plane last night."

"If you don't like what I'm doing, you can go on—"

"I know—without you. I don't think you know what you're doing, but if you stay, I'm staying."

"Then quit preaching at me. I thought we came out to Waterloo to absorb some history."

Perry refrained from pointing out that it was Bea who had made it impossible to "absorb" Waterloo. Instead he rested his arm on her shoulders and directed her attention toward the white stone farmhouse and barn some distance over the rolling terrain to their left, "Listen to your mentor, then," he said with a gentle smile. "Wellington's forces headquartered back there. And Napoleon was behind us, where he had a reasonably good view of the whole area...."

Obediently she watched while he pointed to first one then another landmark, seriously trying to concentrate on his indulgent instruction. But with the overcast skies, Waterloo seemed unreal. It was difficult to believe Perry's claim that more than fifty thousand men died within the few square miles. Even though she had heard the statistics many times from her father, she could hardly imagine that so many soldiers could gather in this place at one time.

For a while, Bea enjoyed listening to Perry. They moved slowly around the huge rectangular monument, climbing to both levels to compare the views, and talking about the intricacies of French politics in 1815. But when he began describing the massing of horses and troops in the battlefield, and the instances when horses actually popped up out of the crowd from the pressure, she was lost again. Her mind was back at the Bastille Day fireworks when the same type of thing happened with tourists. Her eyes were dark with remembered fright.

"I think I've lost you again, Bea." Perry's hand stroked her cheek, and she realized that she must have been staring off into space.

"Oh, Perry, I'm worried about what problems I've caused John Robertson. I feel so... pessimistic! What am I going to do?" she groaned.

"Go back to the hotel, pack and catch the next plane to New York."

"No!"

"Bea, you're just being stubborn."

"I'm not. Truly I'm not. I feel things are. . . unfinished! Somehow I can't go back to New York without knowing what's happening or how I'm to blame."

"If blame is to be placed, then blame me for not showing up in Paris when I was supposed to. If I had, none of this would have happened. I'll never forgive myself for that."

"Let's go on back down." Bea jerked away from his comforting hand and began to skirt the monument to reach the long flight of steps leading to the fields below. As she moved, she realized reluctantly that Perry was right; if John had wanted her to know what he was doing, he would have told her. He wouldn't welcome her help. The only logical thing she could do was behave as if her life was back to normal.

She at least owed that effort to Perry, who had come to watch over her and was sticking by her despite her fractiousness.

"Why did those Belgian women ever decide this hill had to be built?" she asked with forced gaiety as she gripped the rail running down the middle of the steep flight. "Wouldn't it have been more accurate historically to have left the battlefield in its natural setting?"

"Most of those buildings you saw in the distance are the originals." Perry was looking at her thoughtfully, gauging her intentions. He knew her so well. And then as if deciding he would cooperate with her determination to keep up a good front, he flashed an impish grin. "And besides, if you hadn't climbed this hill that the women insisted on constructing as a suitable base for their statue, you wouldn't be able to give the little man at the bottom his tip."

"I thought you said this walk was free." The muscles of Bea's legs were beginning to feel sore from the unaccustomed climbing, and she paused to rest.

"It is. But you still should tip that man in uniform standing at the bottom gate. Didn't you notice him as we came in?"

"Yes. But what has he done to earn a tip?"

"He's watched you walk up these how-many-hundred stairs and back down again."

"Perry!"

"Do you have a better answer?"

As Bea resumed her descent, she glanced back over her shoulder at him following close behind her. He looked so tall. His lanky body was casually clothed in slacks and a soft shirt, and he moved with the lazy grace she always associated with him. She smiled to herself. At times, her affection for Perry knew no bounds.

"How's your pocketbook holding up?"

"What's going through your crazy little mind?"

"I figure since you're out of uniform on this holiday, you can just forget about lawyering and army pay and buy me some lunch."

"I just bought you breakfast," he teased.

"You did not! I know better. That continental breakfast comes with the hotel room."

"I'll buy you some *frites* for lunch," he said cautiously.

"Mmm, lovely! I smelled them from that little stand near where we started up these stairs. You're on!"

When they reached the bottom of the hill, she watched in amusement as Perry dug some change out of his pocket and solemnly handed it to the elderly uniformed man who stood partially barring their exit. Perry didn't crack even a tiny smile in her direction when he expressed his appreciation, and the man just as solemnly accepted the tip as if it was his due. "I'm proud of you," she said softly as Perry caught her hand and led her around the fence toward the food concession. "You are helping wipe out unemployment in Belgium."

"Just for that compliment, I'll be a big spender and buy you a large *frites*. And maybe even something to drink."

They both struggled with their French in placing their orders for two large paper cornucopias filled with the thick, twice-cooked French fries for which the Belgians were noted. But the cheerful proprietor was accustomed to people of all nationalities, and he quickly and accurately prepared their order, managing by pointing to show them the correct amount of money to pay and what sauces they could choose.

For a while they walked around the little buildings surrounding the Lion's Mound monument and nibbled on their *frites*. Numerous others were doing the same thing, for few could resist the delicious odors coming from the man's little stand.

"You know, this place almost reminds me of some of the tourist traps at home," Bea said eventually when they had paused to look in the window of their fifth souvenir shop. "Not at all what I had expected of Europe. How many different statues of Napoleon and the Lion's Mound have you seen, all probably made in Hong Kong?"

"Not as many as the bottle openers of the Manneken-Pis. We'll have to hunt up that little guy when we visit the Grand' Place." Perry idly picked up a postcard from the rack by the open door. "Do you want a souvenir of this place?"

"Of course. Are you buying?"

"I'm in a generous mood. Anything to cheer my Bea up." He handed her his cone of *frites* to hold while he made the purchase. Bea couldn't resist transferring some of his potatoes to her own cornucopia while he was not looking.

"I seem to have been eating very fast while I've been gone," he commented severely as he poured more of his packet of mayonnaise over the remaining food.

"You shouldn't be such a pig." Bea held her own cornucopia awkwardly while she tucked the postcard into her purse, which dangled from her arm. "Perry, when are you going to tell me about your hot date in Naples? You really didn't have to leave her, you know. I was quite safe from John Robertson."

"Would you believe it hurts to talk about

that?'' His tone was not entirely joking. ''Bea, that was the biggest mistake of my life.''

''You mean she was a loser?''

''On the contrary. She was gorgeous—a stewardess from Seattle. But she wasn't Bea.''

''Oh, come on, Perry!'' If Perry had arrived in Paris as planned, and had started such a conversation then, Bea would have been ecstatic. But now he was saying words she didn't want to hear.

''I'll get you something to drink at this sidewalk café down the street.'' Accurately sensing Bea's aversion to discussing their own love life, Perry abruptly changed the subject and led her toward a busy café with many outdoor tables.

''I'm covered with salt and goo,'' she apologized as she tossed her empty *frites* container into a curbside trash can.

''I'll see if I can make the waiter understand we need some extra napkins with our drinks, so we can mop up.'' Perry tossed his own refuse into the can. ''You did get covered, even on your chin. Neat, Bea! I like it!''

''Just get those napkins.''

After passing her a handful of paper napkins, Perry watched Bea wipe off her fingers. ''Feeling better?''

''Yes.''

''We have to talk about *us* sometime, you know.''

''Must we? I appreciate your interest in coming to Paris when you thought I was in trouble. But....''

''You can't forget that I didn't come earlier?''

"Something like that. I was devastated, if you must know."

"I wish I had known you cared whether I came or not. You've always urged me to take this or that girl out. And you have to admit you've stood me up a few times yourself. Always for business, I'll admit, but left me stranded for an evening nonetheless. So when this gorgeous stewardess invited me to a villa for the weekend...."

"You went. Understandable, although leaving someone stranded in his own city for an evening does seem a little different to me than dropping someone for ten days in a foreign country."

"Bea, I love you."

The words were spoken so quietly that Bea almost wasn't certain she had heard correctly.

"I know it sounds strange under the circumstances. I didn't know it myself. Not until I saw your picture in the paper. You looked so gorgeous it tore my heart out, and you were with another man. It should have been me!"

She set her wineglass down carefully, wondering if perhaps she had had too much to drink. The conversation seemed unreal.

"Perry, you don't just suddenly realize you're in love with someone. Surely it happens gradually, after people have known each other a long time?" Subconsciously she knew she was trying to convince herself, not him.

"And we haven't known each other long enough? Bea, I think the same awareness about our relationship was happening to you when you got to Paris, or you wouldn't have cared at all about my not showing up.''

She thought about what he was saying, wondering if it was true. No, realizing it probably had been true. But strangely it wasn't anymore.

''Is it what happened between you and Robertson that has changed things?''

''Nothing happened. I told you. I pulled that stupid act about knowing him and inadvertently got his picture in the paper. Then I believed his cock-and-bull story about family illness and agreed to spend three days with him so—''

''That doesn't sound at all like the levelheaded Bea I know. He must have spun some story.''

''Perry, I'm embarrassed enough that I fell for it without your bugging me about it. That's probably why I feel so involved now. I'm floundering to find some explanation that would make me feel less like a fool.''

''Don't think about it too much, Bea,'' Perry cautioned seriously.

''I can't help but think about it. I've been *took*!''

''That's not what's bothering you.''

''What do you mean?''

''You're a sharp enough lady that if you'd just been 'took,' you'd think of a way to get back at him.''

Bea looked away, not wanting to hear what else Perry was going to say. But mercifully he didn't continue.

''Let's go back to the hotel?''

''I think it's more than time.''

"OUR MORNING OUT wasn't very successful, was it?" Bea's hand rested lightly on Perry's arm as they strolled from their hotel toward the Grand' Place, the famous medieval square of the old city.

"We've had better," Perry admitted, his hand tightening in hers. "You're wrong, you know. I don't think of you as a little sister."

Bea knew she was wrong.

When she had made the remark once they were back at the hotel, Perry had taken her in his arms and kissed her. And she had realized then that his interest was no longer brotherly. Of her own interest, she was just too confused to calculate. John Robertson too effectively dominated her thoughts.

"I wish this Harry Ward thing was clear in my mind," she admitted honestly. "I feel so obligated to John; it's totally illogical, and I don't like it."

Perry didn't like it, either, but he remained silent.

"I'll keep watching the papers," she mused aloud. "Once I know John has settled whatever it was about Ward he needed to work out, I'll probably feel fine again...." Her voice was wistful, almost as if she doubted she could ever feel normal again.

"Do you want to walk down to see the Manneken-Pis?" Perry began shuffling in his pocket for the map of Brussels given him by the hotel. "Everyone says the little-boy statue is the unofficial symbol of Belgian independence, and a must for tourists."

"I think I'd like to reserve him for another day. There's supposed to be a museum here on the

Grand' Place where we can see those hundreds of costumes various countries have sent for him. I think I'd like to wait and see the statue and his outfits on the same day.''

"Hundreds of costumes?" Perry groaned. "I think that will be the day we separate, and I go see the museum of military history.''

They were drawing close to the Grand' Place by then, and the sidewalks were becoming congested with tourists. Mercifully the numbers were nothing like Paris had been during the Bastille Day celebrations, but still the sidewalks were packed with eager visitors. Once Bea and Perry emerged from the narrow streets onto the medieval square that formed the heart of Brussels, they could see why it was attracting such attention.

"I've never seen anything like it!" Bea was all eyes. She and Perry moved slowly into the center of the large public square lined with the ancient Guild Houses, which still maintained their grandeur.

And indeed, it was a sight to see. The tall, narrow buildings were heavy with sculpted ornamentation and colorful embellishment. The large Town Hall, with its golden lacy facade seemed almost too perfect to be real. It was an active square, with elegant restaurants, bakeries, fine-lace and tapestry shops tucked into every available nook. And off every winding, narrow street approaching it were additional shops of every description.

"Would you believe I see a Wendy's down the street?" Perry asked.

"No! I absolutely refuse to eat there. I'll buy you an early supper if you insist, but not at Wendy's. I'm going to eat *moules*, or some elegant French meal when I'm in this lovely place."

Perry just grinned at her and led her across the square so she could see the Guild Houses at close view. While it was true that he was accumulating a nest egg to open his own law practice, Bea's teasing about his miserliness was largely a long-standing joke that he went along with, for he was never ungenerous with her. They both knew that his parents were willing to finance Perry's start in business, but that he preferred to try to take care of things himself. Many times he just let Bea treat him to give her something to fuss about.

"We could try the restaurant in the Amigo Hotel," he suggested. "My army buddies tell me we should at least go inside, just to see what an expensive hotel for executives only looks like. European version, that is."

"The Amigo?" Bea asked faintly, remembering that was the hotel John had wanted to settle her in.

"I think it's just around the corner here."

"No, I don't want to go there." Bea didn't forcefully pull back when Perry guided her in the direction of the hotel. But her reluctance was evident.

"Not interested in a hotel meal? Then let's walk down this way and see what little restaurant we can find nearby." He glanced at his watch. "It remains light so late in Belgium now that we should still be able to see lots after we've eaten."

She couldn't resist looking at the hotel as they approached, admiring the way its new construction had blended into the medieval surroundings. Someone had planned it well. She could see why John had suggested locating her there.

She was staring at the building, not paying much attention to the people around her, when she felt, rather than heard, Perry's grunt of recognition.

"What is it . . . ."

She never finished her question, for chaos broke out.

"There's Bea Allen!"

"Robertson says he's come to Brussels to find you. Are you going back to him? What do you know of his plans for Ward?"

Bea looked around her in amazement, only slowly registering that the trio of people pressing toward her were reporters. And behind them, his expression furious, was a beleaguered John Robertson.

CHAPTER TEN

"YOU'VE RUINED EVERYTHING! I told you to go to New York, Bea." John was livid as he huddled with Bea and Perry around the small table in the cellar restaurant to which they had fled. With the help of his security men they had gained a brief respite from the three reporters waiting impatiently outside, but they were surrounded by customers and still could not talk openly.

"You also told the media you were coming to Brussels to look for me, although you fully expected me not to be here," Bea countered with her own quiet accusations. "Obviously you have your reasons to be here and planned to claim my absence as your cover. I dislike being used, John."

"I thought you realized the importance of getting her out of here." John transferred his harangue to Perry.

"I realized, all right," Perry returned calmly. "But Bea has a mind of her own."

John snorted his disgust and leaned back slightly, his eyes troubled. He and Perry assessed each other in tense silence until John finally whispered again. "Surely you could convince her that she's better off in the States."

"Would you two cretins stop discussing me as if I weren't here?"

"Bea would probably be cooperative if you were open with her." Perry ignored Bea as fully as John did.

"I've been as honest as possible."

"That's a laugh." Bea asserted herself, keeping her voice low as they all hunched even closer around the table, suspicious of anyone near them. "John, I hate to disillusion you; admittedly it's taken me a long time, but I'm finally catching on to what you're doing."

"What I'm doing does not involve you."

"I involved myself, unfortunately, when I claimed you were Perry. Just ask those newsmen out there if they think I'm not involved with this Harry W—"

"You'll find they *don't* think you're involved, except with playing around with me." John stopped her abruptly. "And that's how I intend to keep it. Your clearing out yesterday, as if you couldn't stand this publicity, was the best possible way to get you out of this. I told you I can't play games anymore, and I meant it. I have to be able to count on your being back in the States."

His speech was cut short by the arrival of a middle-aged waitress, somewhat flustered by all the confusion involved in getting the three Americans to their table. The restaurant was apparently one of the few "budget" establishments in the Grand' Place area, and its staff was not accustomed to celebrities of any kind. The agitated woman began chattering in nervous French and pointing to the brief menu, mentioning *moules* several times.

"We'd better order something," Perry suggested, his eyes questioning as he handed John the menu, "if only to pacify the newsmen who are watching us through the door. They seem to think we've arranged this meeting."

"Perhaps if we just order coffee . . ." John ventured, uninterested in food.

"I'll have *moules*—the mussels," Bea insisted perversely. It was too early to eat anything substantial. But Bea was so hurt that John believed her incompetent to help him, she wanted to strike back, if only by being uncooperative. She wondered if he could possibly still suspect that she deliberately set him up for that first photograph. The thought was horrifying.

"That's okay by me," Perry said. "We're going to need a few more minutes here to sort ourselves out. I take it from the waitress's gestures that she's pushing the *moules*?"

"Today's blue-plate special," John verified, after glancing at the handwritten menu. "We'll all have an order of them, then, since Bea insists on eating. At least it will be quick." When he passed on their selections in French, the waitress burst into smiles, relieved that she would not have to spend the rest of her stint at their table fumbling through broken English and sign language.

Bea was disgruntled that John seemed willing to charm everyone else but took so little interest in being fair to her.

"I'll have some wine, too, please," she insisted coolly.

"I've ordered you some wine. Quit trying to make trouble," John snapped. He turned to Perry. "I'll have new reservations for both of you on tonight's flight."

"You'd better make Bea agree to it," Perry replied.

"She's not going to listen to anything I say, because her pride is hurt." John was surprisingly candid. Then he shifted his attention to her. "Bea, I'm giving up trying to reason with you. I simply can't take no for an answer anymore. You're going to get on that plane this evening if I have to assign some of my men to physically accompany you all the way to your apartment in New York."

Bea frowned hostilely. It was obvious John was furious and that he would not be above actually carrying her on the plane himself despite the objections of reporters and airline officials. She could probably raise enough fuss to force Belgian law to come to her aid, but what would it accomplish? There was no purpose in staying if John did not want her help; she could forget about wanting things to "feel right."

"You've made your point," she snapped. "I'll go." But no sooner had she agreed, than another thought occurred to her. Worrying about this situation was fast becoming a hard habit to break.

"Won't the press give you even more trouble if I leave? After all, you've found me, which apparently was what you told them you had come to do."

"My work would be easier if they still thought I was trying to track you down here," he admitted hesitantly. "But under no circumstances will I have you remain in Europe. I'll just have to go with this situation. What I want you both to do now is return to your hotel and pack. I'll send you in my car, and we'll tell the press Bea is rejoining me. They seem to think Perry is your bodyguard, so that should look all right. The driver will come back for you—" he glanced at his watch "—in four hours and take you directly to the airport."

"What about those three gossips outside?" Perry asked.

"They'll hassle her when you start to leave here, but I think they'll opt to stick with me. We'll hope they don't figure out where you're staying before you leave your hotel tonight. When my driver drops you off at the airport, go to the Sabena office; they'll have a place for you to be out of sight until your plane leaves."

"How can you make snap decisions like this and know they'll work?" Bea questioned disbelievingly.

"He's not making snap decisions, Bea." Perry unexpectedly interrupted John's answer. "I called him this afternoon."

Bea stared at him, stunned.

"He had told me he would be in Brussels," Perry said gently, taking her hand. "I think you're in danger in Europe, and while I can't make you leave, I know Robertson can."

Bea's initial reaction was fury. She would never

have suspected that Perry had arranged this "chance" meeting.

"That was a hell of a way of showing your so-called love," she accused numbly.

"If I didn't love you so much, I wouldn't have done it," he replied firmly, his eyes never leaving hers. "I want you first to be safe and second to be happy. Do you want me to go on?"

It was then another reaction set in—mortification. Perry had recognized even before she had that her heart was no longer up for grabs—it belonged to a man who didn't want it.

"I would never have guessed you did this, Perry," she began haltingly, wondering why he had told her. Given time, she might have turned back to him for comfort.

"I know. But I'd rather lose even your friendship than have you make a mistake that will ruin your life."

John cleared his throat gruffly.

"I'll notify your tour guide and the Drakes that we've made other plans for the rest of your holiday," he told Bea with that intense concentration of his, almost as if nothing had been said by the others. "That should make things more comfortable for you in future dealings with your colleagues. Later I'll hope to mend your reputation."

It astounded her that he thought she would welcome his help at some future date. "If you have settled my life," she said coldly, shoving back her chair slightly, "we might as well leave." As she moved she almost knocked against the hefty waitress, who had brought their food.

"Forgotten how starved you were?" John asked bitterly. Then he passed her a huge bowl piled high with the steaming shellfish. The meal included more Belgian *frites* and a salad, and Bea stared at the food distastefully. Almost mechanically the three of them went through the motions of eating, more to postpone running the gauntlet of newsmen than because they wanted the food. Bea forced herself to pick the soft flesh out of the tiny, dark shells, even dipping the *moules* in the steamy broth and sopping her bread in it, too. She thought she did rather well at appearing totally enamored with the traditional Belgian dish. But she couldn't manage to consume anything else, not even the wine.

As she set her fork down and wiped her fingers on her napkin, she glanced over at John and was surprised to see that his face was gray. He appeared in pain.

Perry noticed it, too. "Are you all right?" he asked, setting aside his own partially eaten meal.

"Let's just get on with this." John dug out some Belgian francs and left them on the table. "When we get outside, I want you two to walk on to my hotel with me, then I'll have my driver pick you up from another entrance."

Already feeling nervous about the ordeal ahead, Bea allowed him to take her arm. His hand felt extremely warm against her skin. She wondered if the heat was originating with him or with her.

Once they left the restaurant she knew her nervousness was well-founded. The audacity of some of the questions thrown at them made her face burn with embarrassment, despite her determination to remain detached and let John handle things. She heard him explain tersely that he and Bea had settled their "little argument" and were going to continue their vacation; that he would appreciate reporters leaving them alone. And he fended off questions about Ward, sticking to his statement that he was certain there was no kidnapping and that Ward would turn up when he was in the mood.

Once in the lobby of the Amigo, John couldn't seem to get them away quickly enough. They had hurried into a private room on the same floor, and from there, with not even a goodbye, John had rushed out one door, while some of his men had taken Bea and Perry through another. Perry had been spared any attention when one reporter had seen them slipping out a rear entrance; it was Bea who was shouted at. But the car was able to pull away before the man shouting obscene questions could reach her.

"Do you think he'll try to follow us?" she asked the driver once they were out of sight of the Grand' Place.

"Probably, but I work in Brussels regularly so I know this area well. I have several maneuvers that should lose him." Immediately proving his point he had turned into a parking garage associated both with a hotel and a major office building. At a nod from the attendant, he had taken a ramp marked for private use, stopping in a sheltered area only long enough for a uniformed man to hastily fasten a second license plate over their own identification. "And now, Ms. Allen, if you would just slip down in the seat for a few moments, and Mr. Campbell, if you would sit in the middle of the back seat as if you are the only occupant, I think we will be in good shape."

As they did what he said, he exited the garage on the street opposite from that on which they entered.

"Is this all legal?" Bea asked weakly from her crouched position. "I feel ridiculous, as if I'm playing cops and robbers. Are you sure you didn't arrange this, too, Perry?"

"I wish I had," he said seriously.

They had driven a few blocks before the driver told Bea she could sit up again. She resettled gingerly beside Perry, flinching a little when he took her hand. But he held tight anyway.

"I did what I felt best for you, Bea," he said, reading her thoughts. "Surely you could see that these few reporters still hounding John have no scruples. You're not up to handling that. And there are undoubtedly other dangers, too."

"You two keep passing me back and forth between you. It's degrading to my intelligence and dignity."

Perry looked stubbornly ahead, not answering.

The driver took them to a locked rear entrance of their hotel, and after a knock, they were admitted by a man Bea recognized as usually working at the front desk.

"Did you and John have this all set up, too?" she asked bitterly after the man took them to their floor in a freight elevator hidden away at the back of the hotel.

"Do you want me to come in with you?" Perry asked, still refusing to let her bait him.

"No, I'd like some time alone," Bea said in defeat.

Perry took the key from her unsteady hand.

"Don't make this any harder for me than it is," he said urgently. "I meant it when I said I want you to be happy. It isn't easy for me to bow out to another man."

"I love you," Bea said in a choked voice.

"I know. Like a best friend. At least nothing can ever ruin *that* relationship." His smile was rueful as he kissed her gently on the mouth. Once he had unlocked the door, he handed her back the key. "Behave yourself," he advised, his grin giving only the slightest glimpse of the old Perry. "That means stay in your room until it's time for us to go. If you need anything, call me. I'll get it for you."

Bea pecked his cheek with her own impulsive kiss, then watched him stroll down the hall to his room. Her latest brush with the press had convinced her his advice was wise. She wasn't up to handling that kind of people. In addition to their innuendos about Bea, they had kept on the question of Harry Ward like a dog with a bone.

It's as if they're trying to create an international incident of this thing, she thought, opening the inner door of her entry hall. *They want John to accuse those African revolutionaries....* "What?"

She stood motionless, her mouth open in a gasp of protest. Her room was a shambles.

Her half-unpacked suitcase had been turned out on the bed and her things gone through. Lingerie was strewn all over, books and magazines ripped apart, even the lining of her case torn out. Drawers had been emptied, as had the closets; and from the clothes thrown on the floor, she guessed that many items had been ruined when the intruders had hastily pulled at pockets to see if anything was hidden inside.

Strangely, it did not occur to Bea at the moment to go for Perry. She entered the room gingerly, looking first in the bathroom and checking behind the shower curtain to see if anyone was there. The bedroom was fairly visible at a glance, since closets were gaping, but she did take time to look under the bed before she sat down on the one chair and surveyed the wreckage, confident that no one else was in the room with her. Only then did she become afraid. She could see some of her unused French currency thrown about on the floor with cosmetics and a gold chain necklace, so it could not have been a simple robbery. She had a rather substantial amount of French money, and it could quickly be exchanged for any other currency, so a robber would certainly have taken it. They were looking for something else.... What?

Her first thought was that some reporter had done it. But on reflection, that did not make sense. They had been interested in her only as a secondary issue, since they seemed unable to force John Robertson to make accusations against unnamed Africans. The only value she had was to the scandal sheets, which might be short on illicit Hollywood romances to feature.

Her next thought, and the only one that seemed to make sense, was that John had ordered it done himself. Maybe her intuition had been right in the restaurant. Maybe he still thought she was working for someone—that she was trying to thwart his plans, whatever they were. That thought almost killed her. She wanted to curl up in anguish, distressed that she could still love such a man who had so little faith in her.

"I don't! I can't!" She moaned.

It was then she had to know. She jerked the telephone off the hook, then replaced it while she fumbled with the Brussels directory. Once locating the Amigo, she dialed the hotel. After the expected curt response that Mr. Robertson was impossible to reach, Bea gave the operator her name and insisted that John was expecting her call. It took some continued assertive moves on her part and a good bit of waiting while the operator apparently checked with John himself before Bea was told he was not answering his phone.

She was incensed that he refused her call. That alone convinced her she had been right—that it was John who had ordered her room so destructively searched. Severely disillusioned, she dialed Perry's room.

No answer? She couldn't believe it. Why would Perry have gone out? She tried again, being certain she dialed the correct room, but still he did not answer.

I'm not going to let John get away with this!

It had been her intention to have Perry see John for her, since he had been so insistent that she be careful. But if Perry could not even bother to be available when she needed him, she had had enough of both men interfering with her life. She would handle things herself. Taking only her passport and her purse, she carefully closed and locked her door, and made her way back to the freight elevator. Frustrated that it could not be operated without a special key, she had braced herself for a clash with reporters and gone to the front desk. Prepared as she was for unpleasantness, the rest had been almost anticlimactic, it had gone so smoothly. John's driver had done his work well, or perhaps she had been protected because Perry had insisted that both rooms be registered in his name. No one had appeared to notice her or care who she was as she entered the lobby. She had quickly secured a cab, which had taken her to the front door of the Amigo. And despite some newspeople hovering by the elevators, she had been unnoticed as she walked boldly up the stairs.

She found John's guards on the third floor. They saw her almost as soon as she identified them and it was comical how aghast they were to realize that she was alone. They rushed toward her and took her under their wings, almost like mother hens. She wondered how they could be so protective when they surely must know of the damage in her room.

Upon her explanation that she had to see John and that she would not take no for an answer, they obligingly walked her to his door and knocked lightly. At first he did not answer, and Bea was wondering if perhaps she had been wrong, that he had been out when she phoned. But the guards insisted he had not left, and let themselves into the entry hall where they knocked again. Finally John's voice replied weakly, as if he had been asleep. When they explained Bea was there insisting on seeing him, there had been a long silence before she heard some shuffling near the door and John's voice saying huskily, "Are you certain it's Bea Allen?"

"*I'm* certain I'm Beatrice Allen," she snapped impatiently.

"Get in here!"

The door had cracked open immediately, just enough to let her slip inside, which she did with fire in her eyes. She was ready to do battle.

"What's happened to you?" she cried instead, losing all thought of retribution when she saw the debilitated man before her.

Clothed only in his shorts, a damp towel flung over his bare shoulders, John was leaning weakly against the wall behind the door. His face was a sickly white despite his tan, and his whole stance was one of complete exhaustion.

"John?" she repeated, rushing to him. His skin felt cold to her touch.

"You're not sick?" he asked thickly, leaning his head back against the wall.

"Let me help you lie down."

He did not protest when she led him over to the rumpled bed, removed the damp towel from his shoulders, and drew some covers over him.

"Is it food poisoning?" she asked. She recalled noticing how gray he had looked while they were leaving the restaurant and wished she and Perry had not dismissed it as pressure and fatigue.

"I thought so at first," he said weakly. "It came on so fast. But when I learned you and Campbell weren't sick...."

"How did you know that?"

"Called Campbell, once I could make it to the phone. Panicked when no one answered."

"I couldn't get Perry, either. Are you certain he...."

"I showered and planned to come help you, but couldn't even get myself dressed. So I phoned again, and he answered. He'd gone to a pay phone to ask some army buddy to facilitate customs for you in New York. Didn't want to go through his switchboard. He was okay and was going to check on you."

He closed his eyes; making the lengthy explanation seemed to have exhausted him.

"I'd better call Perry." Bea's stomach knotted when she thought of his getting a passkey and discovering the shambles in her room. He would be frantic.

"John, why did you...."

Even as she dialed she mentally abandoned her question. It simply was not possible that John would show such concern for her welfare had he also been responsible for the search of her room.

"Shouldn't we call a doctor? You look terrible; what do you think is wrong?"

"It's got to be an allergic reaction. I never eat

shellfish, I guess because the one time I tried them as a boy I got violently ill. My family thought it was food poisoning then.''

There was no answer in Perry's room, so she asked the operator to ring her room.

"I thought you'd be sharing a room with Campbell," he said tersely.

"You thought wrong," she snapped. "I save that insanity for you."

"Are you all right?" Perry's voice roared over the line.

"I'm safe with John," she replied. "I came here because I thought he was responsible...."

"You're crazy. Have you told him about this mess in your room?" Perry demanded.

"Not yet. Hold on."

She tucked the receiver between her shoulder and chin and quickly related the thorough search of her room.

"God!" John struggled to raise himself, but it was a simple matter for Bea to push him back down.

"No harm's been done." She tried to reassure him as she stretched awkwardly to soothe his brow with her cool palm. "I doubt that anything was taken, and if it was, it wouldn't matter. I have my passport, so everything else is immaterial."

"That settles it. I'm sending some men home with you, Bea," he said urgently. "I'd hoped to spare you this...."

"John, from now on I'll go along with whatever you want. Just lie there and rest."

She swung the receiver up to her mouth.

"Perry, he's very ill. I think you'd better come over here and...."

"No!" John's voice was authoritative, despite his debilitation. "Tell him to salvage what he can of your things and take a cab to the airport at the time we planned. We have less than two hours left. If you can help me get dressed, I'll bring you and...."

"John, there's no way you can go anywhere today."

"*I have to!* I'm catching a plane, too. We'll make it look as if we're going someplace together. That might get the press off both our backs. Do as I say, Bea. Tell him we'll meet him there."

She hesitated, but finally capitulated, and Perry agreed to her instructions.

After she hung up, John grabbed her arm.

"Give me the phone," he said weakly. "I'll have to risk a call." She didn't bother to argue with him, but dialed the number he dictated and settled his special scramble receiver in his hand. Although she walked around trying to give him some measure of privacy, she could still hear his softly pitched voice talking urgently to a man he addressed as André.

When he eventually hung up, she looked assessingly at him. While you could hardly describe a man of his muscularity as huddling, he did appear to be drawing the covers around himself as much as his weakened state would allow. He seemed to need all the additional body heat he could get. He had closed his eyes again, but Bea knew better than to assume that he was sleeping; he was just marshaling his strength.

Decisively she went to his open suitcase. "You need a warm shirt on," she said.

"Right-hand side of the top section." His ready agreement worried her even more.

Bea located the soft undershirt and shook it out as she walked back to the bed. Compared to her own T-shirts, it looked huge. But once she helped John lean forward enough to slip it over his head she realized it was none too big. The man's shoulders and forearms were immense. Any thoughts she might have had that he was a playboy who spent most of his time on the beach lifting weights were quickly dispelled when she lowered the covers to help slide the shirt down to his waist. She had never looked at his body closely before and it surprised her that his tightly muscled chest and shoulders were relatively white compared to the dark tan of his face and forearms.

"You must wear a short-sleeved sport shirt open at the neck when you're out in the fields," she said lightly, trying to ease the tension of dressing the man. "The sun has left its telltale marks."

"My legs look even more anemic; I always wear long pants." He went along with her ploy, as he too felt the awkwardness of the situation. "Any slacks from the closet will do."

There were only two pairs there, and she selected the brown ones. "Are you certain you're up to trying this yet?" Anxiously she watched him weave slightly back and forth as he tried to sit on the edge of his bed.

"After I get those on I'll have to rest again," he confessed with uncharacteristic vulnerability.

After getting him into his white dress shirt, Bea knelt in front of him and deftly helped him slip a foot into each pant leg. She was reaching a hand across the bed to brace herself for getting to her feet, when she saw the scar.

Her gasp was involuntary.

He looked in the direction of her eyes. About six inches above his knee the jagged gash began and ran diagonally up the inner thigh, slightly puckering the other scars, which indicated muscle and skin grafting along its edge.

"I told you you wouldn't want to see my other souvenir of Vietnam," he grunted as he grabbed the headboard and pulled himself to his feet.

She wondered how she could have missed noticing it some of those other times he had been strolling around their suite in his shorts.

"You must have spent months in therapy to rebuild your leg muscles." She let him lean on her as she quickly slipped the slacks up around his waist. He gripped her shoulders firmly and did not even try to complete fastening his clothing himself. Bea's back ached from supporting him by the time her fumbling fingers eventually completed the top snap.

"You've done a marvelous job of rehabilitating that leg," she chattered nervously, putting her hands under his arms to help him be seated. "You move like an athlete."

"You missed your chance to see the rest of that scar," he surprised her by saying wryly as he resettled gingerly on the edge of the bed.

She moved him back to a lying position. Then

seeing his self-satisfied smile, she had to laugh. It was absurd how he could throw her emotions off balance, tossing a crazy remark her way just when she was wild with concern.

"When you get this...little adventure over with," she said, matching the lightness of his tone as she took some socks from his suitcase and began pulling them onto his feet, "you should put on some shorts and start running around those California beaches of yours. The sun would do you a lot of good."

"Yes, mother," he mumbled. "Ouch!"

She tugged the last sock up over his ankle with unnecessary roughness. "I'm beginning to wonder if you really need any help," she lied.

By then, though, he was too tired to play any more of his little games. He lay motionless, his eyes closed and did not protest when she threw the covers back over him. For a time she busied herself packing the remainder of his belongings. She believed he was fully aware of what she was doing and would have protested had he preferred she leave things alone. She hesitated over whether to fold his sports jacket into his suitcase, then left it out, assuming he would wish to dress as normally as possible for their trip to the airport.

"Do you need anything put into the pockets of this thing?" She walked over by the bed to hold the jacket before him.

"Yes, my passport and—" he contemplated seriously, still unmoving "—and the long envelope and leather packet in my suit jacket."

She made the necessary transfers quickly, careful not to look too long at what she handled. Then she went into the bathroom to check for items left there. The disarray of the towels and soaps convinced her that John had resolutely struggled with his illness alone, instead of seeking help from any of his men outside. She ached to think of him going through that without anyone. His damned independence. She was surprised he was even willing to let her help him. Anxious to get back to him, she hurriedly dropped the toothbrush and few remaining personal items strewn across the counter into his shaving kit.

"Is that everything?" Listlessly he watched her tuck the kit in and close up his suitcase.

"I think so. I put your wallet into your slacks pocket before you put them on." She began rechecking the dresser drawers. "You didn't have anything in here, did you?"

"No. But that scramble phone will have to go. Just unplug it from the jack. There's a slot for it in my briefcase."

"This is madness, you know." She took care of the phone, then walked over to fasten his watch on his wrist. "You're too weak even to speak."

"With your help I'll make it," he insisted.

Loving him as she did, she could hardly argue with that expression of confidence, but she wished the situation were different. Hopelessly she sank into a chair near his bed.

"Bea, about your room...."

"John, please don't waste your energy. We're going to have to leave for the airport in less than an hour now."

"We won't have another chance." He lifted his head. "If you really want to conserve my strength, pull your chair over here where I can see you as we talk."

She quickly did as he asked.

"What do you want to know about my room?"

"Are you absolutely certain it could not have been a burglary?"

"Yes. Too much money and some gold chains were left behind. It looked as if they were hunting for something on paper."

"I'm afraid you're right. I hadn't wanted to tell you anything about this, but—" he had to pause to rest again and her eyes were troubled as she smoothed back his hair "—Harry Ward is definitely being held by some terrorists in Africa. I received a ransom demand, but my advisors have convinced me a rescue attempt is the best way to get him back safely. Carole Ward went to the press before I knew she was worried, so it was too late to reassure her. I can't risk our plans leaking out."

"I can see why. Some of those newspeople seem determined to create an international incident," Bea agreed.

"Luckily most of these scandal reporters hanging on now are more interested in my love life than in Harry, so we may still be able to pull this rescue off. My greatest regret is that you got involved and that I still need you."

He did not seem aware that Bea had cringed at that, and had withdrawn deep into her chair.

"I thought newsmen would be your only possible problem in Brussels, but I was wrong," he continued. "If reporters had searched your room they would have been watching at your hotel afterward. I'm certain somebody working for these terrorists wanted to see if you had written down anything about my plans or itinerary. Although my office is still negotiating with them for transfer of the ransom money, they won't take any chances that I might arrange Harry's escape in the meantime. They'll try to stop me. Did you keep a diary or...."

"I haven't written down a thing, John," she assured him. "And the only printed things with me are some business magazines and manuals I brought along. I've even been pitching tourist brochures."

He seemed reassured by her answer. "I can't guarantee they won't bother you again, so you're going to have to hole up in your apartment where my people can keep you safe until this is over."

"John, if these people are still demanding a ransom, why did they tell you where Harry Ward is being held?" Bea was puzzled.

"That was a different faction, probably someone Harry has bribed. I respect most African nationalist groups, but this group that has Harry are renegades within their own continent. They all seem out for their own gain, and Harry and I are caught in the middle."

"Where are you going to be during all this, John?"

He seemed to hesitate. "Making arrangements."

"Why don't you come with me to my apartment?" she asked quickly, without a thought for
pride.

"Because I have to be free to...." He sighed
deeply as he saw her freeze up with embarrassment
at his rebuff.

"What time is it?" he asked gruffly.

She glanced at her watch. "Five to ten."

Almost painfully he drew back the covers. "I
can't postpone any longer. If you'll help me sit
up?"

Bea did not believe he could make it to the airport, not when each tiny movement taxed his
strength. He had to brace himself against the
headboard just to stay erect while she slipped on
his shoes and tied them. She wanted to shout at
him, to tell him to stop the heroics and let someone else do the job he had in mind for himself. But
she knew it would do no good.

Once she had eased him into his jacket and
combed his hair for him, he asked her to bring in
the man who was head of his security force. Together the three discussed the quickest way to get
John and Bea past the few remaining newsmen.
Making it all look normal was the problem.

The security man was astonished at John's condition.

"He's not going to be able to walk," the
man told Bea with concern. "We can keep people
off this floor the few moments it would take to
carry him down the hall to the freight elevator,
but the sticky part is getting from the elevator
to the car. It would create too much harmful

speculation if we carried him out of the hotel.''

"That last stretch isn't too far. Couldn't we get by if I kind of lounged all over Bea?'' John asked weakly.

The security man looked skeptically at Bea's slender frame. "Those few scandalmongers wouldn't think that unusual,'' he agreed, "but can she. . . .''

"She can,'' Bea said bluntly. "I have a feeling I'm going to wish John had been on a diet for the last month, but let's go!''

It was incredibly difficult. By the time the freight elevator stopped at the lobby level John was weaving on his feet, despite three men holding him up. All of them were dubious as they settled his arm heavily around Bea's shoulders. But they had not allowed for John's determination or for Bea's unexpected strength. Her back was aching, and she thought her leg muscles would knot in spasms by the time they reached the car. But they made it! To the newsmen shrieking for answers, John had managed a few replies which, Bea thought protectively, surely sounded convincing enough. And she even flipped back a few overly sophisticated replies concerning what she planned to do at the hideaway they were supposedly fleeing to.

Not until the car was away from the hotel did John let down. He passed out.

"Are you sure we shouldn't get a doctor to see him?'' she asked the security head, who had climbed into the back seat with them.

"There's no time; he has to meet someone,'' the man said bluntly.

"There'd be time if...."

"I'm not dying," John roused enough to whisper. "Relax."

She flounced back in her seat, trying not to think about how bad his color was, about the uncharacteristic blue circles under his eyes and the sweat breaking out all over him whenever he tried even a simple task such as sitting up straight.

The walk into the airport was worse. A nightmare. But luckily no newspeople caught up with them there, so they were able to move along unimpeded. And somehow the airline managed to expedite their check-in and admission to the concourse area.

During the last long stretch of walking John had to do, his hand tightened on her shoulder, and Bea knew he was approaching total exhaustion. The smile on her face was frozen as she concentrated on putting one foot in front of the other. Right foot, left foot. Smiling. Looking so in love. Hoping the milling travelers around them believed the facade.

They fell into the arms of the guards once they stepped inside the room being held for them near their departure gate.

"Bea, are you sick?"

Vaguely she heard Perry in the background as she felt herself being lowered into a chair. The sudden absence of John's considerable weight had made her slightly dizzy. She thought she could hear him mumbling to someone he called André. And she was certain she recognized the man with them as one of the Algerians she had seen in the sidewalk café. She looked around blearily, wishing her brain would clear quickly, for she thought she saw those two men lifting John carefully to his feet again. Insanity! She shook her head.

"He can't walk anymore!" she protested loudly when she realized they were indeed helping John through a door opening onto a private hall.

John jerked his head around fleetingly, pain in his eyes as he groaned, "It's all right, Bea. I have to do this. André has told Perry what to do." And the men, though looking concerned, ignored her protests as they left the room with John supported between them.

"He can't walk anymore," she shouted again, struggling to rise to her feet. But her legs were numb, and she fell helplessly back into her chair.

CHAPTER ELEVEN

"I STILL CAN'T SHAKE this feeling of doom," Bea confided to Perry as they were landing in New York. She had subsided into worried silence upon boarding the flight, and her reflections had not become any less pessimistic with the passage of time.

"Robertson was all right." Perry didn't bother pretending he thought she was worried about her own safety. "Once his friends got him on his feet he was as anxious to leave as they were."

"I wish the airport doctor you insisted see me could have seen John instead."

"That doctor said such violent allergies to shellfish as you described were not uncommon," Perry reminded her. "He thought that since the retching had already stopped, the worst John could suffer was exhaustion for a few days. He should be fine once he's had enough rest."

Bea had heard similar reassurances from the two guards accompanying them, a Frenchwoman named Suzi Dubois, and a Thomas Gray from John's own staff. But it didn't make her parting glimpse of John forcing his body into action yet again seem any less alarming.

"Did it look as if he planned to rest for a few days?" she asked bleakly.

Perry didn't have any answer for that observation. From the urgency apparent in John's departure with the man named André and the others, Perry had also come to the conclusion that taking care of himself was not high on John's present list of priorities.

Bea sat listlessly while the stewardess prepared the doors for opening. Then, once people began to leave, she tried to freshen up her appearance, self-consciously running her hands over the mouse-brown wig Suzi had insisted she put on when they left Brussels. Not quite recognizing her own image staring back from a pocket mirror, she wondered if things would seem more positive once she got back into her usual routine in her own apartment.

Surprisingly, it didn't take long to accomplish that first step to normality. They cleared customs quickly, thanks to Perry's friend, and were equally lucky in getting a taxi. After Bea had dropped Perry off to catch his train to Washington, it was a simple matter for her and the two guards to get comfortably established in her condominium without anyone else in the building knowing she was home.

"I hope you two are more efficient at maintaining security than my apartment doorman is," Bea told Thomas, not totally joking. Her condominium was noted for its tight security, yet it had been simple for Suzi and Thomas to convince the management that they had permission to use

Bea's quarters. "That telegram I sent from Brussels instructing them to let you two use my place until I returned could have been sent by anyone. They didn't even check on its validity."

"Just be glad the telegram worked. We're here, and the doorman didn't recognize you when you came in with us," Thomas said.

"At least now I can get rid of this wig," Bea sighed as she returned the unfamiliar hairpiece to Suzi.

"Slipping you in here may have been the easiest part of this," Suzi told Bea with a wry smile. "Our orders are to keep anyone from knowing you are here, so that means not letting you go out at all, and keeping the windows shuttered during the day so you won't be seen. You'll have to make a list of things we can buy to help you pass the time comfortably."

Suzi's words had been prophetic. Being cooped up with two strangers, kind though they were, was wearing. And even more wearing was the worry about John that was always there inside her, unexpressed, tempting her to retreat into gloomy preoccupation.

It took a couple of days for her to recover from jet lag, and most of that time her unstated goal was to get information about Harry Ward. She felt once she knew he was safe, she would know John was all right. She watched the television news regularly and spent most of each morning reading the five major newspapers Thomas faithfully purchased for her. Frequently she listened to radio broadcasts, and with the help of Suzi and a

French-English dictionary, checked the Belgian and French papers Thomas would occasionally find on the newsstands.

There had been a few mentions of the missing man that first day home. But as Bea and John remained out of circulation, and other events caught the interest of the press, the story disappeared completely from the media. Bea continued her organized search, but by her fourth day back in the States the only mention of Harry Ward she could find was on the inner pages of one of the yellow-journalism sheets, and that was just a rehash of old information.

It became increasingly difficult to pass the time constructively without fretting. And Bea was determined not to let the others see how deeply she cared about John's welfare. She kept reminding herself that John undoubtedly had a woman of his own who had a right to be concerned about him. Bea had fulfilled her commitment, and further involvement was inappropriate. But her lectures did little good. She had to force herself into all sorts of busy work, just to keep her mind off him.

Although a mediocre cook at best, she insisted on preparing all the meals for the three of them. But even with the newspaper reading and cooking she still was left with large chunks of time to fill. The high point of her routine became the late evenings when they turned out all the lights and Bea could relax for a brief time on her balcony beyond the dining nook.

She was sitting in that dining nook on the fourth afternoon, alternating her attention between trying to see through the cracks of her Florida shades and staring at the thoroughly perused newspapers stacked in the living room to her left, when she found a project to occupy her thoughts. She became fascinated with her couch.

It was literally crawling with flowers.

Not normally interested in interior decorating herself, Bea had agreed with her consultant's suggestion and bought the couch because it was a restful green color with a pretty flower or two on it. If she thought about it at all, she had probably noticed just three designs: the white petunia, a pansy and a small white lily of the valley.

But now that she had nothing better to do than stare at furniture, the couch gradually became the most challenging factor in her day, next to scrounging for news about Robertson or Ward. She counted fourteen different flowers incorporated into the fabric.

Curiously, seven of the designs appeared to be variations of the African violet. That fact alone had morbid fascination for her because she could not get Africa off her mind. She asked Thomas to pick up a flower-identification book at the library so she could reassure herself that indeed African violets did come in shades of pink and white as well as in a wide selection of purples. Once that fact was established, she became obsessed with firmly identifying each of the fourteen blossoms.

Perry suggested that she was going bananas.

Since he knew he was the only person she would be allowed to talk with, he made it a point

to call her every day. And his first question soon
became, ''Are you still staring at that damn
couch?''

''Do you have any better suggestions?'' She
would always ask hopefully, but he didn't. He had
failed abysmally when she had asked him to feel
out Carole Ward's congressman on what was going on with the Harry Ward affair; official Washington seemed to know less than Bea. So without
any news that she wanted to hear, he was forced to
listen to her discourse on what flower she had
identified thus far on her couch.

It was not very difficult to name the rose. And
she had been able to verify the seven different
African violets with the help of Thomas's book.
But for a while the other designs almost seemed to
blur.

Suzi suggested using a magnifying glass, and
once Bea dug that out of her desk, the yellow
snapdragon and yellow daisy were reasonably
easy. But she had some trouble deciphering one
fanciful, distorted shape. Only with the help of the
book and some advice from Thomas had she pin-
pointed an orchid as the fourteenth design.

After spending so much time studying those
flowers, she became amazed that her couch maintained a generally green appearance; there were so
many colors in it.

''Don't you find it fascinating that my flowered
couch looks green, Perry?'' she asked during one
of his regular calls.

''Not particularly. Suzi and Thomas must be
going bananas, too, to be helping you with that.''

"But think how much less expensive this therapy is than seeing a psychiatrist," she said. "Instead of being analyzed on a couch, we're analyzing the couch!"

"That's terrible," Perry groaned. "I'm going to send you a joke book in care of Thomas. You can read it to me next time I call, and spare me your current insanity."

He did send a joke book by express mail, much to Bea's delight. But she would have been much more pleased if he had come up with any information about Harry Ward. She didn't dare call her father in Washington and ask him to milk his contacts. She had already had Perry tell her parents that she had decided to vacation with John and would call them when she got home. There was no need to cause them more worry, and she didn't quite trust her mother's ability to keep a secret.

She wished she knew anyone else who could help her. It didn't seem logical that it could take so long to buy a man's way to freedom when apparently bribery links had already been made. The fact that she had not heard from John himself made her wonder if perhaps she had been wrong in thinking he planned to hide out in Belgium. He had been driven by such urgency when he'd left her at the airport that one might suspect he was going to rescue Harry Ward himself. But upon reflection that idea seemed ludicrous. Professionals would be needed for such work.

As more time passed with no news from John, Bea swallowed her pride and began to pressure Thomas to tell her what he learned in his daily calls to John's office. Other than revealing that Carole Ward was now avoiding the press herself, presumably because she feared the continued publicity might hurt her ex-husband, he claimed the office had heard nothing from John, either. At Bea's urging he had called the hotels in Brussels and Paris where John had stayed, but the management there insisted John was no longer at either of them, nor were any of his staff. Bea was becoming increasingly worried.

As HER TIME IN ISOLATION approached a week, Bea's anxiety had not abated. The waiting seemed hard even on Thomas. Friday morning at breakfast he surprised them all by suddenly dropping his open newspaper on the dining table beside his steaming cup of coffee and exclaiming, "I'm going to call the office again this morning. They should have heard something by now."

Bea's eyes narrowed as she watched him leave, and she curiously picked up the paper he had been reading. Scanning the open sheet, she at first saw nothing that might be related to his sudden decision to call California. But on second glance a headline caught her eye.

EXPLOSION ROCKS STORM-RIDDEN AREA NORTH OF NIGERIA
Investigating Militia Uncovers Terrorist Stronghold

"Suzi, could this be. . . ."

"I don't think it has a thing to do with Harry

Ward," Suzi said firmly, reading over her shoulder. "Look at the dateline; it happened two days ago. We would have heard by now."

"Not if something went wrong," Bea choked. Taking the paper with her, she rushed into the kitchen where Thomas was phoning.

He was just hanging up.

"They haven't heard anything," he said bluntly, his disappointment showing momentarily.

"Are you telling me the truth?" she asked urgently.

"I'm telling you the truth. They said they haven't heard a thing."

"John went there, didn't he? To this place near Nigeria?"

"Why would you think that?" Suzi pushed her way into the tiny kitchen, too. "Why would John go to Africa when he's hired professionals to make this rescue for him?"

"You tell me."

Thomas watched Bea's face whiten with concern while she read the story more carefully. Her hands shook so much the newspaper crackled noisily.

"This says there had been an unusually violent rainstorm with some kind of explosion and flooding in this village near an abandoned mining complex. Government forces who had been flushing out bands of terrorists nearby went in to see if people were hurt. When they got there they discovered the headquarters of some terrorists outlawed throughout Africa. Oh, no!" she said brokenly, "several foreigners there were killed in the skirmish, but it doesn't identify them!''

She looked at Thomas frantically.

"The office did say John called them from Brussels,'' he said calmly, his eyes hooded.

Her face glowed with relief, and she sat down. But her elation was soon replaced with anger.

"Then why hasn't he called us, too? Doesn't he care what we're going through, virtual prisoners that we are? He knows I'm due back at work Monday. Did he plan for me to just sit around while he makes phone calls all over the world, but not here?'' She believed, but did not say, that he had undoubtedly taken time to call *some* woman—one he loved.

"Bea, he probably doesn't want to call until he knows everything is settled,'' Suzi said, trying to calm her.

"Then what about this story you were reading, Thomas?'' she countered. "Obviously you must think it's related? The location is east of where I had been thinking Ward might be, but—''

"It might be related,'' Thomas admitted cautiously. "But then again, it might not. I simply called to see if the office knew anything. I'd suggest we check the radio and television news more carefully from now on.''

"I'm going to call the public library and have their reference department find out if this village—'' she glanced down at the newspaper "—this place where the explosion was has a street named Loglum.''

Thomas's apparent distress that Bea was losing her cool became obvious to her, and with some embarrassment she glanced one last time with morbid fascination at the paper before tossing it on the counter.

She called the library anyway, and within an hour verified that the village did have a street named Loglum. Once she knew that, however, she was stumped. She didn't know anything else to do but wait.

IT WAS ON THE NOON RADIO BROADCAST that they heard the first word.

"Harry Ward has turned up in Algeria?" Bea gasped incredulously, parroting what the announcer had just said.

"Shh." Thomas leaned forward alertly.

". . . said he was unaware that anyone had been concerned about him. He cheerfully admitted to having been on a colossal drunk and apologized for any concern he had caused American government officials. About the concern of his former wife, he appeared equally surprised. John Robertson, Ward's employer, who has maintained all along that Ward would turn up eventually, could not be reached for comment. There is still speculation among the press, who had been covering Robertson's vacation with his current mistress, that the California businessman had paid a hearty ransom for Ward's freedom. But the offices of California Robertson, Inc. firmly deny such stories. They confirm that Robertson and Beatrice Allen are still on vacation together in Europe."

"I'll try the office again," Thomas said as soon as the broadcast was over. But his move toward the phone was merely anticipatory, for it rang at that moment.

Bea stared at him hopefully, then was swept with disappointment when she saw Thomas's face first cloud, then mask with professional lack of emotion as he listened. Once he'd hung up, she did not even ask what he had learned, for it was obvious she was not going to like the news.

"We're going to have to stay put a little longer," he said.

"Who did you talk to?" Suzi asked steadily.

"The office in California. Harry Ward is free and fine, but they...André and Blanco...are held up in Africa. Someone was slightly hurt, and they don't want to move him for another day or two."

Suzi was watching him silently, her face equally unreadable.

"You're speaking of the men John hired? Are they and this injured man in Algeria now?" Bea asked.

Suzi was now looking anxiously at Thomas, her intent expression reflecting the concern voiced by Bea.

"Yes, in Algeria. Mr....one of them is under hospital observation for a suspected blood clot, but as soon as he can be moved, the whole team will leave. We can't risk publicity until they are all out of Africa."

"I understand. I suppose John won't surface in Belgium, either, until they're out. Still you'd think he might have called us now; surely he realizes we'd be worried. He looked like walking death the last time we saw him.'' Her voice was anxious rather than angry.

Thomas turned away as if annoyed with her wistful statement, and she noticed that Suzi appeared equally chagrined. It bothered her that she had let her own self-control lapse.

''I must call Perry.''

''I believe it would be better to wait until. . . .''

Again the ringing telephone anticipated the deed. And the caller was Perry. When Thomas saw Bea's stricken face, he relented and calmly handed her the receiver.

They didn't talk long. Bea told him that Ward had been freed and explained her plans to continue her isolation.

But Perry knew her so well he could sense her worry just by the tone of her voice. ''You'll be seeing Robertson soon,'' he had reassured her huskily. ''Now that this is almost over I won't be calling for a while. But if that Robertson doesn't treat you right, you get in touch with me.''

''I love you, Perry,'' she had said sincerely.

''I know, dear. . . friends always?''

''Always!''

When Bea hung up she thought about Perry's prediction that she would be seeing John soon. Darling Perry. It wouldn't occur to him that anyone Bea loved would not return the sentiment.

She decided she would be lucky if she ever heard from John again, even by phone. Her face must have revealed her desolate thoughts, for Suzi and Thomas were watching her with such sympathy that she turned away in confusion. She realized it was time she got on with the serious business of forgetting John.

And it was going to be serious business. She hated to admit how much it had hurt to hear herself described on the news as Robertson's "current mistress." That description alone told her where she stood in his past, present and future. With a pang of self-pity she almost wished that the mistress part had been accurate, too. At least she would have had that memory of him.

On Sunday John's office was late in making its daily call, and Bea was deeply resentful.

She began to rehearse an assertive speech in which she would tell them she had to return to work Monday. If they objected she was going to insist on learning the injured man's identity and talking with his doctor in Algeria. Only a real case of life and death would keep her doing John's bidding any longer.

But when the call from California Robertson, Inc. finally came, she didn't get a chance to start her complaints.

A man who identified himself as Phillip Robertson, John's older brother, was thanking her profusely and telling her the waiting was all over, that the injured man was safely out of Africa. He sounded jubilant. His voice was so much like John's that Bea hardly registered anything he said after that. She was too mesmerized by the intonation of his words, the texture of the gruff sound. The lure of John, even in memories of his voice, was frighteningly strong.

Bea did manage to register one caution Phillip made—she was to avoid telling the press how she got back to the States or how long she had been home.

"We think you're safe now from any faction within the terrorists; they've been pretty well broken up," he explained. "However you may get some flak from the press once you go out. We would not be surprised by a good bit of media interest immediately, but public attention should die down soon. If you'll just wait a few more hours before venturing out, we'll have released a press story by then. That will make it easier to avoid answering questions; just refer them to our press release. Remember that we still have lots of African sources to protect."

"I'll be discreet," Bea replied. "And luckily I know very little, anyway. Now you want me to remain at the apartment until late afternoon?"

"That would be fine. And again, we appreciate all your cooperation, Ms. Allen; we know it hasn't been easy. Thomas and Suzi will be staying on with you for a few days just in case you need any help."

There was a muffled sound in the background before he added, "Hold on a minute—someone here wants to talk with you."

Bea's hand sweated as she gripped the phone tighter, certain the next voice she would hear would actually be John's. Her tongue felt heavy and her heart was racing like a child's erratic wind-up toy.

"Ms. Allen, this is Harry Ward." The man's

words had a cheerful quality directly contrasting to her own leaden reaction.

"Ms. Allen?" Her disappointed silence made him think he had lost connection.

Bea recovered herself enough to quip, "You sound sober to me."

She was rewarded with a hearty laugh from the other end of the line. "John said I would like you, that you have a clever tongue."

"You've seen John Robertson?"

"Ah, well, talked with him. Phone, you know. Look, Ms. Allen, I just wanted to tell you I appreciate your help. Things were pretty sticky there for a while, and if you and John hadn't carried this off as well as you did...."

"I'm just pleased you got out safely. Have you seen your wife?"

"Now *that* may do me in." He sounded shamelessly ecstatic. "I hadn't seen my ex in more than two years and yet she creates a fuss like that when I'm missing. *Now* she says she doesn't want to see me ever again. Does that make sense to you?"

"Absolutely. If I were she, I'd be tempted to lock you away myself for all the trouble you've caused," Bea said lightly.

"I do like you. Well, I'll be back in touch, if I survive seeing Carole. Thanks again!"

Bea hung up the phone, both satisfied and disappointed. Harry Ward sounded like a man worth saving. But he wasn't John.

"Is everything all right?" Suzi had been watching her.

"Yes, Harry Ward is back. I talked with him

and he sounds fine. I can go out by this evening. Would you two like to be my guests for a genuine restaurant meal tonight?''

"Not to criticize your cooking—" Suzi grinned, running her tongue across her lips "—but the idea sounds long overdue!''

However, they didn't eat out after all.

For it was only two hours later that John Robertson walked into Bea's apartment.

CHAPTER TWELVE

LATER, UPON REFLECTION, Bea was ashamed that she had fallen so readily into John's open arms. She should have had more pride.

But at the moment, his unexpected arrival seemed like heaven, and reticence had never crossed her mind.

When he came she was out in her kitchen returning mustard and a bag of fruit to the refrigerator. Lunch had already been carried into the dining nook, and she planned to join Suzi and Thomas for the meal as soon as she finished her chores. Her black hair, freshly washed and brushed dry to a glossy shine, hung loose down her back. She was barefoot and had on her oldest pair of slacks with, incongruously, an expensive designer blouse she had bought during her one brief shopping trip to the Galéries Lafayette.

She had chosen the vibrantly colored blouse more to cheer herself up than anything else. After talking with Phillip Robertson and Harry Ward, she was living in a curious mixture of anticipation that John might soon call, and of dread that once he had called, her contact with him would be irretrievably finished.

It was Suzi who let John into her kitchen, then

discreetly disappeared, closing the door behind her. At first Bea was stunned and stared at his grinning, wonderful face as if not certain he was real. Then in her surprise she reacted exuberantly and threw herself laughingly into his arms.

She covered his drawn face with joyful kisses, ran her hands over and over his shoulders in her need to be certain he was actually there, hugged him, then kissed him again.

He was all smiles and appeared to relish every aspect of her attention.

"We did it! We pulled it off," he finally said when she gave him opportunity to draw a breath.

"Yes, we did it!" She smiled back at him foolishly. He had never looked so good to her, despite the tiredness lining his face. "You must be exhausted," she fussed. "Did you come straight here from the airport?"

"Yes. But I'm not too exhausted to enjoy a little welcoming kiss!" And she had enthusiastically kissed him again before drawing away. It was only then, as she realized how surprised he was by her uninhibited welcome, that she decided she should have exercised more self-control.

Laughing at her obvious embarrassment, he fondled her bare arms, then captured her hands and brought them to his mouth, nibbling on each fingertip. Eventually Bea could stand the exquisite pleasure no more, so she set aside her pride and stepped within his embrace.

Safe against his strength, comforted, she had a hundred questions about the rescue on the tip of her tongue. She could hardly think what to ask first.

"I talked with Harry Ward." John's actual presence there still seemed so beautifully unreal that she had to hug him again. "He sounds like a wild man."

"A safe, live wild man thanks to you," John said with satisfaction, kissing her thoroughly.

"I'm glad that I could. . . . Oh!"

Only gradually, while still hugging him, was Bea aware that his hands were wandering all over her body. His touch was affectionate—heartbreaking in its gentleness. Being caressed by him felt marvelous; it introduced such a different emotion than her impulsive welcoming kisses had done that she was tempted to let the new development take its course.

But once she'd recovered from her shock at seeing him, the lectures she had been giving herself during the two weeks of waiting returned to mind. She had to accept that she was just a temporary necessity in John's life, that he had no deep interest in her. Resolutely she again tried to move out of his embrace.

"You should be explaining to Suzi and Thomas. . . ." she objected breathlessly when he insistently kept her against him.

"Surely not explaining this," he teased, his mouth roving to her throat.

"John, we can't. They've been penned up in this apartment with me for days."

"Lucky Suzi and Thomas." He slipped his hand under her loose silk blouse. She could feel his fingers splaying across her back when he pressed her closer.

"Then explain this Harry Ward rescue to me," she tried to insist, despite the temptation his determined lovemaking held out to her. "John, you've stayed in Belgium so long. Why didn't you at least call us and let us know how things were going with you?"

He seemed so startled by her words that he drew back to stare incredulously at her, leaving her with such a feeling of deprivation that she allowed herself the luxury of being the one to pull him close. Since explanations had to be made, she reasoned, she might as well enjoy the telling from the security of his arms.

He sighed with satisfaction. "There isn't a lot I can tell yet." His breath was warm against her hair.

She leaned her head against his chest so she could listen to the rumble of his voice through his shirt.

"You were worried about me?" He seemed to be distracted, and his lips were playing with the wisps of hair around her temples. Mindlessly giving in to temptation, she held her face up to him so he could better continue his devastation.

"Of course I was worried," she murmured. "I kept wondering how long it could possibly take to complete your payments. I knew you needed secrecy, but I couldn't understand why you...."

"Bea, you talk too much."

Hungrily he shut her lips with his own. And she returned his kiss as fully, not even stopping when she felt him awkwardly unfasten her bra and begin rubbing the whole expanse of her back underneath her soft blouse. His other hand tangled in her hair as his warm, eager fingers moved around her side, then eased her away from him slightly so he could discover her breasts. And as he stroked her gently, she kept right on kissing him, moaning slightly as she did so, loving him, loving the way he made her feel.

"How does this thing open?"

She came out of her daze only slightly when he released her to fumble with the tiny buttons that made a neck opening across the shoulder of her blouse.

"It's a designer blouse," she babbled, her lips throbbing with desire. "I bought it in Paris."

"Bea!" he warned, impatient with the fastening.

She began releasing the buttons from their intricate loops, her love-drugged gaze lost in his ardent look. It was not until she had finished the last button that she realized what she was doing.

"I can't take this blouse off. Suzi and Thomas are right outside."

He didn't even try to argue with her. Dropping his hands from her waist, he strode through the swinging kitchen door. When Bea did not hear any talking she cautiously stuck her head around the door herself, automatically holding her blouse together at the shoulder. Surprisingly, the room was empty except for John, who was opening the front door of the apartment. The tray of food she had placed on the dinette table was even gone. She saw

John take one glance outside, then close the door quietly and meticulously lock it.

Still clutching her blouse at the shoulder, she stepped gingerly into the room. "What's happened?"

He was walking toward her slowly, his expression pleased, his desire undisguised. Her eyes were wide as she watched him approach.

"They seem to assume we have a lot to talk about. I think they're settled for a long afternoon of guard duty. They're enjoying lunch in two comfortable chairs right outside the door and even have some newspapers and the phone on a long cord out there with them."

"Oh." She didn't move, not even when he stopped directly in front of her. "Are you hungry?"

"Not for food. Where is it?"

"What?" she asked breathlessly, her skin heating in a rosy flush as his arm went around her waist.

"Your bedroom." He leaned over and kissed her behind the ear, then, not seeming to be able to stop, on the throat and eyelids as well. He was urging her along, moving her toward the hall as he continued to drift little caresses across her face.

"I'm so full of the need for you I wish I could carry you off in my arms like some returning hero," he apologized huskily, "but this hasn't been my best week. . . ."

She turned her head just slightly so his lips could touch hers as they walked along, now embracing each other rather awkwardly.

"You seem to be limping. Are you still weak from that allergy?" Given their present preoccupation the question was absurdly mundane. But important to her.

"No, a water tower fell on me."

She pulled away slightly. "I don't find that very funny."

"I didn't, either. Bea, are you going to talk all day?"

So relieved was she at his safe return that she didn't even question his assumption she was going to bed with him. Immediately. With no arguments.

It was what she wanted, too—urgently, despite her lectures to herself for the previous two weeks, despite having no assurances for the future. She felt as if she had belonged to him so long that expressing her love for him in this way was the most natural thing in the world. She reasoned, if indeed it could be called reasoning for she was so unreasonably in love, that if she had to belong to him, she deserved to possess him once no matter what his commitments to her would be.

Her only concern at that moment was the obvious....

"I must stop in the bathroom a moment. I'm not in the habit of, I mean I don't normally...."

He kissed her gently, interrupting her halting, embarrassed explanation. "I know you don't. And you're right. We have some things to settle before planning a child." He kissed her several times again, then pushed himself away.

"Don't take long."

She didn't. He was still waiting for her in the hall when she returned, although he had apparently at least located her bedroom, for he led her there unerringly. The spread was already turned down. She heard him click the lock behind him, then felt his hands going to her shoulders.

"John?" Fleetingly she wished, after all, that she did have some assurances... that he would tell her she was more to him than just his "current mistress." But as he began to undress her, even that concern was overcome by her need for him. She had to love him, just this once, if only to try to get him out of her system so she could survive the loss when he was gone.

When he stretched out, naked, on the bed beside her, she turned unquestioningly into his arms.

His sigh of satisfaction equaled her own. It was beguiling to touch each other, a wish long overdue. They smiled, almost laughing aloud at such an uncomplicated joy. Bea let her fingers trail across his chest, tracing the line where his open shirt collar had allowed the tanning of his throat, then across the lighter shades of his skin beyond. Her hands ran under his arms to his back, up to the shoulders, then slowly down to his hips.

She could feel him shudder, sense him pausing in his caressing of her so he could fully enjoy her own tentative lovemaking. Obligingly she again ran her hand across his shoulders and broad back, smiling like a cat with cream as she watched his pleasured response.

'Do you know, I've been dreaming about

you," he murmured against her lips. "Even before we left Paris...."

The feelings he was creating deep within her
were so much sweeter than any dream that she
could not even answer. He drew her tightly against
him as they kissed deeply, lying against each other
along every line of their bodies, yet wanting even
more closeness. It was strange to Bea that they fitted so perfectly together. Strange because she visualized him as a giant and had thought she might
feel overpowered in his arms. But rather, there
was the sensation of blending. Her firm fullness
beautifully complemented his hard muscularity—
the age-old affinity of male and female. He was so
right for her.

"I love you," she sighed as his hands shaped
her waist and hips, and he slid deliciously down
along her body so he could taste her breasts. She
restlessly caressed his head, the crispness of his
hair stimulating her fingertips. But suddenly she
fell still, aware of something wrong.

"What is it?" He raised his head, his voice
drugged as he focused on her startled face.

"You've been hurt!" Again she touched his
head gingerly, slipping her fingers through his
thick thatch of hair, barely outlining a swollen
freshly scarred area.

"And your leg.... There's something...." Almost frightened, she let her hands slide along his
nakedness to discover what it was that she had
become so gradually aware of—along his thigh,
the large bandage taped across part of his old scar.
Immediately she began to cry.

"My God, Bea," he groaned, gathering her in his arms and rolling over so that she lay almost on top of him. "You do pick your times...."

He tried to soothe her, tried to kiss away her grief, but she was crying all over him, her tears moistening his face as she kissed him with little fluttering pecks.

"You went after him yourself, didn't you?" she accused breathlessly. "You could have been killed. Why didn't you tell me?" She kept gasping between sobs and kisses.

Finally he began to laugh, all the while teasingly stroking the rounded buttocks, which so conveniently filled his hands. Her silken hair draped around him when she raised her head tearfully and ordered him to stop.

"It's not funny! If you cared at all about me you would have told me," she almost shrieked, elevating herself above him to see his eyes, to force his attention to her seriousness.

"You're always jumping to the wrong conclusions." He grinned affectionately, drawing her face toward his and beginning to lick her tears. But she strained away from him, her frightened concern not yet spent.

"If you weren't in Africa, why didn't you call us? You were hurt and didn't let us know!" The tears rolled down her face afresh while she angrily berated him. And he laughed all the more.

"Stop it!" She shook him as hard as she could while still sprawled across him, wanting to make him feel the fear and pain she was feeling. But when she noticed that he was not at all bothered by her punishment but rather was gleefully enjoying watching the movement of her body as she elevated herself above him, tugging at his shoulders, she stopped in shock.

"John?" she murmured weakly.

His lips curved as he slowly raised his eyes up to her face.

"My darling Bea."

It was a statement, not an answer. Once made, he liked the sound of it, and he turned his head slightly so that her hair dragged across his lips when he murmured it again. As if addicted already, he again restlessly shaped her buttocks, caressing, loving. Eventually one hand glided forward, exploring ever higher. His fingers went round and round, thoughtfully, and the emotion he stirred shocked her into breathless silence. Her body remained motionless, but her eyes widened in wonderment.

"Can't we talk later, Bea?" he asked thickly, closing his eyes and raising his head to rub his lips gently against first one, then the other breast. "I've waited so very long for you."

Her hair curtained his face as she remained suspended above him, her hands on either side of his broad shoulders. Almost disbelievingly she watched the satisfaction and pleasure on his own face as his fingers played her body like a musical instrument, stroking, encouraging. Her breath came in short gasps, and she could feel herself filling his hands, moving eagerly. It was as if she were singing inside, responding to each cue of the ardent instrumentalist. Shyly she watched him, marveling at his concentration. He looked as if he believed he was performing the most urgent task in the world—his discovery of the shape of her body. She seemed to bloom under his attention, to soften and shape to his own design. When he lowered a hand to her thighs, she could stand their remaining slight separation no longer. Slowly, deliciously, she sank down against him and curved her arms beneath his head, burying her face in the curve of his neck.

"It took a lifetime to get back to you," he moaned. He forced her chin up, his hand tangling in her hair while he kissed her deeply. "I needed you so much!" She could hardly hear the words as he kissed her again and again, his arms tightening around her.

At that moment Bea thought she would drown in the depth of her love. He had given her such a gift—that need of his for the comfort only she could supply.

"I love you, I love you," she sighed, kissing him almost frantically. But he seized her head and held her still, his lips softening hers, slowing her down, not letting her rush him. When he finally released her lips with a breathless sigh, he ran his hands through her hair, letting it sift through his fingers as he watched. She still felt a frustrating urgency, but when she slid lower on his body and began to kiss his hard muscle-strung chest, her toes curling sensuously against his, she absorbed his own need to take time.

No longer did she feel as she had at Versailles, when they both had been so hurried, so anxious to memorize something they thought they might never experience again. In growing amazement, she realized that her discovery of this man she loved could never be memorized, never completed; it could take a lifetime and still give pleasure.

The curly hair covering his body teased her, making her want to caress more of him. She slid her hands along his sides, down to his thighs, under his body, so she could press more fully against him, and she was rewarded with his own gasps of delight. Feeling almost powerful in that haze of loving, she continued to kiss him slowly, hungrily, knowing that she was giving him as much pleasure as she was receiving.

One hand moved up to his strong jaw, ran along his eyebrows, then strayed into his thatch of sandy hair, avoiding the area where he had been hurt because she wanted nothing, certainly not pain, to intrude on this moment. He was touching her just as lushly, reveling equally in the indulgence.

They turned onto their sides to give themselves more access to each other, to hands and lips and the feasting of eyes. But gradually their excitement could not be absorbed by caresses any longer.

Sensing John's growing urgency and building to heights of frustration herself, Bea let him roll her beneath him and carefully lift her hips.

She adored the way he adjusted her to him, as if she were so delicately special that despite his need he could take all the time in the world. Their union was gentle and slow, allowing them to shape to each other. Bea's body fitted to his as if intended only for that purpose. Instinctively she moved with him, letting his lazy motions swamp her with an increasingly heated response. It was so beautiful!

But quickly the intense need grew. Unbearably. They began to move together more anxiously, then desperately, their hunger so unsatisfied that they both ached with the demand for fulfillment.

And then it happened, the surprise of loving— that slow, spiraling passion so overwhelming that they could only cling to each other blindly and let it engulf them in great cyclical waves.

Her breathing was suspended, her muscles gripped with inertia as ecstasy filled her, straining against the depths of her body.

"I love you!"

Bea heard John's hoarse whisper as if from a distance, her body so absorbed with what was happening to her that she did not have the strength to clasp him tighter in response. She could only let the passion complete itself, dominate her, take over her body and soul for long moments before both she and John shuddered with release.

Even the aftershock was beautiful.

Helplessly they trembled against each other, fitting together in sweeter intimacy than either could have dreamed possible. They could not bear to move apart.

John recovered first, but only to ease Bea into a more comfortable position. He was too spent to caress her, but he kept her pressed warm against him with his hands spread possessively around her shoulders as he lay back in utter relaxation. Groggily she looked up at his face, her heart lurching at his tender smile as he laid his lips almost reverently against her temple. Closing her eyes in response to his own satisfied weariness, she nestled against him, almost feeling her pulse beat in sympathetic harmony with his. Before long, despite the hint of afternoon sun creeping around the edge of her window shades, they both fell into deep sleep.

BEA TIPTOED TO THE SHOWER. She was grateful that her bathroom was not between the two bedrooms, but far enough down the hall to somewhat mute the sound of running water. For she did not want to waken John. He needed the sleep.

She laughed to herself and hung up the clothes she had rescued from the bedroom floor, then tucked her long hair under a shower cap before stepping under the warm water. As it ran over her skin, she luxuriated in the gentle cleansing, feeling full and rounded—beautiful.

Yes, John definitely needed the sleep now! She felt ecstatically happy that despite the pressures of the past week and of his travels, he had sought her out. Hungry for her. Surely there were other women friends he could have turned to—she couldn't rid her mind completely of the conviction that there must be a special woman in his life elsewhere. But at this moment, in his need, he had turned to her. And when they had fallen, spent, into each other's arms for sleep, he had left her in no doubt that she had satisfied him fully.

Surely that was something to build on.

She ran her hands over her body, soaping herself, then rinsing lazily, wondering if she would ever come back down to earth. She tingled all over with a new awareness. It was impossible to believe that she could have experienced this fulfillment with just any man. Her love for John had transformed her reactions, making her lose her self-consciousness and want to give and give and give....

And take a little bit, too. She grinned, flipping off the water and beginning to towel herself dry. She could hardly deny the satisfaction she herself had felt.

When she had shaken her hair loose and slipped back into her clothes, she tiptoed back to check on John.

Her heart felt full to the breaking point to see him resting in her bed, his shoulders bare above the sheet she had draped around him when she had left his arms. As in Paris, he seemed to take up all the space, and she wondered why she had not felt crowded when she had lain with him. Her face flushed at the recollections, and she eased the door almost shut again and padded quietly out to the living room.

Suzi and Thomas had not returned inside. In fact, they probably couldn't come in even if their discretion had not kept them from trying, she suddenly realized, for the night latch was still across the entry. Bea slipped it off, but very quietly, because she wanted a little more time alone.

She had never been in this position before, intimately sharing her life with a man and knowing that others were aware of it. Living together in the hotel in Europe had been different because they had only been pretending. Now it was real. Even if only for an afternoon.

As she wandered over to a chair and settled somewhat stiffly, her body still adjusting to the demands of loving, she thought how satisfying it was to relax in her own home, knowing her man was resting nearby. With a pang, she wondered how she could possibly face the reality of this being their only afternoon together.

But of course you must face it, she reminded herself. *You knew what you were getting into when you let him lead you to bed.*

The honest appraisal didn't help her spirits. Now that she had had this much of him, far from feeling satiated, she was greedy. She wanted all of him—his body, his love, his commitment, his loyalty.

The sad fact was that once they had made love, parting from him was going to be even harder.

Mulling over this unexpected development, she half heard the telephone ringing out in the hall where it had been carried, and she was grateful she did not have to answer it. She did not feel like talking to anyone.

She wondered if all women who entered their first serious affair felt as confused as she, as engulfed in ecstasy mixed with regret.

First serious affair? Even the term sounded offensive to her. She loved the man! She belonged to him, whether or not he wanted the responsibility of her loyalty. Perhaps if she cared less, the idea of an affair would be easier. But without his own commitment to her, she wondered how long it would be before her love would become too demanding, making her lose her self-respect.

He had said he loved her. But you could hardly count on whispers of love made in the height of passion. She had only a slight hope that she was imagining her future problems, that when John rose from her bed he might come looking for her to tell her he wanted to be with her forever.

Still feeling the unsettling emotions of their lovemaking softening and taunting her body, she got up restlessly, determined to find something to keep her occupied until John awakened, and they could talk.

As she wandered into the kitchen she heard the phone ring again. But she made no attempt to let Suzi and Thomas know she could accept calls. She needed to be alone and busy. Completely forgetting her earlier suggestion that they eat dinner at a restaurant, she began looking in her refrigerator for something to cook.

The insistent knocking at the front door forced her to turn her thoughts to other realities.

"John, we need to see you." Thomas's voice, hushed but urgent, followed up his tapping on the door.

Bea started to call out that they could come back in the apartment, then unable to completely shake her protective instinct, rushed to the door to open it quietly.

"John's still asleep," she explained, strangely without embarrassment as she stepped aside to let an apologetic-looking Thomas and Suzi come in-

side. Suzi was holding the telephone receiver
against her shoulder, looking troubled.

"What is it?" Instinctively Bea responded to
Suzi's expression. "What's wrong?"

"We've tried to put them off as long as we
could," Thomas explained gently, his eyes taking
in her blooming appearance, but revealing no reaction. "Newsmen have learned John is here.
They are thronging the lobby, and other residents
are having trouble getting in. Your management is
insisting that someone come down for a press conference so they can get rid of them."

"John's office is on the phone now and has
called twice before." Suzi pointed to the receiver
on her shoulder. "They're also being swamped by
the press. They did as John instructed and announced that he has been with you all along, but
they're afraid if they delay much longer releasing
the joint statement he promised from you
two...."

"He's planned we would announce that we've
been together?" A chill swept over Bea and her
eyes hardened thoughtfully.

"He must protect his African contacts, Bea."
Suzi pushed the phone hard against her shoulder
so the conversation could not be heard.

"Of course," Bea agreed too quickly, her voice
sounding controlled, even though ice was per-
meating her soul.

And she had thought he had nothing to gain by
coming to see her, that he had come because he
needed her understanding in his moment of success and relief.

What a fool she was!

She suddenly understood his sudden appearance after such a long silence. He had needed a final alibi to finish this Harry Ward episode up properly. And what better proof that he had been vacationing with her all along than walking directly out of her bedroom into a press conference?

Her chin lifted in hurt pride.

Womanlike, Suzi was sensitive to Bea's train of thought.

"Bea, it isn't what you...."

"What's happening?" John entered the room hurriedly, partially dressed. His shirt was half open and he was slipping his watch onto his wrist. His hair was still tousled and his eyes half open.

"I heard you knocking."

Bea watched him expressionlessly as Thomas repeated his explanations.

She saw the annoyance sweep across John's face and was somewhat surprised that as he listened, he did not glance guiltily in her direction. She wondered if the man had no shame. Her face, however, reflected none of her reactions.

She did not even blanch when he said matter-of-factly, "Bea, we're going to have to go down there to make a brief statement together. But you don't need to fix up. The more casual we look, the better. After we get rid of the press we can come back up here, and I'll fill everybody in...."

There would be no need to fill her in, she thought wearily. She knew it all now.

Of course he would want her to look casual—casual enough to have just been in bed with him.

He had even gone to the trouble of making her look blooming and fulfilled. Then the press would believe anything he said about the past two weeks. She felt as if she were dying inside. The pulsating fullness of awakened love was shriveling into raw agony at his betrayal. Numbly she moved toward her bedroom.

"What shall we tell your office?" Suzi indicated the telephone.

John quickly took the receiver out of her hands.

As she entered her bedroom Bea looped her lush hair in a rope and automatically began twisting it against her neck. She wished her hearing was not so acute, that she need not know what he was instructing his office to say to the California press. But his voice carried well.

"Just repeat that I'm pleased my friend Harry Ward is home safely, but I never doubted he would be. Tell them Bea and I had a delightful vacation together and that we have no intention of telling where we spent it. No! Deny any marriage plans. Get the press off our backs...."

Bea shut the bedroom door, then stood in front of her dresser, thrusting pins into her hair to hold it in place.

She told the stone woman reflected in the mirror that she was not going to cry. But it was alarming how her body, which only minutes earlier had been throbbing with a new, ecstatic sense of life, could be so quickly and ruthlessly drained, so cold and empty.

She pulled off her slacks and tossed them across her rumpled bed.

"Ready, Bea?" John walked into her bedroom without even knocking, and she thought resentfully that he was making himself very much at home in her own quarters.

Her bikini panties were little covering below her blouse as she walked past him to get a half slip from a dresser drawer. She sensed that her long, bare legs were the object of his attention, for he did not bother to hide his obvious appreciation while he watched her every move. Hurriedly she stepped into the slip, buttoned a skirt around her waist and put on her sandals. She had intended to look as businesslike and cold as possible for the press conference, but with him standing in her small bedroom, wolfishly watching her dress, she didn't want to take the time to complete the career-woman impression.

She wanted this press meeting over and him out of her life.

As she walked slowly toward him, her face was set in cold, angry determination.

"It won't be too bad, love, I promise."

Misjudging her frozen expression as fear, he took her arm protectively when they left the apartment, flanked by Suzi and Thomas.

The impromptu press conference went quickly. John and Bea stood on the raised hearth of the lobby's fireplace, so they could easily be seen. Perhaps discouraged by the restrictive presence of Suzi and Thomas, or perhaps because with the reappearance of Harry Ward the story was all but over, the newspeople had remained under rather good control.

John's statement was basically what he had told his office to say. Only when they kept pursuing his plans with Bea did he cut questions short and display some irritation. But to Bea's surprise he did pause for her to make a statement, too.

She thought she did remarkably well.

"Although I do not know Mr. Ward," she said coolly, "I am happy that fears for his safety were unfounded. I am looking forward to returning to work tomorrow. This has been—" her voice broke only slightly "—a different kind of holiday. Quite different." She smiled wryly at the reporters, and they chuckled in rare sympathy.

The inevitable one or two voices made innuendos in attempts to force an impulsive, newsworthy response. But at that point Suzi and Thomas began making a path, and John insistently guided her to the elevator.

Once back in her living room John abounded with enthusiasm.

"You were perfect, Bea! You said exactly the right thing! Now they'll quit following us around."

"I'm glad you were satisfied, John," she said with stiff formality. "I believe you left your tie on my dresser. You'll want to get it as you leave."

He was instantly wary, his eyes narrowing as he studied her, warned by the tone of her voice as well as her pointed words.

Suzi and Thomas, who had been standing close by smiling widely in the enthusiasm they shared with John, suddenly seemed to disappear out the front door. Their hasty reaction would have been funny to Bea if the whole situation had not been so horribly cruel.

"What's this about, Bea?"

"It hardly needs explaining, John. I want you to go."

"The hell I will! After what we shared...."

"I'd hardly call it sharing. You took! No! Don't say it," she objected as he opened his mouth in outrage. "I don't deny I was as eager to hop in bed with you as you were to get me there. But there's one big difference, John. I *love* you. You came here wanting an alibi. But when I was so damned glad to see you, you got greedy—you took my alibi and my love."

He was obviously shocked by her accusations. But she didn't believe she could stand any more of his convenient explanations and rushed on before he could respond.

"When you got here, why didn't you just say you still needed me to cover up what you had arranged in Africa? It would have been a lot more honest, John. And who knows? I just might have been lonely enough, and impressed enough with your truthfulness, to go to bed with you anyway."

"You're talking crap!" John didn't mince words as he strode toward her.

"Leave me alone!" She fought his hold wildly. "Go back to your own woman."

"There isn't any other woman. You're my...."

"We're not in the press conference now," she sobbed. "Get out of here!"

"Bea, Harry and I had to protect some contacts in Africa. They might be able to resume normal lives there once this terrorism ends. We can't jeopardize their safety by admitting what really happened. Some idiot reporter would try to find out who helped us.''

"Don't you think I appreciate the danger of retribution by local Africans? Why do you think I cooperated with that press conference?'' She glared at him, her distaste for his touch so evident that he let her step away from his grip.

"Then what is it?''

"My God, John, you dare ask? I love you! I'm not ashamed to admit it. But I won't have that love manipulated. You're not using me anymore.''

"Bea, listen to me. When I first arrived I intended to explain what I had to tell the press. I've had enough experience with your pride already to know how important that was. But once I held you in my arms, I wanted you so badly I couldn't make myself take time to . . . .''

"I've let you trample on me enough. Get *out* of here!''

He seemed to consider arguing with her. But as he studied her flushed, distraught face, his own expression hardened. "There's no reasoning with you when you're like this,'' he said harshly. "I'm not even going to try.''

He gathered up the suit jacket he had thrown on the couch and opened her door.

"Don't forget your tie,'' she said emotionlessly, wanting all traces of him out of her life.

"Keep it for a souvenir,'' he bit out harshly, his look condemning before he shut the door firmly behind him.

CHAPTER THIRTEEN

GOING BACK TO WORK became Bea's salvation. For almost a week she was kept frantically busy from the moment she arrived at seven each morning, until she left well after six. The exhausting schedule was necessary to catch up on the things Bea's replacement had not been able to handle, but it suited Bea fine, for then she had little time to think about John Robertson.

Every day Thomas accompanied her to the office and settled in a chair near her desk to prevent problems with the media. His presence had a secondary effect, which was to discourage any overly curious questions by her colleagues, thus leaving Bea free to do her job.

Initially, of course, there were the accumulated stacks of correspondence and phone messages to answer. She took care of what she could while at the office, but frequently she was so rushed handling current business that she had to take some of the backlog paperwork home and dictate replies on her recorder well into the night.

She also systematically reviewed the investment portfolios of her clients, and computer-checked trends and predicted problems in all corporations they held. In several cases she felt that immediate investment changes were needed, and so she had to contact those clients to discuss the situation.

Their friendly speculation over the telephone was something Thomas couldn't control, but Bea was relieved that most people's interest seemed good-natured enough. They were satisfied to tease her a bit about her public romance with John and were content with her vague, airy replies.

Such unavoidable conversations, though, shattered her hard-gained composure and seemed to reopen her raw wounds. So she became more determined to put all possible reminders of him behind her.

It had been a simple matter to rid herself of the most personal reminder by mailing his necktie to the home office of California Robertson, Inc.

But she could not mail away, send away or wish away the memories.

It didn't help that her bodyguards insisted on remaining with her. While she knew that she needed Thomas those first few days back at work, and she was grateful that Suzi was there to handle the too-numerous telephone calls to her apartment, their very presence reminded her poignantly of that afternoon she had spent in John's arms while Suzi and Thomas carefully guarded their privacy.

Bea suspected that the two remained several days after the press had lost all interest in her simply because they had not yet received clearance from John to leave. But she had not asked. When they did finally go, she bade them a tearful good-bye, which had been a curious mixture of regret because she had grown quite fond of them both, and of relief because their departure would sever her last link with John.

She wanted so desperately to forget him.

He had called twice when Suzi was still answering her phone, but Bea had refused to talk to him. A few days later he had called her at the office, and it had so alarmed her when she was instinctively overjoyed to hear his voice, that in reaction, her refusal to listen to his explanation had been brutally firm. He had not tried calling again.

For a few days after Suzi and Thomas left there was still plenty to do at work. Two investment clubs that Bea advised were to meet that week, and she spent a great deal of time researching her presentation for each group. They were both composed of young career women with relatively little money to invest, but Bea took seriously their interest in becoming knowledgeable about stocks. As she told the women, she was confident they would be in a position to make large personal investments at some later point in their careers, and she would be pleased to handle their accounts.

Once she had those club meetings behind her, however, things slowed down. She faced a traditionally slow investment month with nothing major to break the routine. And it was then that John would intrude on her thoughts at the most unexpected times.

For one thing, with Thomas gone she had to face the curiosity of her colleagues. Her brazen behavior in Europe had taken them all by surprise, and many of them approached her with questions that ranged from genuine interest and good-natured teasing to propositions.

"Ms. Allen, we all hoped you'd bring that Robertson man to the office and introduce him around," the secretary for Bea's investment unit confided the first day Thomas was gone. "He looked so handsome!"

"Sorry, but he's back at work in California," Bea replied discouragingly, her head bent over her work.

Other secretaries also hung around Bea's desk on unnecessary errands, but finally gave up on learning any confidences worthy of the office grapevine.

But Bea's male colleagues were not so easily discouraged.

"We never had such perfect business opportunities on the incentive tour I won two years ago," Kelly Boles, the cheerful head of their agricultural stocks department informed her, tongue-in-cheek. "Now tell me, Bea, did you talk Robertson into going public? I need a new stock offering to tempt some fresh money out of my clients, so I could use an accurate tip."

"Get lost, Kelly," Bea returned calmly.

"Just a little tip, then, Bea," he grinningly pleaded. "What are the corn futures going to do?"

Bea knew she should bat her eyelashes and coo that she and John had never got around to discussing corn. It was certainly the type of answer Kelly was fishing for; he loved witty repartee. But her feelings about John were still so ambivalent and raw that she could not bring herself to joke about their relationship.

"Get lost, Kelly," she said again, this time with a trace of irritation.

That was a mistake.

Others found they could get under her skin with a little teasing in the same vein, and they were quick to do so. It seemed to delight them that Bea, who had always seemed so cool and unapproachable, could blush and be left without words. The quips ran all the way from, "Hey, Bea, you look gorgeous today. If you ever get tired of your California farmer, I have a hideaway cabin in Maine," to "Don't ask Bea to research that pharmaceutical stock. She's so taken up with the farm world she'll probably confuse orange-flavored aspirin with Robertson's orange juice concentrate."

The propositions from a couple of married men in her office were the least acceptable of the office reaction to her affair with John, and she put a stop to that sort of thing very quickly.

But she couldn't stop the unintended, unpredictable reminders of him.

Sometimes the trigger was something obvious, as when her boss asked if John had ever said anything about using avocados for dog food. The question turned out to be a serious one because he was pondering the prospectus of a company that was hoping to purchase excess avocados cheaply and market them for animal food. But Bea had felt that he intentionally opened her wounds. She overreacted with a scathing remark, which required some further explanations on both their parts before the air cleared.

Other times the reminders were totally accidental and indirect. There was the man who took a booth next to her at a restaurant one day when she and two other women from the office had run out for lunch. His voice was so like John's that she began trembling and was unable to finish her meal.

On another occasion she was devastated to receive a hand-addressed letter from California. She left it unopened on her desk for two hours, certain the masculine hand had to be John's and torn between wanting to throw it away and dying to hear from him, after all. When she eventually forced herself to read it, it was a request for a contribution to a Sierra Club conservation project. The letdown was tremendous.

The hardest time was late in the evenings, when she had washed up after her solitary meal. Then the memories would not stay away.

She avoided going into her own room until the very last minute before exhaustion claimed her, for she could not approach her bed without feeling again the emotions John had created in her there. She kept remembering what it had been like to wake up with him warm against her in the shaded room. Even in the kitchen he entered her thoughts, for it was there they had stood longingly in each other's arms, so overwhelmed at being together again that nothing else seemed important.

Only in her living room was she free of memories of him. And so she settled there each night to read the business periodicals she brought home with her. Occasionally she made an effort to go out to a concert or art preview in the evenings, and once she met a college sorority sister for dinner. Bea enjoyed herself tremendously because her friend had discreetly avoided asking anything about John. But unfortunately Bea had few friends or colleagues who were as thoughtful, and so she spent most of her time by herself.

She was so lonely she was tempted to call Perry just to chat. But she knew that would not be fair to him, not as long as she had the plaguing conviction that she belonged to John Robertson.

I feel married, she admitted to herself. The realization was shattering.

It became her goal to make it through just one day at a time. She worked hard at the office, exerted her best concentration on useless activities in her leisure time and by the beginning of the fourth week after ordering John from her apartment finally believed she would succeed in forgetting him.

JOHN WAS DRIVING HIMSELF to exhaustion with equal fervor. But his fatigue was more from necessity than intention. August was the midst of his busy season. And it took almost three weeks of intensive labor before he was even caught up enough to call a staff conference.

That first meeting was a small one. Only John, Phillip, their sister Marlene and Harry Ward were there. But together they represented some of the major decision-making for California Robertson, Inc.

Marlene had come to the meeting mostly to listen. Although her university accounting degree was only two years under her belt, she was already demonstrating a quick understanding of the financial end of their business, and enjoyed a strong confidence from both her brothers, as well as their father. She was being groomed to take over more of the managerial responsibility presently loaded on John and Harry Ward.

For Harry, the meeting was an opportunity to familiarize himself with business developments that had occurred during his absence in Africa.

Phillip, a biologist by training and head of the corporation's research staff, spent a good bit of time updating them on the status of their plant health activities. He was particularly concerned about his discovery of mineral depletion in the soils of their new variety of orange trees and suggested that a research contract be granted to a small firm that had done work for them before. He did not believe his own staff could study the development quickly enough, because they were at a critical point in testing the effects of some new pesticides being used on their sugar-beet fields in Colorado.

"If no one objects, we'll go ahead and hire that research firm." John looked at those around him to be certain of their agreement. "I think we're all in accord with Phillip's position right now—more needs to be done than we have human energy to complete. In fact, I wanted to get you together now to analyze our current status, because I'll be headed out to Colorado with Phillip tomorrow, and it may be several weeks before all of us can match our schedules up again.''

He looked down at the mass of papers piled before him, as if choosing what developments he wanted to discuss himself.

"As you know, the lemons have been of greatest concern to us. Now that the long-range weather forecasts are promising, we're predicting the crop will be slightly below average this year. I feel lucky to settle for that. The protective measures we took during that late spring frost at least saved our trees. Some of our neighbors have lost half their groves.''

He handed around typed statistics of their current production in many commodities, which they all studied silently for some time.

"The canning vegetables look almost too good,'' Harry observed.

"You're right. We're contracting to distribute some of the excess to local produce suppliers for the home canning market. We don't want too high an inventory.''

"Animal feed is unbelievably good. Grapes should be a bumper crop. It sounds as if all of you can cope very well without me.'' Harry grinned at them, obviously not as insulted as he liked to make it appear.

"I've been back in the States three weeks now, and you haven't let me take on my full load yet. You make me feel unnecessary.''

"Don't you see the rings of exhaustion around our eyes, Harry.'' Marlene leaned toward him dramatically and gave him a woeful look. ''We've all worked double duty, and even had to talk dad into leaving his roses and come help us while John was chasing you down. We're just giving you a little time to rest up before we shove everything back on your shoulders!''

"Your absence even stirred Louis to action for once," Phillip said wryly. "When you guys couldn't account for that fertilizer, he got off his academic duff and helped us out."

"That may be a trend we will see continuing," John said quietly, not looking dissatisfied with the development. While they had all accepted Louis's preference for scholarly work, they had been disappointed that for a time he had seemed to lose complete touch with the family business. "I was supposed to attend the official opening of our vineyards in France tomorrow. But Phillip wants me to check on a problem in the sugar-beet fields, and I'd like to see those pesticide tests myself, so this morning I called Paris and prevailed upon Louis and Mathilde to represent us."

"He agreed to do that? He's tearing himself away from his last weeks of research at the Sorbonne?" Phillip was astounded.

"He did! That leaves me free to spend several days in Colorado with you if necessary. Making some of the decisions about this fertilizer scare got Louis to considering the food we provide to the world and the variety of expertise we need to keep the firm operating. It staggered him. And with Mathilde pregnant now, he figures it will be just his bad luck that one of his children will decide they want to enter this business instead of the world of books. He claims he wants to be sure there's a going concern for his kids to join.''

Marlene burst out laughing. ''Poor Louis!'' she sputtered. ''That his children might dare sink to such mercenary pursuits!'' They all enjoyed the development. Even Harry.

''It just could happen to him, John,'' Harry said. ''Take you and Louis—you look like twins, but are so opposite in skills and interests! And yet Phillip and Marlene, who are the tall, spare type like your father's side of the family, are so much closer to you in temperament.''

''I don't like that 'spare' description,'' Marlene objected heatedly. ''Tall women are supposed to be called 'willowy.' ''

''Willowy, then, dear. If Phillip doesn't object to being called that.''

''Be my guest.'' Phillip grinned.

''I don't think I have much more we have to go over right now,'' John said wearily, enjoying their nonsense, but beginning to feel pressed for time. He still had much to do before leaving for Colorado.

''I just wanted to update everyone and take care of that research problem.''

''Can you spare another few minutes, John?'' Harry asked casually. ''I have a couple of things I need to check with you. I'm going to start the inspection of the canneries tomorrow, right?''

''If you feel up to it. Marlene can try it, if you don't.''

''I'm healthy enough to work. Probably more so than you.''

"John needs a real holiday," Marlene agreed.

"The whole family is fussing over me too much. All I need is about three extra hours in each day." John's smile of healthy confidence was almost convincing. "So if there's nothing else you two Robertsons need, I'll talk to Harry?"

"We can take a hint," Phillip said agreeably, throwing his arm around his younger sister's shoulders.

"Buy you a cup of coffee, kid, before we head off?"

"WHAT IS IT, Harry?" John asked quietly, once they were alone. Sensitive to his close friend's moods, John knew he was worried about something.

"Have you heard anything from Nand yet? I didn't want to ask in front of Phillip and Marlene; I didn't know how much you've told them."

"I'm glad you didn't. They know the gist of it, but there was no need to go into all the gory details. I got a telegram from Nand this morning. The government forces seem to have cleared out most of the terrorists in his area. The few who escaped the fighting at that mining camp have apparently dispersed, for things have been so quiet that he hopes to resume farming in a few days."

"He has a lot of displaced people depending on him for food this season. Would you consider shipping in a large supply of free canned goods?"

"The order is already on the books." John grinned at him. "But no fertilizer this time."

Harry smiled his own appreciation of John's remark.

"If things are that much quieter, he can get his old European shippers to cooperate for spring pasturage anyway. Now let's talk about you.... Don't pull that 'I'm too busy right now' crap on me anymore, John. I saw you limping this morning, before you realized any of us had come in for the meeting."

"The leg's giving me some trouble," John admitted slowly. "The splinters from that wooden water tower pierced the same muscle that was botched in Vietnam. It's healing all right, but I guess I'm going to have to get some therapy again."

"Don't neglect it."

"I'm just pressed for time right now."

"Turn some of your work over to the rest of us. There's always a way people can get by in an emergency," Harry pointed out. "And I'm completely functional now. You've given me more rest and steak dinners than I needed. They hadn't fully starved me, you know."

"You looked like a scarecrow," John snapped. "André and I didn't believe you could manage that seven-mile hike we had out of there after we blew up that water tower."

"We must have been a sight," Harry admitted. "André with his wrist sprained from splitting open all those bags of fertilizer. Blanco swollen up from that bug infestation. And you with your head cracked open and hobbling along on that stick, not telling us your leg was all cut up when the tower collapsed.''

''My biggest problem was that I hadn't been able to rest since eating those damn mussels. I still felt as weak as a baby. We made it though!''

''We sure did!'' The two friends said little for a while, as they pondered the chilling experience they had survived together, able to be proud of the final conclusion and thrusting the worst memories behind them. ''You haven't had any more problem with clotting in your leg?'' Harry finally asked.

''No. It really wasn't necessary to keep me under observation in that hospital in Algeria; the diagnosis of a possible clot was uncertain. André is getting to be an old woman.''

''Speaking of women, how would you like to give me some free advice?''

''I knew there was something *really* serious on your mind,'' John said half humorously. Then, sensing Harry's intentness, he added bitterly, ''But you're coming to the wrong person for advice. My record with the woman I love is abysmal.''

''Wouldn't you think,'' Harry pursued, ''that if a woman stirred up half the press in the country because you hadn't come home on time, she'd be willing to at least talk to you once you did return?''

''You and Carole aren't back together?'' John was shocked.

''When I went to see her she was barely civil,'' Harry admitted ruefully. ''I told her I had had a business problem come up that had delayed me in Africa, but I think she believes I really was drunk. She's embarrassed that she raised such a fuss.''

"And you didn't feel free to tell her what really happened," John deduced. "If you're waiting for my consent, go tell her now. Nand's situation seems safe enough. Of course we still don't want to publicize your escape, but from what I remember of Carol, she can keep a secret.... ''

"She's so damn stubborn when she's embarrassed that I'm going to have an uphill battle," Harry bit out.

"I don't understand women and their pride." John agreed. But it occurred to him that if his woman had made it as clear that she loved him as Carole Ward had done for Harry, he would run right over her pride.

"I'll tell you this," John added. "Giving them time to cool down is a damn frustrating route to go. I'm seriously beginning to consider caveman tactics."

BEA SAW THE PICTURE quite by accident. The business newspaper in which it appeared was not one she normally read; it had somehow been placed among the publications she had brought home from the office. Before starting to cook her dinner, she had sorted them out for later reading and on impulse had carried that particular paper in to glance over while heating up a can of soup.

But the soup can never even got opened. For there on the front page of the *Wine Growers' Journal* was that picture. The caption read:

John Robertson clips the ribbon at the gate of
the new vineyards just dedicated as a joint research project of the French-American con-
sortium in which he is a partner. The joint
venture was....

She didn't read further. Instead she stared at the
picture. The husky man was facing the camera,
looking distinctly uncomfortable as he held up the
two edges of what had apparently been a decorative ribbon across an ornate exterior gate. Some
very official-looking men were standing to his left,
smiling at the camera. Simply seeing the name had
made her grow flushed. The jog to her memory
destroyed any illusion she had that she was suc-
ceeding in forgetting him. But the worst reaction
was yet to come.

There was something wrong about that picture.

She looked at it again, trying to figure it out. At
first she wondered if after almost a month away
from John, she was just reading too much into the
image. The picture had been taken the day before.
It was apparently a sunny afternoon in France.
The caption indicated that the location was somewhere in the wine-growing region, and that John
was there representing his firm for opening celebrations. The project was viewed with great favor
both by the French wine growers, who were anxious to see if California varieties could flourish in
some of the more troublesome growing areas of
France, and by the Robertson staff, who felt their
research in France might help them select other
areas of the United States in which they could ex-

pand their production of grapes for fine domestic dinner wines.

John did not look comfortable participating in the ceremony. She could understand that cutting a fancy ribbon was probably better suited for a politician than a businessman, but after seeing John's deportment in front of the press so recently, she did not believe he could let such a thing unnerve him. Feeling uneasy, she studied the picture again.

It hurt to see his face. Her fingers tingled as she recalled how she had touched every inch of that beloved face and then had followed her touch with kisses, pressing her naked body against his as she examined his strong features. She had traced his eyebrows, held that strong jaw in her curved hands, kissed his laughing mouth.

He had been so carefree then, despite his fatigue. And when her attention had moved to his hands, he had let her pull them from her own body and stroke them. She had adored the contrast of his roughness with her own soft skin. She had kissed each finger, giving special attention to the tipless one, which had so frightened her on Bastille Day. Then she had. . . .

"Oh, my God!"

She ran back to her spare bedroom, which housed her desk, and flipped on the bright reading lamp. Looking carefully at the picture, she knew what was wrong. And yet she couldn't believe it. The proof was there, but. . . .

Frantically she shuffled in her desk drawer for her magnifying glass, thinking that perhaps she could be wrong. But she was not. Through the lens she studied the man's hands holding up the ribbon. They were perfect. Every single finger. Perfect.

"That's not John," she gasped.

She had sensed it all along. She knew John's body. There was something wrong about the way that man held his head, about his smile, his demeanor. And the proof was there. His incomplete finger was suddenly, miraculously perfect.

With morbid fascination she unfolded the newspaper so she could read the whole story associated with the picture. But it told her nothing. She waded through boring facts on declining production of French grapes in three depressed areas of the country. Read quotes from numerous public officials. Statements from John's corporation.

It sounded so businesslike. But why would someone else claim to be John?

She groaned in frustration. She had thought with the African problem behind her she did not have to be concerned about what danger John was getting himself into. She regretted that they had never got around to talking that afternoon they had made love. Perhaps the Harry Ward incident was not finished after all.

For a long time Bea stared at the terrible photograph and pondered the situation. She could think of no logical reason why someone would be impersonating John. That left two sinister possibilities. Either he had arranged for an actor to take his place so he could do things elsewhere without being missed. Or he had been kidnapped and for some reason his captors were covering up his absence. In that case, it was improbable that his family would have received a ransom note, but still. . . .

Decisively she reached for the phone.

California information gave her the number of John's ranch, but she got no answer there, so she tried California Robertson, Inc. The only person she could reach at the office was a night watchman. He must have recognized her name, for once he learned who she was he seemed cooperative. He had all sorts of numbers to give her in case of agricultural emergencies on Robertson property or problems with customers' orders. But he was no help at all to find John personally.

"I've been on vacation for a week," the man said, "but last I heard he was scheduled to be in France for several days."

Bea's heart fluttered at that information. She had been hoping to learn that the picture was a mistake. "Could I reach Harry Ward or Phillip Robertson?" she asked on impulse.

"I don't have access to anyone's home number, and I wouldn't know where they're working right now. Ward planned to inspect some canneries, and Phillip was to be in Colorado for several days. Their secretaries will both be in tomorrow, though, if that will help you?"

"What about Thomas Gray," she asked, knowing her former guard would surely help her. But the man had no idea how to reach him, either. Bea hung up in dejection. It didn't sound as if anyone connected with John's office was aware of trouble or they would have made some arrangements to take emergency calls. This bothered her even more, for it would be so like John to go charging off on some mission without telling anyone, not wanting to worry them.

Of course if he had been kidnapped.... But the more she thought about it, the more she doubted that was the case. At least not kidnapped for money, because there would be no need to try to hide John's absence. It just didn't make sense.

The only thing certain was that John was undoubtedly in trouble, and apparently no one realized it. Either he had purposely disappeared, hiring someone to take his place in France to buy him some time. Or else he was being held for the information he knew. And the only way to find out soon enough to be any help was to locate that impostor in France.

She forgot completely that she never wanted to see John again. Forgot that because he had betrayed her trust and love she was determined never to allow him an opportunity to manipulate her again. Narrowing her eyes with decision, she reached for the phone. This time her business was conducted quickly.

It only took her three minutes to arrange booking on an early-morning flight to Paris.

JOHN WAS KNEE-DEEP IN MUD when Louis's call reached him. Although he and Phillip had finished their observations of the pesticide tests, they were concerned about one particular field of sugar beets. The depleted condition of the plants seemed to go beyond damage that could be caused by insects. He and Phillip were inspecting the irrigation ditch that fed the field, theorizing that the water movement might be sluggish enough in Colorado's dry climate for evaporation to cause harmful salts to accumulate. Over the years they could be gradually leaching into the fields.

The messenger seeking John had said the call was an emergency, and John had climbed hurriedly out of the ditch and limped across the field as fast as his aching leg and the newly dampened terrain would allow. It was so unusual for Louis to call at all, much less to claim he had an emergency, that Phillip also slogged his muddy way to the nearby farmhouse where the telephone was located.

"You'd better get yourself on the next plane to Paris," Louis said with obvious glee when John answered.

"What are you up to, Louis?" Relieved at the cheerful sound of his brother's voice, John glanced out at the afternoon sun. "It's got to be late evening in Paris."

"I have an extremely angry Beatrice Allen here accusing me of kidnapping you."

"What?"

"She thinks you're up to your old tricks trying to outwit experts in international intrigue." His voice rose dramatically. "And that I am a nefarious villain impersonating you while you're being held in some far-off torture chamber...."

"Louis, what the hell are you talking about?" Phillip impatiently snapped into the extension.

"John's lady friend saw my picture in a paper

after that research-vineyard dedication,'' their youngest brother recounted more sensibly. "When she realized I wasn't John, she flew over here to demand his safe return."

"Why would *your* picture make her do that?" John barked.

"Well, it wasn't exactly *my* picture."

"Wasn't your picture?"

"I know I told you I would 'sub' for you at that ceremony,'' Louis said somewhat sheepishly. "But when I actually had to cut that ribbon I was ready to back out of the whole thing. These functions just aren't my style. It made me feel a hell of a lot better that the photographer assumed I was you and didn't tie my name to that ceremony. So I didn't enlighten him.''

"You mean they ran *your* picture, but identified you as me?" John asked.

"That's it. I don't know how she could tell the difference from a bad news photo. How well did you say you two got acquainted?"

"Shut up, Louis." It was Phillip who barked the order.

"Why did she say she came to Paris?" John tried to control the exultation sweeping over him. Bea was beginning to act like Carole Ward. But he had to be certain.

"As I said, she came to rescue you. She thought you had gone off on one of your escapades again, unbeknown to anyone or that you were being held for information. Mathilde and I finally managed to convince her that I'm really your brother and that you're not being held for ransom somewhere.

That took some talking. She was ready to go to the American Embassy. We have her settled in our hotel for the night, but she's embarrassed as hell and is clearing out of here tomorrow.''

"Keep her there. Do anything you have to. Lock her up! Louis, I take back every bad thing I've ever said about you—I love you!''

"I guess that means he'll be on the next plane,'' Louis said with satisfaction, despite hearing one phone receiver slam down.

"Undoubtedly. He just went running out the door, covered in mud,'' Phillip replied.

"If he comes down to earth long enough to check back in with you, tell him we're at the Royal as usual. I'll meet his plane if he lets me know when he's arriving.''

"How did the lady track you down?'' Phillip asked curiously.

"Either she's got pull, or there's nothing to the claim that journalists protect their sources. It took her less than a day after arriving in France; she found out where I was staying through the journal that published the picture. That woman can pack a wallop with words. I'm glad she can only rave in English. Lord, if any of my French colleagues could have understood the things she accused me of. . . .''

"Louis, quit enjoying yourself so much. You were the only one of us who ever doubted John was human.''

"You should see this woman, Phillip.'' Louis was suddenly quieter, his voice rich with appreciation. "She's a looker. But very understated, lady-like. She's shy, I would guess. But it's hard to tell when she's on this kick about saving John. ''

"I'm sure we'll all love her." Phillip answered indulgently, trying to decide which of his two younger brothers was more trouble. Upon returning from Africa John had been so stubbornly silent about Bea Allen that they had all given up hope he was seriously interested in her.

"This means we'll have to plan on attending a family wedding soon," Louis predicted.

"If I know John, none of us will be invited to meet the bride." Phillip grinned as he added, "Not until later. John won't want us to scare her away."

CHAPTER FOURTEEN

THERE WERE CROISSANTS, as usual, and mounds of hard rolls, huge oranges, soft-boiled eggs and yogurt. Bea stared at the display distastefully. The Royal Hotel's small dining room offered the same late-breakfast fare Bea and John had frequently shared in their suite. And it brought back so many memories she was certain she would choke on each bite.

"Surely you must eat before making such a long flight again." The lovely blond woman standing patiently in line behind her with an empty plate spoke encouragingly. "You ate almost nothing last night, either. You will make yourself ill."

Not wanting to hold up Mathilde Robertson and the rest of the line any more, Bea helped herself to one hard roll and broke off a section of orange someone had left half peeled on the otherwise perfect display of fruit. But that was the most she could face.

Her high heels clicked lightly against the tiny white hexagonal floor tiles as she followed the waitress to a corner table on which the woman placed a large pot of steaming coffee and a smaller one of hot milk. Bea and John had never eaten in this room reserved for hotel guests who preferred to have their breakfast in the company of others, and for that she was grateful. At least the room itself brought no reminders of John. She could let the peaceful atmosphere sweep over her. Gingerly she settled on one of the delicate-looking antique chairs, then, finding it more sturdy than it appeared, she gratefully relaxed into its unexpected comfort.

"I think you must be suffering from—what does Louis call it—jet lag?" Mathilde looked at Bea's almost empty plate as she placed her own heaping one beside it on the white linen tablecloth.

"I suppose so. And embarrassment," Bea admitted readily, for she found the Frenchwoman likable and amazingly easy to talk with. "I wish I had realized you spoke English when I first saw you. Then I would never have got myself into this mess."

Mathilde smiled in understanding and began to eat, so Bea shook out her own napkin and placed it on her lap. But still she did not begin on her meal. "It was kind of you to meet me this morning for brunch. But I'm relieved your husband had an appointment. I don't believe I could face him again."

"Oh, he hopes to be back before you must leave for the airport," Mathilde said breezily. "This was all his fault, as we have said. He should never have let that photographer go on thinking he was John. I suppose since Louis had arranged for them to exchange places last time John was in Paris, he didn't think it mattered."

Bea was puzzled. "You mean they were to exchange places when I was here before?" she asked.

"Of course. In fact they had just done it when you walked by and tripped over my suitcase."

Bea poured some coffee, then, seeing how very strong it was, she added a half cup of the hot milk. She stirred it carefully, over and over.

"Don't you want to drink that before it gets cold?" Mathilde's question interrupted Bea's reverie, and she glanced up, startled at how much time had passed.

"I was just thinking about Louis and John exchanging places. Do they do it frequently?"

"Only that one time. It was Louis's idea, so John could have secrecy in Paris while he arranged Harry Ward's rescue."

"Then you were just a cover?"

Mathilde laughed at the word. "I have heard that on American television. Yes, I was a cover. Louis and I checked in here, then Louis moved in with André and John came to put me on the train for Strasbourg."

"And I fouled everything up."

"I guess you did. But you see, everything is fine now. Harry and John both made it safely out of Africa, and the fertilizer is—"

"You don't mean that John went after Ward himself?" Bea couldn't absorb the implication, couldn't believe she had heard correctly. When she had accused John of going after Ward, he had told her she was jumping to wrong conclusions.

"Oh, yes. Louis was furious because the situation there was so precarious. But you know John.

There's no stopping him when he makes his mind up.''

Bea couldn't answer as she tried to adjust to the fact that John had not been safe in Belgium throughout the Harry Ward rescue as she had thought. He had lied to her again.

"Then John's leg, the one he hurt...."

"I believe it will be all right once he goes through therapy again," Mathilde said soothingly. "It was because the doctor feared a clot that André wanted to keep him in the hospital in Algeria longer. But his circulation is perfect now."

Bea remembered with growing horror that John had told her a water tower had fallen on him, and she had berated him for teasing her. She felt as if she had jumped off a tall building, and her body was falling too fast for her mind to keep up. She had not learned any of this information the previous night when she had been berating Louis Robertson.

"Are you all right?" Mathilde's concerned voice came faintly through Bea's struggle into this new terrible reality.

White-faced, Bea stared at her companion momentarily. "I hadn't realized all that was going on," she said weakly.

"I only know what Louis helped plan, and he didn't tell me that until it was all over. John, as you know, does not...."

"Tell anyone anything," Bea finished ruefully. She picked up her coffee cup and tried to drink. It was a useless attempt at normality and she immediately gave it up. She was plagued to know everything, had a self-destructive obsession to wallow in the stories of his danger. But dejectedly she remained silent, ashamed to ask her questions, ashamed to expose even more of her love than her foolish flight to Paris had already done. She toyed with the idea of asking Mathilde not to ever tell John she had come.

But as she watched the woman enthusiastically enjoying her heaping plate of food, the idea was obviously ludicrous. Only Bea placed such great, mortifying importance on the situation.

They said very little as they continued their meal. Mathilde seemed to respect Bea's preoccupation and was unbothered by her reticence. Since it was almost noon, Bea knew she should have something, so she did manage to eat half of the roll she had taken. It seemed to her that she had worked on it for an eternity, and yet, when she finally looked up, expecting Mathilde to be long since finished, she saw much food still left on her plate.

It occurred to her that the French must be extremely slow eaters. Mathilde was just starting on her ample selection of fresh fruits. Bea tried not to fidget as she watched Mathilde slowly make her way through an orange. But she did sneak a look at her delicate wristwatch when Mathilde meticulously sliced through a plump pear and then began to nibble at it, tiny piece by piece.

Bea was feeling pressed for time. She had meant it when she said she didn't believe she could face Louis Robertson again, and if he was trying to make it back to see her to the airport, she felt it

was even more important to be long gone. But it
did seem rude to leave Mathilde still eating. The
woman had confided that she was two months
pregnant, and Bea hated to rush her if she was
determined to be eating for an extra little person.

Bea was wondering how it could possibly take a
woman so long to finish a single piece of fruit,
when a hand fell heavily on her shoulder.

"Let's go," a husky, no-nonsense voice ordered.

In alarm she turned around, then gasped, for
she was looking directly into the eyes of John
Robertson. There was no doubt about his identity,
even if she had not then seen Louis Robertson slip
smugly into the empty seat beside his wife. For
Bea's heart told her who the man was. She felt
filled to capacity with the knowledge, her whole
body overflowing with conflicting emotions.
There was the frightened emptiness she had felt
since learning John had actually endangered himself by going into Africa, but she also felt the contrasting fullness of joy just seeing his beloved face.
Safe! Thank God, safe! And the humiliation
because now he knew of her love but didn't love
her in return. She was spilling over with conflict.

And John was staring back at her with such anger. She hadn't anticipated that.

Vaguely she was aware of Louis expressing
amazement that his wife felt like eating again...of
Mathilde laughing in that almost musical lilt of
hers, asking why it had taken them so long to come
from the airport, complaining that had he delayed
one moment longer their infant would be doomed
to looking like a stuffed pig.

"Thanks for your help, Mathilde." Only John's voice had the power to snap her back to total awareness. She saw him pick up her purse from the empty chair but wasn't fast enough to prevent him from harshly drawing her to her feet.

"Just a minute!" she objected in confusion, trying to pull away.

"No minute, no nothing, Bea. Let's go."

He pulled her behind him as he strode out of the breakfast room. At first she kept trying to tug free. But when that proved impossible unless she literally dug her heels into the floor, she angrily followed, stumbling awkwardly in her haste to keep up with him. They were attracting an embarrassing amount of attention from the other patrons, who were astounded to see her meekly scurrying after a man who carried a feminine violet handbag over one arm.

"There's no need for this drama, John," she gasped once they were in the relative privacy of the hall outside the breakfast room. "I intended to go straight to the airport, anyway."

"The hell you will!"

"Let me go!" she insisted, angered that he still didn't trust her, didn't believe he could count on her leaving without embarrassing him further. But she was addressing the back of his head, for he was leading her toward the elevator.

"Let me go," she protested again when he pushed her inside the familiar little cage.

"Not likely. We're going to have a talk, and this time you're going to do some listening for a change."

"John, I swear I don't intend to inconvenience your family any further. I—"

His kiss effectively stopped her protests. There was no fumbling for her mouth, no scuffling to embrace her as there had been the first time he had silenced her in that same elevator. This time he forced her body against his unerringly and honed in on her babbling lips with practiced skill, as if he knew just what to anticipate from her even before she decided what to attempt next.

His passion was not faked, either. It was so real that it frightened her with its angry aggression. She was quivering helplessly when he finally released her from his arms and pushed her in front of him out of the elevator.

Even so, he was soon striding ahead of her, and she had to run to keep up with him. His greater strength kept her an unwilling captive as he dragged her by her wrist.

"My room isn't on this floor. I've got to get my suitcase before I leave. Dammit, John!"

She was given a brief respite when he opened up a room and pushed her ahead of him while he locked both doors behind them. But then he pulled her back into his arms, and when she tried to struggle free, he became incensed. His angry kisses were even more forceful, and only when he felt her trembling did his fury seem to subside.

"Hell, you've almost got me dragging you off to bed again," he literally shouted at her, his control not extending to his speech. "I'll never learn."

Uncaringly tossing aside her purse, he walked

her backward until her legs bumped into the seat of a chair, but when she started to sink into it he changed his mind and jerked her against his chest with a groan. She fell against him listlessly, trying to find her bearings in the storm of his bewildering behavior. She didn't know what to expect next.

His hands stroked her hair, then fumbled with the pins until her neat braid fell down her back. She felt him separating the strands, sensed the growing passion replacing his anger, and she tried to wriggle away. But he loosened her hair anyway.

"John, I'm mortified enough that I came to Paris for you. And I promise to leave you alone from now on," she moaned, trying to deny the warm longing his embrace was creating deep within her. "Why are you doing this?"

"Doing this?" he asked huskily, running his lips along her throat as his hands roamed over her back. His touch felt so pleasing that she hated herself, was disgusted with her inability to control the situation.

But amazingly he rescued her himself. Drawing a shuddering breath, he held her slightly away from him.

His look of obvious affection was a shock to her delicately balanced emotions, and she stood motionless where he had placed her, her eyes wide.

"Sit down, Bea," he sighed, gently lowering her to the red velvet chair before hauling up the nearby desk chair for himself. He sprawled in front of her, so effectively blocking any exit that she wondered if it was intentional. His muscular thighs bulged against his slacks as he stretched his legs near her and took her hands in his own.

If he was trying to keep her captive, his precautions were unnecessary. She was enervated, unable to think, much less move. Her hair streamed wildly over her shoulders, strangely at odds with the precision of her muted violet tunic outfit. Her face was vulnerable yet flushed with anger at herself because she was unable to keep the tears from running down her cheeks.

"I wish you'd quit crying," he groaned, grasping her face in his hands and kissing her moist eyes. But his soothing only made her feel worse, and she began to sob. She didn't know if she was happy, unhappy or relieved. But the tears flowed just the same, no matter what the cause.

"Stop it, Bea!" John insisted, covering her face with kisses. "I'm determined not to get sidetracked into bed with you this time. We have to talk."

"Why do you keep accusing me of luring you to bed?" she objected painfully.

"I'm the weak one, not you." His expression miraculously lightened with a boyish smile as he caressed her face with his big hands. "Don't you remember the last time in New York?"

She remembered it all too well—her bleak expression testified to that.

"But don't you understand? When I came to your apartment I fully intended to go to bed with you if you were at all agreeable; I'd fought the desire to since you first sprawled at my feet. But you've got to believe me, I did plan to tell you all about this Harry Ward mess first."

She moaned, wishing he would stop.

"It was too late for explanations, though, when you gave me such a warm welcome. I had to have you first. I had gone to Africa never expecting to come back. Then to make it, to succeed and to have *you* to come home to! My life was so full I was almost drunk with the sweetness of it. I woke up in your bed, thinking I was the luckiest man alive. No man had ever been given anything more precious than the love you shared with me."

"How can I believe you? Everyone has been lying to me. Thomas, telling me you had called from Brussels, you telling me...."

"Thomas worried about that, but he wanted to relieve your mind. And it wasn't exactly a lie. I did call the office, just before I left for Africa."

"But you! You told me in my apartment point-blank that you had not gone to Africa," she said angrily.

"No! I said you had jumped to the wrong conclusion. You thought I didn't care about you enough to tell you I was going after Harry, but I cared too much. I really didn't think we would make it back, Bea."

She shuddered as she looked at his earnest face, and he immediately kissed her, trying to comfort her.

"After we made love and I had slept awhile, I thought I would burst with happiness," he continued with determination. "No man had a right to be so foolishly happy. I rested in your bed listening to the soft sounds of your moving about, savoring the knowledge you were nearby, that I could see you any moment I wanted with no barriers between us. I was just pulling myself together to come find you and explain all that was still ahead of us when I heard Suzi and Thomas coming in.''

''And by then it was too late. I had found out *why* you had come back to me,'' she finished bitterly, still afraid to believe the implications of what he seemed to be saying. She clung to her old beliefs in a final attempt at self-preservation. ''Don't tell me you didn't need my cooperation for an alibi about what really went on.''

''Bea, I *did* need your alibi. I still do. Terrorists in Africa don't settle for dirty phone calls and poison-pen letters. They kill. The government forces have cleared out most of them, but we can't take a chance that the few remaining free will find out how we accomplished that rescue. I can't jeopardize the lives of people who helped us, not even for you.

''If I'd realized what you were thinking, I would have explained before the press conference. But I swear I didn't! You looked shaken, but I thought you were just dreading facing the media again. I was so damned glad this thing was almost over that I wanted to finish it up. I wanted to tell the press goodbye forever, then take you back to bed.''

She protested at that lusty declaration, but he firmly silenced her with a hand over her lips.

''I came here determined to make you understand. And I'm not giving up until you do.''

When her mutterings subsided he let his fingers move languorously to her throat in a nonthreatening, almost possessive gesture.

She revealed all her insecurities. "I don't understand about fertilizer or why you went to Africa yourself. Those were things Mathilde assumed I knew."

It seemed to stun him momentarily that she had not realized the urgency behind his dilemma.

"What do you know about ammonium nitrate?"

She frowned slightly as she tried to recall. "That it's an extremely effective fertilizer for specialized needs, of course. And it has additional uses as a potent explosive, which gives it a marketing advantage. Oh!"

He grasped her hands tightly.

"But you shipped dry herbicide to Africa," she said almost hopefully, not wanting to believe what was taking shape in her mind.

"That's what we wanted people to think. Actually it was a large quantity of ammonium nitrate.

"We took a calculated risk for a close friend. His people are near starvation, and he must increase beef production. Harry hoped to get the fertilizer down on the pasturage before the terrorists endangered the area."

"You were afraid the terrorists would use it?"

"That's it. The one hope we had was that we could get it destroyed before the natives realized what it was."

"I would have understood if you had told me that from the start."

"At first I didn't know what you were up to. I had already received one ransom note for Harry, and I was suspicious of everyone. I never wanted to involve you. But the number of human lives at risk was so potentially high that once you blew my cover in Paris, I had to. Then I thought your greatest protection from France-based terrorists would be ignorance."

"It also meant I couldn't give them any information if I got caught." She didn't know why she made that accusation. She realized it wasn't true, even before John hauled her to her feet in outrage. His strong hands gripped her shoulders as he shook her.

"How could you believe I ever took your safety lightly, that I wasn't frantic to think someone might...." He was so incensed he could not even finish his thought. She bobbed before him like a rag doll until he realized how forcefully he was shaking her and released her in horror.

"John, what are we doing to each other?" she sobbed, forcing her way back into his arms. It became Bea consoling him, holding him.

Only when he groaned against her hair did she pull away. "Tell me what happened in Africa." She wiped at her tear-stained face with her bare hands.

She knew her demand upset him because he began pacing around the room, taking short steps which ill fitted his caged strength.

"Harry was missing. I got André's help, and we

went after him. Then we found the fertilizer and destroyed it." He snapped out the words in hot succession, uncompromising in his succinctness. Obviously he expected her to settle for that.

"Do you have any idea what I went through waiting to hear from you?" she asked slowly, trying to express her need to know more. "I couldn't forget your look of near death when those men were helping you leave the Brussels airport. I screamed, but you left me anyway. It's unbearable how much I love you. The only thing that kept me functional was convincing myself you were reasonably safe in Belgium. You could have been killed in Africa, and I would never have known what happened!"

"I was conceited enough to believe you loved me as much as I loved you, and I didn't want to put you through the fear I was going through," John argued. "Even though security people were watching you constantly, I was haunted that terrorists might still get to you."

There was no doubting his sincerity. "I believe you," she said quietly, not knowing where the admission would lead, but ready to take the first step. "Now please, John, tell me what happened in Africa. I have to know your danger is really over."

Talking about it seemed to be so difficult for him that she was fleetingly tempted to try to make her mental adjustments without his story. But she felt that some verbal catharsis was necessary for both of them. She laid her hand on his knee encouragingly.

He looked down at her fingertips, his lips up-turning a little as he saw how much the nails had grown, how neatly manicured they were. His hand covered hers, and he began to force out the words.

"We had everything ready for a rescue attempt when Carole got the ransom note, and all hell seemed to break loose in Paris. The publicity made it impossible to get out of France secretly, so André had to shift our rescue operations to Belgium."

"André is your old friend whom Suzi mentioned?"

"Yes. He is a professional, so I had the best of help. He arranged our commercial flight out of Brussels and our transfer to a chartered aircraft."

John seemed to be exhausted with the brief explanations. "Bea, there's so much I can't tell you, people we still have to protect."

"But in Africa. Your leg, the water tower. You started to tell me that at the apartment, and I foolishly ignored you."

He laughed in self-deprecation. "You didn't ignore me—the two of us just got sidetracked. But that part I can tell you about. It's funny to me now, since we were successful. But not so funny then. We were such a useless crew! I was still debilitated from eating those *moules*. Harry was close to starvation, and Blanco was covered with bug infestation. Only André was fully functional, and he didn't stay that way long.

"After we rescued Harry, we located, with his help, the fertilizer still loaded on the trucks that delivered it. Unfortunately it was also still in its hundred-pound waterproof bags.''

''Why was that a problem?''

''We couldn't blow it up. Too dangerous to control. The safest thing was to dissolve it in water.'' He was looking better, as if he was finding his own relief by talking about it.

''So you had to get it out of the waterproof bags?'' Even to her it sounded like an impossible job.

''Harry and the trucks were both at the rebel headquarters in a two-bit abandoned mining complex outside this little village. That tip you helped me get at the Bistro d'Oiseau was right on that score. The site had a good-size, full water tower originally built for the mines. So we figured we could effectively flood the bags if we could get them sliced partially open. The force of that much water would do the rest.

''There were the four of us, plus only one native. We had left most of our crew outside the camp both to facilitate secrecy and to help get us out of there. Anyway, once we got Harry free it was night, and the camp was asleep, so we got on those trucks and started slitting bags. We wanted to expose as much fertilizer as possible in the time we had to work.

''Luckily there was a torrential rain and thunderstorm that night with gully-washing sheets of water and noise with lightning like you've never heard or seen in the States. Unusual for that arid land, too. It covered our rescue of Harry and kept up with such force no one heard us working.

Eventually I left André and his crew to finish up, and I took some of the dry ammonium nitrate and set it up to blow the water tower. Everything seemed to be going in our favor. That rain helped loosen the fertilizer and even muffled our noise when we drove those trucks right through the camp and under the tower. Then André and the others jumped out of the trucks and ran like hell, and I detonated my explosives and took off myself.''

"But you got hurt."

"The charges were timed to split the bottom of the tank just after all the legs went. But one of the charges on the legs was slightly late, and the tower fell at an angle. It still worked like a charm; the water came out with maximum force, while the tower literally crushed down on the trucks. Africa will be fertilized downstream for miles!''

He was smiling in satisfaction. But Bea was not.

"But the tank fell on you." Instinctively her hand was seeking the damage done to his leg.

"Only a portion." He drew her toward him. "They pulled me out and we walked to freedom. I was a little dizzy from a head wound, and Harry and Blanco were in pitiful states. But André was strong except for his sprained wrist. So it was just a matter of following him. The storm confused the terrorists so much it was hours before they realized anyone had been there, and by then the government forces had arrived to investigate the storm damage. We were lucky.''

"You were still a long way from safety," she said, not needing a map to figure that out.

"But we made it. André's natives helped us. End of story. Kiss me."

She didn't.

He was fast becoming boyishly jubilant, and she could tell he felt it unnecessary to relate anything more. But things felt unfinished. She turned away, unable to erase from her mind the unbearable pain she had suffered thinking he had made love to her just for an alibi.

"John, I want to go home," she said quietly, tensing as his hands fell on her shoulders.

"I love you, Bea, then, now, always," he said softly, his lips pressing against her hair, parting it, seeking the back of her neck.

She shuddered with longing. "I wish I could believe that, but somehow I can't."

"Your pride won't let you. I couldn't believe you loved me, either," he admitted, his hands flowing around her waist to draw her against him. "Otherwise I would have stayed in New York. I thought that if you really cared about me you would have been willing to listen to my explanations."

"You didn't try very hard," she claimed unfairly.

"I got tired of the games you played—ordering me out of your apartment, refusing to speak to me on the phone."

"So you gave up." She sighed in regret.

"No, I bided my time. I remember thinking that if I knew you really loved me, I wouldn't let anything stop me from making you listen."

He could feel Bea's silent sobs against his chest.

"It took this crazy trip of yours to Paris to convince me." He turned her toward him. "You raised a sillier stink than Carole Ward!"

"But you seemed so angry down in the breakfast room." Her confusion was evident.

"Nothing short of caveman tactics seem to work with you." He was smiling fully, his happiness uncomplicated. "You're not the world's best listener except under duress."

She didn't go willingly into his arms. He had told her a few brief sentences of his brush with death, said he loved her and thought she should forget all her concerns. He made no promises for the future, but she was supposed to be happy, too. He was an insane man.

Because he was so insistent, she let him hold her but ignored his kissing her below the ear. She wanted to get everything straight—into the little compartments she was accustomed to in her life.

"I don't see how my coming to Paris changed your mind." It seemed to her that if anything, he would have been mortified by her behavior.

"When a beautiful woman comes all the way to Paris just because she gets the crazy notion the man she loves is being—"

"You told me once I wasn't beautiful!" Bea interrupted. She remembered it well. It was among the first insults he had unwittingly thrown her way.

"I lied." He began unbuttoning the violet tunic.

She watched him absentmindedly, trying to get a clear understanding. She needed desperately to know about the future. There were so many problems.

"John, we're so different."

"I've noticed." His eyes roved over the fullness of her figure beneath her brightly patterned blouse as he tossed the tunic on a chair.

She watched him bend over to slip off her shoes.

"For one thing, there are all these lies you've told me. I couldn't live with lying. I think people must always be honest with one another."

"Okay, I'll be honest, trustworthy and true from now on." He was slipping his hands under her skirt, and she knew he was not taking her seriously.

"I would always try to be honest with you," she asserted, wriggling while he slid down her panty hose, then automatically balancing a hand on his shoulders as she stepped out of them and watched him toss them alongside the tunic.

"I should probably tell you the truth about me right now," she continued earnestly. "My bad habits, I mean. My shortcomings. You can't know about them—not in just a week of living together in a hotel. For one thing, I am not a good cook. Suzi and Thomas were polite about it, but I'm dreadfully clumsy about preparing meals other than simple things for myself. I don't even like to cook."

"Terrible."

He appeared to accept her out-of-context confession philosophically. The violet skirt joined the tunic on the chair.

"And I'm not a good housekeeper, either. I've

always hired someone to clean up after me.'' She studied him in confusion, wondering why he was running his hands under her half slip. But curiosity did not stop her strange confession. ''Although I've noticed I'm much neater than you are.''

''You're right. You are.'' He managed to get her panties off with her half slip.

''Even if we hired a housekeeper, you deserve a woman to nurture you, to fuss over you. I don't know if I could give up working.''

''You fuss enough as a career woman; you'd do me in if you were home full-time,'' he said humorously, unbuttoning her blouse and sliding his eager hands around to work on the fastening of her bra. ''You can get a broker's license in California and make lots of money for us. I've used most of my personal funds on this rescue deal, so it will take us a few years to recover.''

He got the blouse and bra off next.

''Beautiful,'' he sighed in satisfaction.

''Don't act as if you think I couldn't really help you recoup your losses. I'm an excellent businesswoman. I could make good profits for us.''

''Just beautiful,'' he said almost reverently, bending to press his face against her breasts.

''You're not listening to me.'' Insulted that he still didn't take her seriously, she tugged at his hair.

''Right,'' he admitted, easing them both carefully onto the bed before again burying his face against her softness.

''John,'' she wailed in anguish, ''are you going to marry me or not?''

"If you'll take me on." He nodded against her peachy skin before kissing her breasts lightly. Then he propped himself up on an elbow to look at her. "I have reservations for us to fly to New York tonight, and I hoped you'd want to get married in three days. I figured it would take us that long to get the legalities straightened out. But I've asked both our parents to plan on coming to New York for the ceremony."

"Oh, good," she sighed, feeling that things were finally shaping up. "Three days will be fine."

It was when she looked into his face and saw that he was looking up and down the length of her as if he could never see enough that she became aware of her total nakedness. In broad daylight, with him fully clothed beside her on his own bed.

Only for a moment was she flustered. Then she smiled at him with happiness surpassing his. Her eyes widened with desire, and she pulled his head down to meet her eager lips.

CHAPTER FIFTEEN

THE LONG HALL WAS HUSHED, as if those tenants who had gone out for the evening had deliberately taken all the potential noise and confusion with them. There was no one to notice that the elevator stopped on Bea's floor, its heavy doors yawning open, waiting impatiently to disgorge its two passengers. Inside the shiny steel box, Bea seemed puzzled and was motionless in her white lace dress until John slipped his hand into hers. As the elevator began noisily complaining, he ushered her out. But the moment its heavy doors closed behind them she gasped in pleased comprehension and turned in his arms as much as was possible with the bouquet she was carrying and the two suitcases he was gripping awkwardly in his huge hand. Their kiss was long and sweet.

"I never dreamed this was your surprise honeymoon location," Bea eventually murmured. "So perfect—my own apartment." She let her lips slide around his chin and tease the edges of his mouth before kissing him again.

"I hoped you wouldn't be disappointed, Mrs. Robertson." He smiled in satisfaction at the name, liking the sound of it. "I've had enough of plane flights to last a lifetime."

The suitcases dropped to the floor with a thud, and he drew her completely into his arms as if he could not tolerate the slight separation in their embrace.

The effect on Bea was shattering.

"John, I think we'd better get inside," she finally said shakily as her breath quickened against his throat and the now-familiar warmth of passion stirred the depths of her body.

Gripping the suitcases, he unlocked the door of her apartment and watched anxiously as she entered the room from which they had left for the church scant hours before. The sweet smell of blooming flowers greeted them and Bea's eyes brightened in delight. She walked around slowly, awed, not believing she was in the same place she had so carefully closed up earlier that day, thinking she would be leaving it for a week. She was literally surrounded with extravagantly colorful blooms, their fragrant beauty welcoming the bride.

"Are these all from you?" She turned to look at him, her eyes full of love.

"Every last one," John answered softly. This time he set the suitcases down carefully. "Don't I get a kiss for thanks?"

"You're becoming spoiled," she laughed, and raced into his open arms. The bouquet of tiny white rosebuds she still carried from the church hung over his shoulder while she enthusiastically expressed her gratitude. Over and over. She could never get enough of kissing him.

"I'll have to remember to send flowers every

anniversary,'' he said huskily when he drew back for breath. ''This expression of gratitude could get to be addictive, you know.''

''I thought nothing could be more beautiful than this bouquet you gave me for the wedding,'' she whispered, ''but now you've created a garden heaven for me.''

There wasn't a table or flat surface in the room that did not have a bouquet. There must have been a dozen or more.

''I can't believe how many varieties you've sent.'' She began to walk around the room again, first sniffing one sweet bouquet then touching the delicate petals of a plant because they looked so perfect it was hard to believe they were real. ''Here's some more white roses, an African violet, yellow snapdragons. Another African violet....''

Her eyes widened, and suddenly she swung around in triumphant surprise. ''My couch! You remembered!''

''How could I forget?'' he smiled lovingly as she flew delightedly back into his arms. ''You talked about nothing else in Paris but the cruel lengths I drove you to while I was in Africa. Counting flowers, no less. I figured I had to make it up to your poor couch.''

''John, you really are ridiculous. If you made all these plans for us to honeymoon in my apartment, why did you have me pack a bag and bring it along to the ceremony this evening?''

''No one else knew we were coming here except Thomas, and I wanted to keep it that way. We can use the privacy for a change.''

"Thomas knew?"

"Sure. He and his wife slipped in after you left and did the last-minute cleaning and placement of the flowers."

"You asked them to fly to New York and do all that without inviting them to our wedding?" Bca was aghast.

"If we'd invited Thomas, my whole damned family and staff would have had an excuse to come, too; they were all badgering me. But the two sets of parents were enough of a crowd. Besides, Thomas is a gourmet cook. Usually he won't even let his wife in the kitchen. I figured if he would eat your cooking for more than a week without complaint, he was fond enough of you to do us one little favor. And I was right."

"I can see I told you much too much our last day in Paris." Bea snuggled against him, savoring the feel of his mouth tracing the outline of her lips. "You had me in a weakened state."

"I remember you told me you loved me. I intend to keep you in that weakened state for years." He moved his attention to her eyelids. "Because that's all I'll ever need to hear."

John started to pull her closer, then realized he was almost crushing her bridal bouquet.

"Do you want this any special place?" he asked as she reluctantly moved out of his arms.

"In the refrigerator. I want to try to press it later."

She led the way into the kitchen, noticing as she did that there were even flowers on the dining table and the kitchen counters. Her heart felt as if it would burst with the fullness of her love and the knowledge that she was loved in return.

"Oh, look, your stomach is safe for a few more days," she exclaimed when she opened the refrigerator door. "Thomas has left tons of food in here."

He watched her move aside salads, casseroles and sliced meats to make room for the bridal bouquet. "It looks good, but I have a feeling I'm not going to want to eat much for a long time. You are all I want."

His arms slid around her waist, and she leaned against him happily, but only for a moment.

"John," she said seriously, forcing him away from her so she could close the refrigerator. "Don't you feel funny? With jet lag or something, I mean? I don't feel real."

"I feel real. Let's go to bed." His smile was wolfish.

"We should eat; my stomach is growling. And I know you haven't had a meal all day. Your biological clock is all off."

"Is that what's wrong with me?"

She laughed aloud. "I don't know what's wrong with me. I'm so happy I want to burst. Our candlelight wedding at the chapel with just our parents sharing our happiness was perfect. And even coming here. Crazy! But so right. There are lots of my favorite things in New York I'd like to show you." Her eyes glowed.

"I'd like that. I wanted this time just for us. That's why I wouldn't let my office say anything about wedding plans,'' he said seriously. "We've had enough publicity to cope with.''

He looked at her lovingly, then seemed to visibly hold his passion in check. "If you're going to insist on eating, go change that dress while I set something out for us.''

She didn't argue with the offer. In her bedroom, she paused only long enough to take in the effect of the bouquets decorating even that room, then hurriedly changed out of her wedding dress, into her favorite long caftan.

He had everything all ready and was in his shirt sleeves, relaxing with a glass of wine in the dining nook when she returned.

"Is it an insult to the bridegroom to say he looks tired?'' she quipped as she let him seat her and fill her wineglass.

"An insult, but true.'' He grinned ruefully, taking a seat across from her. "You were right to insist we eat. As I looked at Thomas's food, the pace of these last few days began to catch up with me. I can't count how many meals or how much sleep I've missed.''

They both ate heartily, not saying much, just pausing every so often to smile crazily at each other and occasionally to touch hands. It had been wearing for both of them to fly home from Paris so soon after John's arrival. And for the ensuing three days they were rushing through the legal necessities for a marriage, getting acquainted with each other's parents and making arrangements for Bea's transfer to California. The time for the wedding ceremony seemed to come too fast.

"I'm relieved this is all behind us, Mrs. Robertson," John said, as he helped her clean up after their meal. "The wedding foofaraw, I mean. We can take this week to unwind, before getting you settled in my apartment in L.A. We can have your furniture shipped to the ranch later. You'll love it—the ranch—on weekends. It's not Versailles, but there's lots of ground and some gardens. I might even rig you up a few fountains."

Bea hadn't been listening too carefully past the Mrs. Robertson. It amused her how much he seemed to like saying that. Almost as much as she did. Bea Robertson. Beautiful name.

"It shouldn't take you long to get your broker's license in California," John continued seriously when they had settled down on her couch in the living room. "You'll have to take your California tests, of course. And then we'll see if you like this branch of your firm that's so close to my office. If not, you might want to go into business for yourself."

"For myself? I hadn't thought of that." Bea toyed with the unexpected suggestion. When she sold her condominium she would have a sizable amount if she combined it with her savings. But it took a good bit to hang on in business until you got yourself established. Her indecision showed in her face.

"My wallet is thin right now, but not completely busted." John continued his train of thought. "We'd have to do without redecorating the ranch house, or a new car and fur coats for a while, but everything I have left is yours, if you want to start your own firm.''

Her eyes were misty, more from his unselfish consideration than from excitement about a brokerage business of her own. ''I'll have to see how things go. . . .''

''I want you to be happy, Bea,'' he said, his arm going around her shoulder. He looked slightly worried. ''It's just begun to occur to me how much I'm asking you to give up by marrying me. My business responsibilities require me to stay in the west. But you've always lived in the east, and your family is here. You've worked hard for your success.''

''I don't think I need the accolades of being the tops in some firm, even my own. It's the thinking challenge I need,'' she admitted, fitting herself against the hardness of his body. ''And I'm lucky. The work I like can be done anywhere. Maybe if we have a family, I might want to put that money into our own investments, which I could manage from our home. My father has been pressuring me to take over some of his finances, too.''

She fell quiet as she pondered it all, and for some time they remained wrapped in each other's arms, but with their own thoughts. Eventually, though, he stirred restlessly.

''Mrs. Robertson?'' His hand was roving down from around her shoulder toward her waist.

''Hm?''

''Do you have anything on under this caftan?''

"Not a blessed thing," she said smugly, stretching provocatively.

"Let's go to bed."

She rose immediately and drew him to his feet. "I thought you'd never ask."

THEY WERE LYING FLUSHED AND NAKED in her bed, lazily caressing one another as their ardor slowed from its ultimate fever pitch, when his urgent whisper broke the quiet surrounding them.

"Bea, will you promise me one thing?"

"What's that?" she murmured against his shoulder, too beautifully exhausted after their lovemaking to even raise her head. Sensuously she ran her hand over his bare chest, luxuriating in the feel of his hair tangling against her fingertips.

He was drawing the sheet up around their waists, settling them for the night even as he spoke. "If you awaken before I do, don't get up without me."

She lay still against him a moment longer, aware of his hard warmth against her throbbing breasts, along her trembling thighs. She knew that he had been as satisfied as she in the passionate depths to which their recent lovemaking had drawn them, yet there was a curious, different tension developing within him. Exerting the ultimate effort, she propped herself up on one elbow to study his face.

"You mean wake you up?"

"Yes."

"But why? You need the sleep."

"I don't want to awaken in your bed alone. The

last time I did, everything went wrong with us."
His voice was rough with hurt.

Touched by the unbelievable depth of his feeling, she started covering his face with kisses, her
hands slipping under his shoulders to press him
even closer against her warm body.

"But you know I love you." She pecked more
kisses on his lips, trying to coax a smile.

"The most devastating moment of my life came
in this bedroom," he insisted, "when I awakened
to find you gone and all hell breaking loose with
our love. I have to erase that memory."

Her eyes darkened, and she let her head fall
down on his chest, her hair streaming over him.
She could feel his hand brushing it away from her
face, his fingers memorizing the outlines of her
eyes, her mouth.

"Bea, promise me!"

She let him pull her higher, frame her face with
his hands as he looked urgently at her.

"Is that why you wanted to come back here?"
she asked softly. She didn't even need an answer.
She could tell by his eyes. Her heart tightened at
the realization of what trust he had placed in her
hands by giving her his love.

"Oh, my darling!" She turned to lie fully against
him, her toes stretching to curl around his ankles,
her hips pressing into his manhood, her arms twin-
ing in his.

She kissed him deeply before giving him the
answer he desired.

"I won't wake you up," she said huskily, easing
to his side and drawing the sheet to their shoul-

ders. "But I promise I will be here, right beside you. You won't have to fear any more misunderstandings."

With that reassurance, they melded to each other and fell into the deepest of sleep.

Much later the next morning, their awakening was everything that a man and woman passionately in love could ask for.

ABOUT THE AUTHOR

Sharon McCaffree has led a very busy life. In addition to her present career as contemporary romance author, Sharon has been a professional proofreader, a newspaper wire editor, a personal-interest columnist and a community college history teacher.

She's also busy at her home in St. Louis, Missouri, with her husband, Douglas, and her three active teenagers, Anna, Kurt and William.

Sharon's first novel, which she wrote for "fun," has just been published by Harlequin American Romances and is entitled *Now and Forever*. She's now decided to devote her time exclusively to her writing. *Passport to Passion* is Sharon's first Superromance, but she assures us there's plenty more where this one came from. We can't wait!

Begin a long love affair with
SUPERROMANCE.
Accept LOVE BEYOND DESIRE **FREE.**

Complete and mail the coupon below today!

- -

Enter a uniquely exciting new world with

Harlequin American Romance ™·

Harlequin American Romances are the first romances to explore today's love relationships. These compelling novels reach into the hearts and minds of women across America... probing the most intimate moments of romance, love and desire.

You'll follow romantic heroines and irresistible men as they boldly face confusing choices. Career first, love later? Love without marriage? Long-distance relationships? All the experiences that make love real are captured in the tender, loving pages of **Harlequin American Romances**.

What makes American women so different when it comes to love? Find out with **Harlequin American Romance!**

Send for your introductory **FREE** book now!

Get this book FREE!

Mail to:

Harlequin Reader Service
In the U.S.
2504 West Southern Avenue
Tempe, AZ 85282

In Canada
649 Ontario Street
Stratford, Ontario N5A 6W2

YES! I want to be one of the first to discover **Harlequin American Romance.** Send me FREE and without obligation *Twice in a Lifetime.* If you do not hear from me after I have examined my FREE book, please send me the 4 new **Harlequin American Romances** each month as soon as they come off the presses. I understand that I will be billed only $2.25 for each book (total $9.00). There are no shipping or handling charges. There is no minimum number of books that I have to purchase. In fact, I may cancel this arrangement at any time. *Twice in a Lifetime* is mine to keep as a FREE gift, even if I do not buy any additional books.

Name   (please print)

Address   Apt. no.

City   State/Prov.   Zip/Postal Code

Signature (If under 18, parent or guardian must sign.)

354-BPA-2AC4

HARLEQUIN
PREMIERE AUTHOR EDITIONS

6 top Harlequin authors — 6 of their best books!

1. **JANET DAILEY** Giant of Mesabi
2. **CHARLOTTE LAMB** Dark Master
3. **ROBERTA LEIGH** Heart of the Lion
4. **ANNE MATHER** Legacy of the Past
5. **ANNE WEALE** Stowaway
6. **VIOLET WINSPEAR** The Burning Sands

Harlequin is proud to offer these 6 exciting romance novels by 6 of our most popular authors. In brand-new beautifully designed covers, each Harlequin Premiere Author Edition is a bestselling love story—a contemporary, compelling and passionate read to remember!

Available wherever paperback books are sold, or through
Harlequin Reader Service. Simply complete and mail the coupon below.